THE JEHOVAH CONTRACT

THE
JEHOVAH
CONTRACT

VICTOR
KOMAN

Franklin Watts
1987 / New York / Toronto

Library of Congress Cataloging-in-Publication Data

Koman, Victor.
The Jehovah contract.

Translation of: Der Jehova-Vertrag.
I. Title.
PT2671.0425J4413   1987   833'.914   86-28950
ISBN 0-531-15043-7

Originally published in 1985 in Germany by
Wilhelm Heyne Verlag as *Der Jehova-Vertrag*
First published in the United States in 1987
by Franklin Watts

To my parents,
Igor Petrovich and Alexandra Pavlovna,
who showed me what possibilities
life, liberty, and love could bring.

THE
JEHOVAH
CONTRACT

1
ASSASSIN

I've seen it all and I've done half of it. Frankly, I was ready to cash it in. So the word from the doctor didn't hit me too hard. I was halfway through the *Times* when Evangeline, his nurse, poked her gorgeous head into the waiting room and glanced toward me. Her fawn eyes misted as though she had just said good-bye to a beloved teddy bear.

"Mr. Ammo? Dr. La Vecque will see you now."

I switched off the newspaper plaque and slipped it into my breast pocket. Passing by her, I reached to pat the small of her back just about where her avalanche of platinum hair ended in a cloud of curls. She didn't smile this time the way she used to. That clinched it.

"Learn to take it colder, Evvie. See?" I grinned at her.

She looked me in the eye, her tension unwinding. I gave her another pat and made my way to the examination room.

Dr. La Vecque treated most of the aging bums that hung around Figueroa and Fourth. I included myself in the clientele mostly because his office was just a few floors below mine.

The office reflected the social status of· his patients—all

the needles and drugs were kept under lock and key, same for even the most inexpensive equipment. His office and mine were located in the worst section of Old Downtown—the Arco Tower. The one that's still standing, so to speak.

After about twenty minutes of moist palms, I heard La Vecque rummaging for my file in the little tray outside the door. He entered with less of a greeting than a mortician gives a stiff.

"Sit down." He eased his birdlike frame into a ripped swivel chair next to the examination table.

I sat on the butcher paper that covered the table and stared at him.

He was bald, beak-nosed, and looked as if he didn't take much of his own medical advice, or maybe he took too much of it. He gave the impression of being a practiced, controlled drug user. He tossed the folder he carried onto the counter, rubbed the bridge of his raw nose, and sighed.

After a moment he said, "Do you want me to ease into this, Dell?"

"No."

"You've got about three to six months. It's a form of cancer called osteogenic sarcoma, and it's metastatic. All through your bones."

"Sounds painful."

"It will be. More and more as time goes by. I can give you something to help ease it—"

"Forget it, Doc. I won't end my life as a junkie."

He looked hurt for a moment, then let it slide. Shaking his head, he leaned back to stare at me with a technician's impartial gaze. "The State Institute for Cancer Research has a center for osteogenic sarcoma. They could treat you for free. You probably wouldn't get treatment with something as expensive as monoclonal antibodies, but I'm sure—"

"Yeah," I said. "I'd wind up wearing a plastic skeleton impregnated with cobalt sixty. No thanks. I'll go when I go."

He raised what eyebrows he had. "You're a religious man, are you?"

"I'm a man. I believe in staying that way till I die." I scooted off the table.

He looked up at me as though I'd robbed him of some petty cash. That expression reminded me of why he chose to conduct his practice in the middle of Skid Row.

"It's this building, Dell. They never did get rid of all the radiation."

"Yeah," I said, "but the rent is sure reasonable." I headed out. "Thanks for the prognosis anyway, Doc. Now I can plan my retirement."

I waved to Evangeline on my way out. She blinked as she waved back. I could tell she wasn't cut out to be a nurse. I figured I knew why La Vecque kept her around.

I climbed up eight floors to my office, wondering how long it would be before the pain and effort became unbearable. How long until I'd be forced to depend upon the jury-rigged elevator. How long it would ride me up and down before I died or it dropped and killed me. Falling twenty stories in a stainless steel box seemed cleaner than lying awake at night feeling my bones rot.

I was getting depressed. In my opinion, drunk was better than depressed any day. I opened the door to the stately office of Solutions, Inc.—Dell Ammo, sole proprietor. My shoes scuffed at the holes in the rug. The place smelled of the years it had served as both an office and a dwelling.

I flopped down in the cracked remains of a black vinyl executive chair and pulled a bag of whiskey from my desk drawer. I proceeded to get drunk as per request.

It was always then—during that buzzing, whirling spin of intoxication—that I wondered why I bothered. With ten million Panamerican dollars in cash waiting for me, I was living like a maggot. I squirmed around in a decaying corpse with all the other maggots, trying not to be as maggotlike as they.

Ten million saved up under dozens of names as false as my current one. And I couldn't touch it until A.D. 2000.

A.D. 2000 was roughly two months away.

I felt like a marathon runner who drops dead right before hitting the ribbon.

I'm in a business that pays very well if you're unobtrusive and keep your mouth shut. Excessive spending is generally a bad idea. Sudden, unexplained increases in wealth will sometimes get noticed. Sometimes a nosey fed or a rival with a contract will start poking around. If he's on the wrong side of the fence from you and finds out enough . . .

People in my profession usually don't go to trial. They wind up with blades in their backs in crummy dives—their fingerprints etched away, their retinas seared, their faces practiced upon by amateur plastic surgeons.

Don't ever believe that an assassin's life is exciting and glamorous. It's a marginal risk at best.

Memories flowed with a couple more swigs of Professor Daniel's. I'd been an assassin for thirty-seven years, earning my living exclusively in the field. At fifteen, I had been setting off firecrackers behind the grassy knoll in Dallas. It was a glorious job, and my first. Sure, the Secret Service boys gave me the firecrackers and told me that it was all part of a salute to the President.

I learned right there to keep my mouth shut and disappear after the job—they had their own ideas on how to repay me for my efforts. From then on, it was strictly cash—up front.

The sixties were a fabulous time to be young and building a career in political murder. The one nuisance in my business was that all the publicity hounds stole my thunder. I didn't dare go public, but that suited me just fine.

The closest I ever came to fame was when they had cameras in the Ambassador Hotel in '68. You can almost see me duck behind that football player to slap one of the guns into Sirhan's hand right after I'd finished with it. I was also the one who gave Bobby the rosary. He would have wanted it that way.

A lot of people thought that one was political. I know different. It was a whole big flap over that actress and what he'd done to her.

That job got me a clientele, and I moved on to bigger and more lucrative jobs. Johnson, Mao, Moscone, Sadat, Brezhnev, Andropov, Chernenko, Gorbachev (it was like a revolving door there), that Gandhi dame, Duarte, Botha, Doc Rock— I can't even list them all.

Sometimes an assassination doesn't even require any killing on my part. Putting the right person in the right bed with the right blabbermouth is all that's needed. A well-placed scandal can usually result in an assassin from the other side of the fence receiving a contract to clear up the embarrassment with bullets or poison or a nasty case of cancer.

La Vecque had implied that my cancer was caused by the radiation in Old Downtown. Cancer is also the preferred weapon of some of the more patient people in my trade. It's usually employed by those who can lure their victims into a medical room or prison. Government assassins use it a lot. I think it's unsporting. And it takes too long.

Could someone have gotten to me? Bone cancer wasn't the trademark of anyone I knew.

Did it matter? I was done for, no matter how it had come about. So what if someone saw me living it up here and there? A garrotting cord around the neck in a stinking L.A. alley would only save me the trouble of having to cash it in myself when the pain became too great.

I'd made up my mind.

The next morning I woke up with a thousand overweight pixies tap-dancing on my skull. Dragging my head off the desk, I stumbled through a personal kaleidoscope of light and pain toward the hall bathroom.

Bennie the Dipso lay sprawled there, one elbow in the urinal, snoring merrily. I moved him to a more dignified position and used the convenience for its intended purpose. L.A. smog drifted in through the vent shafts. I was glad I hadn't developed any lung diseases.

I finished up and returned to my office for a breakfast glass of dog hair. I needed a shave and a bath. Or just a quick swim through carbolic acid. Instead, I tucked the .45 Colt Lightweight Commander into my waistband holster and headed for the stairs.

I could feel it this time. Maybe I was anticipating it. A sort of dull agony spread all through me by the time I got to the lobby. I sat down for a moment. It made no difference. At least I finally knew what all those little aches and pains over the past few months had been. I almost felt relieved. It wasn't as if I was getting *old*—I was merely dying.

I surveyed the ground floor. The lobby served as a repository for all the old, degenerating losers in the Arco slum area. They sat or lay or piled themselves in dirty heaps of gin and old clothing, waiting for that ultimate assassin to fire his fatal round. Men and women left behind by the spirit of uncaring time.

And I was one of them.

I felt like an old sick dog and knew it. I adjusted my foulard—the hottest design ten years ago, as was most of my ensemble—and pulled myself up to my full five-ten to step over the other derelicts.

I beelined to my nearest bank, over on Seventh. This one contained about five hundred thousand Panamerican dollars from a job I did on a senator who'd opposed private ownership of solar power satellites. He'd been one of those quirks you sometimes run across in politics. He wouldn't stay bought.

I'd decided to be poetic on that guy. He was driving up to his cabin in Vermont one summer day. Secluded country road. Lovely.

I was waiting along the way with a dazzlingly polished parabolic reflector. At a sharp bend in the road.

Easy money. Getting it out of the account turned out to be a lot tougher.

The line at the bank stretched almost the length of the building. The tellers had been shut off—a bad sign. Human substitutes had taken their place at tables set up at the far end of the floor. Guards with neural interruptors and backup revolvers formed a threatening line between the customers and their savings.

Even with a staggering hangover, I figured something was slightly amiss. Pulling my newsplaque with yesterday's *Times* from my pocket, I punched up page one, column one. Since I usually started at the comics, then went to the obituaries, followed by sports and finally the news, this minor item had escaped my attention.

There'd been another devaluation.

The lady with the wheelbarrow full of cash should have tipped me off.

I sighed and pulled out my passcard—a slip of plastic with the bank's logo on it. I'd been through this before. The feds always called it a "revaluation." That's a fancy term meaning "the shaft" for anyone on a fixed income.

My foggy brain couldn't remember the date of the last deposit. '94? '95? I ignored the babble of impatient customers and the jostle of spectators while waiting my turn.

"Next," the man behind the table said. Someone leaned too far over the counter, causing him to shout, "Come on, everyone! Calm down. We're converting all currency. There's no shortage."

"That's the problem," someone whispered. "Too damned *much* of the stuff!"

I dropped my card onto the table. A gangly youngster in a red jumpsuit took it and popped it into the aluminum box beside his elbow. Yawning, he pulled the card out to hand back to me.

"Any deposit or withdrawal?" he asked.

"All of it," I said as cordially as possible. "Now."

"Cash or debit card?"

"Cash."

He looked at me as if I'd asked for beads and bearskins. From a drawer under the table he pulled out a packet of orange scrap paper with pretty swirls engraved on it surrounding a drawing of some stranger in clothes more out of date than mine. He counted out ten of them.

"Four hundred, four-fifty, five hundred." He reached into a sack by his other elbow to pull out some clear plastic poker chips with squiggly colored strands sealed inside them. They fell into my hand with a dull, sad clack. "And fifty-eight cents."

I stared at the Monopoly money in my hand, then eyed the weasel behind the table.

"I had half a million Panamerican dollars in there!"

"Which you deposited in April of '92. There's been seven revaluations since then. You now have five hundred Panpacific dollars and fifty-eight Panpacific cents. Next." His gaze darted to one of the guards.

A sudden feeling of porcine enclosure coursed through me. I nudged past the tightening circle of federal bank police and didn't look back.

Great. That deposit had been one of my more recent ones. A quick mental calculation gave me a revised estimate of my total worth.

Between seven and ten thousand Panpacific scraps of paper. *Sic transit pecunia.* The rest of my savings had already been wiped out in the Great Gold Seizure of '93.

Oh well, die and learn.

The walk back seemed longer and hurt more. Overhead thundered the sonic clap of a Phoenix spacecraft returning to Earth. The sound of it lifted my gaze up from the trash-clogged sidewalks. Arco Plaza commanded my attention.

I remembered when both towers stood tall and black like a pair of stone idols against the blue. Now the sky was slightly brown *all* the time. And only one tower stood, if you could call it standing.

A few years back, the Red Twelfth of November Revolutionary People's Brigade for the Liberation of the Third through Sixth Worlds had detonated a small fizzle fission explosion in the women's restroom on the twenty-sixth floor of the South Tower.

The whole southern structure had collapsed, taking with it a good portion of the North Tower and blowing out most of the facing windows for a few blocks around with secondary projectiles.

Instant property depreciation. The ultimate in block busting.

None of the survivors cared to risk living or working near the radioactive mess, so—in spite of superior decontamination efforts—Old Downtown became an instant slum. It promptly filled up with the ignored scum of life. It made a perfect hiding place.

Solutions, Inc., served as my legit front. I even did some minor detective work—recovering stolen property, finding lost daughters, and the like. No divorce work, though. It made a good cover. A cover I no longer cared much about blowing.

I found a phone booth and slammed a callcard into the slot. When it verified, I punched up the number of a fellow tradesman. The line buzzed three times.

"Yeah?" demanded a bullhorn voice.

"Pete—check your stash. The lobby scheme's inoperative. Pass it on." I rang off.

Several people in the same line of work as mine were saving up some of their money to push for a statute granting a blanket amnesty for all political crimes committed in the twentieth century. We'd even gotten to the point of killing the major legislators standing in our way. We'd hired a hotshot lawyer to figure out the tricky wording and were all set with the bribes. Only now, most of us were out of money.

The amnesty idea vanished from my thoughts, to be replaced by a desire to forget everything and live out my last months as pleasantly as I could.

There was an area near Old Downtown where the law was most conspicuously absent. Under a tenement slum that even rats ignored lay a labyrinth honeycombing all of Bunker Hill. Inside it, every illegal substance, act, or commodity was available for a price. But this place was different from every other rathole of vice throughout history.

A blind man could stroll through with a fistful of gold and not be bothered. A mother could send her daughter to the ice cream store on the first level and see her return with her ice cream, change, and virginity all intact. The people who devised Auberge had a pleasant philosophy—if something's illegal, there must be a market for it. If it's marketable,

—9—

they'd attract a much better clientele with a hotel or shopping mall atmosphere.

The armed guards in tuxedos served as the crime deterrent. The managements were eager to retain their wealthy customers from Malibu, the Valley Rim, and Disney County.

The same guards also prevented unwelcome intrusions by such spoilsports as the feds and the LAPD. Since half of City Hall frequented the casinos and cathouses there, such precautions may have been unnecessary. They patrolled the corridors and establishments anyway, each armed with a laser, a neural interruptor, and an automatic pistol of choice.

They never lost arguments.

I walked across the unpaved field that served as a parking lot. Expensive cars covered every square meter like party night at the Rockefellers'.

A blatantly obvious cavern served as the entrance to Auberge. Just past the stylized mouth of the cave, a door whirred open to let me in. A knockout redhead smiled from behind a mahogany counter.

"Welcome to Auberge, sir. May I take your coat?"

I surrendered my trench coat and asked for directions to Casino Grande. Though I'd been there a few times in the past—mostly as a guest on business outings—I'd never gotten the hang of the underground's three-dimensional layout.

I listened carefully and set off. Despite her directions, I took what became either the rightest or the wrongest turn in my life.

2
SILVER ANGEL

I hadn't noticed that the crowded, classy joint I'd entered was the Casino of the Angels, not the Grande. To me, it wouldn't have mattered anyway. I just wanted to gamble away my dough.

The blackjack table wiped out half of what I had with me. I took the rest and drifted to a craps table. People milled around. Rich people, mostly. And a good portion of losers, such as yours truly, dressed up and ready to lose even more while feeling like a part of the diamond and dashing crowd.

I watched the game in progress, shifting my weight from leg to leg to ease the dull pains that poked at my bones. It was then that I saw her.

I had just muscled in between two kibitzers who looked as if they wouldn't let go of a dime to bet on the sun setting. The rest of the crowd around the table bet fast and loose. I saw why.

She stood at the head of the table holding the dice in her hand. Blond hair the color of unalloyed gold hung past her shoulders to touch the low-cut back of her silver evening gown. She tapped dark, blood-hued nails against the little green cubes. They rattled in her hand for a moment before being cast forward across the table. They landed near me. A two and a three.

"Bicycle tricycle," the croupier said in a tired voice. He looked as if he had once weighed a few hundred pounds and lost the weight but not the skin. He raked the dice back to the woman.

"Five again," someone marveled. The onlookers, especially the men, applauded. The croupier stoically shoved some chips her way.

She smiled. Not with the smile I usually associate with blondes. If there's one thing worse than the dull, brainless expression I see on most blondes, it's the faked look of intelligence I see on others. There were exceptions, and this lady was one.

She appeared unimpressed by her luck, though not bored —she seemed to be whiling away her time, not really paying attention.

The men, oddly enough, didn't pay much attention to her, either. Sure, the oily gigolos greedily eyed her mountain of chips. An occasional wolf gave lustful notice to the dress that clung skintight to skin that deserved to be clung tight to. And I could tell which of us sitting at the table knew we had no chance with her. We were the few who just stared at her arctic blue eyes and their blizzard gaze that never seemed to touch on anyone. Mostly, though, the crowd behaved as if she weren't much more than a mannequin propped up at the end of the table.

I broke away from watching her long enough to scan the room, and I noticed two interesting occurrences. First, one of the pit bosses appeared from behind a mirrored door to approach the owner of the establishment. He pointed toward the lady in silver.

Second, a trio of nervous weasels with *hood* written all over them strolled through the main door separately. They reunited as soon as they were inside. Amateurs.

I let my gaze wander back to the gaming floor. The owner and the pit boss were approaching the craps table.

Just before they got there, as if she had eyes in the back of her head, the golden lady scooped up most of her winnings and nodded courteously to the table. She made a straight line for the cashier.

To get there, she had to pass the owner. I braced myself for the quiet scene about to occur. It didn't. Instead, the owner and the pit boss drifted right past her, a sort of glaze coming over their eyes.

Reaching the table, the owner simply glanced around with a dull expression, counted the remaining chips, and quietly berated the pit boss. The fat man ran a hand through his toupee and shrugged. They went their separate ways.

The silver lady glided toward the cashier at about the same rate as the three jittery thugs in monkey suits. I looked around for guards. The only two visible were on the other side of the room taking care of a drunk.

When the unwholesome trinity reached to their waistbands, I knew what had to be done.

I shouldered my way over to the cashier, getting there ahead of Blondie to place my hulk between her and the approaching hit team. A calculated misstep permitted her to collide with me, spilling her chips.

The hoods had their guns out by the time the chips clattered to the floor. They clustered around the cashier, propositioning him. Blondie stooped to recover her goods.

"Next time why don't you watch—"

I crouched down, drawing my automatic from its waistband holster.

"Keep down, beautiful, we're in for fun."

One of the little men socked somebody who had stepped up to the booth. A woman screamed, and the crowd surged backward.

The crooks panicked. One whipped about and pointed aimlessly at the bystanders, stark terror showing behind his eyes. Another one joined in, while the third continued to fill a sack with orange paper. The guards tried to push their way forward from the rear without catching the crooks' attention.

They were too busy to notice me, so I drew my aim upward. At about that time, the ugliest, most ill-dressed of the three slowly shifted the aim of his muzzle in my direction. I figured that the cloudy look in his eyes arose from his amateur standing.

Blondie gasped behind me—more in disbelief than in fear. I fired.

The first creep fell, a bloody gap blooming red like a rose in his lapel. I snapped my aim over to the second squirt just as the guards used my diversion to rush forward and point their neural interruptors.

We were on the fringe of the field effect those things emit. I went numb. I would have been sure it was a heart attack or a stroke if I hadn't known better.

The two remaining thugs dropped, their lights knocked dim by the interruptor beams.

"We've got to get out," a voice behind me whispered.

Suddenly, *out* was what I wanted to get above all else. I rose up. Determining that I could walk without too much effort, I made tracks for the exit.

The guards seemed too busy to notice me, even though a crook lay dead at their feet and a .45 dangled in my right hand. One of them looked blankly at me, then turned back to the corpse and its snoring partners.

At the doorway, I turned to Blondie saying, "Hey—your chips—"

She was gone.

I scanned the casino for a moment. Not there. I turned to look down the hallway. A silver figure strode unnoticed down the corridor.

"Hey, lady!" I shouted. If she didn't want her chips, I thought, to hell with them. But she deserved some thanks for getting me out of there.

Bullshit.

I was irritated because she hadn't had the decency to thank me for saving her life. Why I ever expected decency from anyone hadn't occurred to me. I jammed the pistol back into my waistband.

Did she think she'd have a gunman at her side every time she needed one?

She heard my shout and turned around to stop dead in her tracks. She stared at me with the queerest expression I'd ever seen on a dame. She looked shocked. If I hadn't seen her up close under the previous circumstances, I would have chalked the look up to simple snootiness. Yet I think she genuinely expected no further notice from me.

She spun about in a swirl of glimmering silver and walked away, her haughtiness losing some of its cutting edge. She glanced back just before turning a corner, stared at me again, and vanished out of view.

I shrugged and headed for the exit from Auberge. Security was lax, as usual. The exit guards probably didn't even know that something had happened inside one of the casinos. They patrolled the corridors, leaving internal affairs to the owners of each establishment.

The redhead at the cloakroom had been replaced by a lovely black woman in a topaz-hued harem outfit. I retrieved my coat and strolled out into the night air.

Walking down Hope Street toward Flower, my thoughts drifted back to the blonde. Who was she, to watch one man kill another and take it in stride?

Ah hell, I thought, maybe she figured I worked for the club or something. Considering how handily she won those chips, maybe she didn't want to stick around to retrieve them, let alone carry on small talk.

I jammed my hands into my pockets and headed back to my office. The night air was warm for the end of October. I let it waft around me and carry my worries away. Before I knew it, I had reached the tower and climbed to my floor.

Lights glowed in the waiting room.

Normally, I leave my office door locked and my waiting room open. I find that I get more business that way. Sometimes, I just get Bennie the Dipso curled up on the couch.

This time, I had company.

He stood as I entered. Not more than an inch or two taller, he towered over me in that psychologically intimidating manner that marked him as a hustler of vast experience. I decided to counter by playing it tough.

"Mr. Dell Ammo, I presume?" He wore the most well-tailored suit of the finest beige material I'd ever seen. His dark brown hair exploded around his head in a loose shag style. Even though he was in his mid-forties, the style suited him. Everything about him fit to perfection. Even the soft brown eyes suited him. In body, clothes, manner, and self-assurance, he radiated perfection.

I disliked him already.

"So maybe you know me. And maybe I know the Reverend Emil Zacharias." Some name—it sounded as fake as the one I'd picked for myself. I opened up the office door and pocketed my keys. He followed me in after I'd switched on the lights.

"I seem to have a reputation that precedes me."

"I watch the news. Your breakdown got a lot of airplay. Not many other evangelists announce on live television that the earth is occupied territory and challenge God to meet them in battle to take it back."

"It was a momentary lapse, I assure you." He looked about my office with amused disdain. "Are you trying to create an image with this decor?"

I eased myself into the swivel chair. My bones felt like fragile-stemmed roses with the thorns turned inward.

I pointed to the chair across the desk. He preferred to stand, leaning forward on an expensive-looking antique walking stick. It would have suited his image if it housed a sword dipped in curare. He seemed nothing like an evangelist.

"So," he said, turning to look me in the eye. "We both know each other. Perhaps you can guess why I'm here."

I leaned back and frowned. "It's not my business to guess."

He sat down, laying the stick against one leg. He folded his arms and took a deep breath.

"I understand, Mr. Ammo, that in the past you have provided solutions to rather, ah, *difficult* problems."

"That's what the brochures say."

"Yes." He fiddled with his walking stick, tapping it against one of the less worn spots on the rug. He seemed enormously troubled. Every trace of self-assurance dissolved in the midst of some internal battle. His words caught in his throat like fishhooks.

He stared directly at me. "I want someone . . . " He hesitated. The same look of struggle ran across him. I knew what word he wanted. I refrained from supplying it. He eventually realized that I wouldn't write his script for him and said, "Killed. I want someone killed, more or less. I want someone out of the way." With that, his confidence returned and he relaxed.

"Sorry," I said, "I don't operate in that field. I'm just a gumshoe."

"Oh?" He pulled a cigarette from a polished ebony case, tapped it, and stuck it between his lips. His motions employed a practiced slowness intended to hold my attention. He replaced the case in his pocket and raised both hands to his cigarette.

I didn't see what sort of lighter he had hidden in his fist, but the flame it put out danced red and yellow at the tip of the coffin nail. He inhaled deeply, then let a cloud of smoke escape through his mouth and nose.

"I have the ability to pay very well. The job will entail great difficulties, but the reward will be commensurate, I assure you."

"Out of the pocketbooks of the faithful, I suppose?" Before he could get too insulted, I continued. I was too conscious of my age, my health, and my emotions.

"Sorry, Zack. I'm not able to take on any clients, regardless of price. I'm taking an extended vacation. Maybe if you came back in a year—"

"That would be too late!"

Wouldn't it, though. "I'm sorry." I opened the last bag of whiskey I had in the office.

"Well." Emil stood, holding his walking stick loosely. "Perhaps I may leave you with something to think about during the next few days."

I automatically rose to shake his hand. His grasp was firm, not fishy as I'd expected.

"Thanks, but I don't accept advance considerations. Makes for misunderstandings. Good evening." I sat back down and clomped my feet on the desk.

"As you wish. However, I still think you shall find my offer foremost in your thoughts in days to come. Good night." He turned and walked out of my office.

I didn't like him. I didn't like his confidence, his total faith that I could be bent to his way of thought.

I didn't like getting drunk, either. It was preferable to thinking about him, though. I loosened my shoes and foulard and poured a glassful of the bourbon.

Halfway through my drunk, I staggered up to shut off the blower. I figured the ventilation system had screwed up again. I fell asleep with the distinct impression that the place smelled like an oil refinery.

I woke up in the same position in which I'd fallen asleep— feet on the desk, hands in my lap, my chair leaning against the stacks of books behind me.

I felt like Dante waking up in Hell.

A sick rushing sensation coursed through me. The dream I awoke with faded in my effort to reach the bathroom in the hall. I wasn't nauseated—I merely felt as if my insides had been shish-kebabbed.

The door slammed open under my urgings. Bennie the Dipso sat in one of the stalls, singing old sailor chanteys. I headed toward the wall. A certain portion of me was so filled that I thought it might burst. I faced the urinal and nearly fainted.

It felt like pissing thumbtacks. Blood and milky strands swirled around in the drain.

The room spun back and forth. My fingers clutched the edge of the urinal and held tight.

I wondered whether I'd make it to Dr. La Vecque.

I didn't notice any pain as I hurried down the stairs. My brain was working overtime on suspicion. Maybe Doc had lied about how much time I had. Maybe Zacharias had slipped me a contact poison—it was possible he knew what I had had to do with the murder of Pope John Paul I. I considered everything.

La Vecque frowned. "Doesn't look good. Aside from the blood, there're cancer cells and proteins. The cancer may have reached your kidneys. If so, it's metastasized further than I thought."

"And?"

"And I'd like another body scan. Tomorrow at the hospital. And I think you should stay there awhile."

"No, thanks." I stood. "If I go, I go. I'll see you tomorrow, but that's all. I've got a lot to do."

"I'm glad you feel that way."

He watched me leave as if I were walking into the Outer Limits.

Back in my office, I half-fretted about dying, half-wondered why I thought it mattered. A cog in a machine never wonders whether it can be replaced or whether its failure will stop the machine. My universe ends with me, sure, but all the other universes go on.

I spent the day and evening rereading an old book called *The Dice Man*. One of the lines that I remembered enough for it to bother me when I read it again was, "Life is islands of ecstasy in an ocean of ennui, and after the age of thirty land is seldom seen."

Except for those brief moments during an assassination—when I could feel the tides of history flow around me like a palpable, living stream—I'd been adrift in that featureless ocean.

I spent the night getting drunk.

The next morning—afternoon, actually—I rolled off the couch, poured myself breakfast, and made my way down First Street to Belvedere Hospital. I had a date with an NMR scanner. The walk took over an hour. I considered it a bad sign that my bones didn't bother me at all during that time. Maybe even my nervous system had entered the breakdown stage.

I reached the desk breathing heavily and wheezing. The short, fat girl behind the desk popped her chewing gum and handed me a plaque of forms to fill out. She stuck her thumb at a cracked coffee cup that held three styli. I picked out the cleanest one and punched up an image. The top right-hand corner read, "Page 1 of 17."

An hour later, I lay naked on a table that had the look and feel of a block of ice. I was still beefy, I observed dispassionately, though a lot of my muscle had turned to flab in recent years. When I realized in what direction that line of thought led, I quit and turned to La Vecque.

"How's it going?"

"Shut up and turn your head back. Breathe normally. It's going fine." He looked even more birdlike, hovering over the tech's shoulder.

"Dr. La Vecque?" A scrawny kid with glasses stuck his head through the doorway, followed by a folder and a plaque. Doc took both from the boy and read through the reports.

"My latest sample?" I asked.

He waved his hand around as if a palsy had struck him and then sat down by the scanner technician. The tech showed him a readout of my condition. Beady eyes narrowed in interest.

He said nothing for a long time.

"Can I get up, Doc?"

"Sure, Dell, sure." His fingers tapped against his jawline like a dancing spider.

"Is it something worse?" I reached for my slacks.

The tech moved around the two of us, preparing the machine for the next patient. I dressed and kept an eye on the good doctor. He looked like a sinking ship.

His first words in five minutes were, "Have you had a bowel movement today?"

His skill at charming banter was exceeded only by his taste in conversational topics.

"No," I said. "I haven't."

"Go to the lab."

The whole process was growing repulsive. With a sigh, I went to the lab to do what he wanted.

La Vecque told me that the computer analysis would be ready the next day.

"Go home and get some rest." He shook like a youngster commanding a firing squad for the first time. Or a man standing before one. His bedside manner instilled little hope for my future.

I hardly noticed the walk back to my office except to observe that my wheezing had eased up a bit. I stopped in the garment district to buy some evening clothes with money I'd taken from another bank under another name. I have that sort of build upon which even new clothes look as if I'd slept in them. I felt better, though, strolling to Auberge. If the news was as bad as La Vecque's demeanor indicated, I figured I should have some fun before I cashed it all in.

And maybe I had another reason to go there.

The redhead was there at the cloakroom again. As I headed toward the Casino of the Angels, I was aware of a feeling of . . . anticipation.

What if I saw *her* again?

The thought stopped me in midstride. What was I looking for—a final adventure? A last fling with a woman half my age?

Someone bumped me from behind. A sensation of enormous rage radiated from about two feet below my eyes. I turned around to see a kid. Not a normal kid, of course. My luck's not that good.

She wore a slinky peach satin dress that clung to what would in a few years be called her body. Her makeup, expertly applied, made her look mature and sensuous. Her long nails mimicked the color of her dress. I guessed that she wore high heels from the audible scuff they made on the carpet. She brushed back her long mane of tousled auburn hair and spoke in a low child's voice.

"Watch your fucking step, asshole."

I looked at her for a confused moment, then broke into a bellyful of laughter.

Her orange lips pouted. "Whyn't you watch where you're going?" she demanded. Small fists rested angrily on her hips; innocent green eyes stared up at me, filled with a child's fury.

"Why don't *you?*" I snapped back. "You were behind me." I expected her to run off crying. I wasn't in any mood to coddle.

"Ah, shut up." She whipped ahead of me and walked with womanly grace down the hallway. In a few steps she quickly vanished from sight in the twists and turns of the maze. I shook my head—half in amusement, half in pity.

I turned a corner and the kid stepped in front of me, her arms folded. The cigarette nipped between two of her small fingers looked as big as a cigar.

"Aren't you on the wrong level?" I asked. "Hooking is two floors down."

"Rules are made to be broken for a price. I've got a couple of the guards up here on the take. I walk around till someone picks me up, then we go down to Three."

"In that case," I said, "I'm restricting your business by hanging around. So long." Stepping past her, I noticed a look of amazement that her youth left undisguised.

"Hey, mister!" She trotted up behind me to pull at my coattails. "Don't you want to go to bed with me?" She struck a sultry pose.

"I'm not a politician, kid. I don't kiss babies."

"But every man I talk to wants to make it with me. And give me things."

I shrugged. "Consider me your first strikeout."

She pulled close enough to me that I could smell the heavy scent of Opium perfume. Her voice dropped half an octave lower.

"I can do anything you want. I can take it anywhere you want to give it to me."

"Can you take it out of here and bring it back when you've grown up?" I resumed my walk. She kept up with me, two steps to one, trotting alongside me like an unwelcome puppy.

"I give really good head."

"Good." I pointed. "Head in that direction and get lost."

She stopped and glowered. "You're supposed to want me!"

"Says who?"

"They *all* want me!" Her eyes narrowed in fierce concentration. Her face scrunched up like a bulldog's.

I felt a tremble inside me, as if the cancer were eating deeper. I looked at her. She wasn't wearing a satin dress anymore. An image appeared to me of how she would look naked except for stockings and high heels. She squatted astride me, her hands on my chest. Moving slowly, with an expert's skill.

We both looked ludicrous. Hideous.

I fought to shake the picture from my mind and regain my bearings. I glared at her. "Someone ought to give you a spanking."

"You can," she said with a smile. "Let's talk price."

I clammed up, figuring her to be hopeless. With a muttered curse, I muscled my way through the crowd toward the casino.

She practically yelped in shock. Her gaze shot daggers into my back. That satisfied me just fine.

The interlude distracted me so much that I followed a crowd of noise and people into the wrong casino.

Or maybe the right one.

3
THE
CONTRACT

I stepped into the Casino Grande, realized my mistake, and turned to go. At the edge of my field of view shimmered silver and gold surrounded by a crowd of onlookers. A gasp of amazement escaped from them.

The lady was at the craps table of the Grande tonight.

I wandered over to watch her for a few moments in her deep concentration. She laid down her chips. In a blur of action the rest of the players faded the bets. The dice rattled in her hand for an instant, then scampered across the felt.

Seven.

She let the money lie. It took a little longer for the crowd to cover her bets, but newcomers arrived every few seconds to add to the crush of gawkers and gamblers. She rolled again. The red cubes knocked along the table to stop at six and four.

"Ten," the croupier announced, sliding the dice back to her.

She rolled again. Ten. Several frustrated bettors left the

table, looking at her as though she'd robbed their babies of pabulum. She ignored them and scooped up some of her winnings. I scanned the table, found a bet of hers that wouldn't wipe me out, and faded it.

She rattled the dice carelessly in her slender hand and let them loose. Boxcars.

"Twelve," the croupier said with relief, raking in the dice to give to someone else.

Blondie looked directly at me as if it were my fault. One of the boys handed her a tray with her pile of chips. She tipped heavily and left the table.

I picked up my share and sauntered to the bar.

While watching a whiskey sour fill up before me, a familiar metallic sheen approached and slipped into the chair at my right.

"Margarita. No salt." She spoke slowly. A low, intimate tone.

When the bartender slid the drink over to her, she handed him a couple of chips. He looked at them for a moment.

"Lady," he said, "there was a devaluation two days ago. A hundred new dollars is quite a bit."

She smiled and shrugged her lovely shoulders. The barkeep argued no further. A grin spread across his ruddy face.

"Thank *you*, lady!"

She ignored him to turn to me. "You don't belong here," she said in a quizzical voice.

"Okay," I said, "I don't. And what's a nice girl like you—"

"You're different. You notice me. You *see* me."

I eyeballed her up and down. Her long legs, as far as I could see, possessed the sleek lines of a professional dancer's. From there on up, she pulled in at the right places and flared out at the righter places. Her piercingly blue eyes imparted a startling power to her defiant visage. Anyone who trifled with her, it read, paid the price.

"You're hard to overlook." I turned back to my drink.

She sipped at her margarita. Her eyes continued to watch me.

"I want to thank you for what you did the other night." She smiled with friendly ease. "Things such as that don't usually happen to me."

"Me neither."

"What's your name?"

"Ammo. Dell Ammo."

She nodded. "It fits." She returned to her drink.

She wasn't going to tell me her name—that much was obvious. I gave the whiskey my undivided attention.

After a few minutes of nursing her drink, she spoke without turning to face me.

"What do you think they did with them? The robbers."

The thieves most likely had been sold to the kink caves on Auberge's lowest level. Both the living and the dead. I didn't think she wanted to hear that.

"I don't know," was all I said. "If you think they're after you, don't worry. They won't bother you again."

She set her glass down. "And what makes you think they were after me?" Her baby blues gazed at me with penetrating force.

"Someone's after you." I leaned back and groped around for a cigarette. "If it wasn't the little rat that happened to point his rod in your direction, then it must have been someone else. Why were you in such a hurry to leave?"

"Wouldn't most people try to run away from a shooting?"

"Most people last night stuck around to watch."

She shuddered. "Death . . . repels me." She took a long sip of her drink, then gulped the remainder down. The glass returned to the bar with a resounding clank. She stood, gazing toward the craps table.

I grinned. "Going to risk the management's curiousity at this casino, too?"

"Not after the way you changed my luck. I'm going to watch *you* play."

I shrugged and followed her over. It wasn't as if I'd had any plans for the money. I edged into the playing order behind several quick losers. She moved behind me to watch.

My turn came up fairly quickly. A lot of losers haunted

that table. I asked for a new pair of dice, got them, twiddled with them awhile. What money I had went on the table. The crowd faded the bets, and I cut loose with the cubes.

"Nine," said the croupier—a woman my age with an expression of Stakhanovite gloom about her. She slid the dice back to me.

I rolled again. A three and a six. The money piled up, but I let it lay. The onlookers plunked their chips down. I glanced behind me to see Blondie watching me. Her beautiful brow frowned in vague puzzlement, as if the numbers the dice generated were some secret code she had to break. I grinned and returned to the work at hand.

I rolled a seven and left the chips showing. It took longer for the bets to get covered. More rubberneckers drifted to the table, drawn by the noise the others made every time I won.

The dice bounced across the green again. Seven. The crowd gasped. So did I. This time the covering bets came faster. I had to lose sooner or later, didn't I?

Roll. Seven!

A mania seized them. Chips clacked on top of chips, and paper rustled onto the cloth. I grinned at the lady behind me. She smiled and nodded at the dice, urging me on.

A pair of threes. Carefully maneuvering between the piles of chips, the croupier slid the dice back to me. I threw them down the emerald field, a pair of rubies dancing.

"Again six," the woman said.

I was beginning to amaze myself.

I picked up the dice, checked that my bets were faded, and rolled. Two and four.

The crowd had polarized into two factions. The bettors desperately wanted me to crap out. The onlookers cheered for me to roll another six. An intoxicating amount of wealth covered most of the table.

I rolled.

When the crowd gasped, I peered at the dice. A one and a five.

"Jesus Christ," I muttered. As I said it, the five tipped on its side to expose the two spot.

"Little Joe," the croupier announced with smug finality. I'd been obliterated. Sort of the way I'd be in a few months.

For the moment, though, I had a hundred friends. The gamblers all loved me. They gathered up their huge winnings and offered to buy me drinks, dinners, women.

The lady in silver laughed, her voice tinkling like small clear ice cubes in a glass of purest crystal.

I smiled at her over the heads and shoulders of the happy crowd. "The old man's had a big night and has to go to bed now." I pocketed what little money I had left.

"Don't fool yourself, Mr. Ammo. You're not quite as old as you think. Take a long hard look at yourself when you get home."

"Yeah, sure, dollface." She would take the opportunity to get away right about then, I thought. And sure as clockwork she turned away. She hesitated, though, like a vixen curious about a strange creature she sees before her.

"I—" She turned back to look at me, a desperate decision forming behind her eyes. "My name is Ann Perrine. I work at the Bautista Corporation on Cordova. If you ever need help, give me a call."

"What makes you think I'll need help?"

Her smile said it all. "I'm in charge of Final Accounts. Extension four-eighteen."

With that, she spun around in a swish of silver and gold. She walked quickly away, leaving me with a snappy reply left unspoken.

I cashed my few chips, found that I'd only just broken even. I retrieved my coat from the cloakroom and stepped into the cool L.A. night.

On the way up to my office, I decided to stop at La Vecque's floor. A puddle of light spilled out from under his door.

I rapped a few knuckles against the rotting wood veneer.

"Who the hell's bothering me at this hour?" He paused. "I've got a shotgun!"

"Relax, Doc. It's me."

"Dell? Get in here." The door unlocked.

I pushed it open and entered to see La Vecque duck into his record room. He emerged a moment later with a plaque and a file folder.

"Take a look at these." He punched the tiny keys on the plaque, calling up two nearly identical body-shaped images. Their only difference lay in their coloring.

"Me, right?" I balanced the plaque on my fingertips.

"Right. Last month's scan and today's. Notice the changes in coloration where your bones are? And the changes in places such as your intestines and prostate? They correspond to absorptive and transmissive differences in the oscillations of the magnetic waves we used to make the scan."

"Of course," I said with as much authority as I could. He had me stumped. The pictures seemed to be almost exact opposites in coloration.

"Your lab reports show large amounts of cancer cells in your urine and feces. I was sure it meant that the cancer had spread to your vital organs. The scan says otherwise. The incidence of cancer cells in your body has sharply declined. I don't understand the mechanism, but somehow you're excreting your sarcoma."

"What?"

"Damn it, Dell, you're pissing out your cancer. I couldn't be totally sure from the scan, but your lab reports and blood tests show it. You've gone into some kind of spontaneous remission and you're rapidly expelling both your metastatic cancer cells and the osteogenic cells." He ran a spotted hand over his bald, sweat-dappled head and waved his other hand around in helpless circles.

"I don't know what's causing it, I don't understand the transport mechanism, I don't even know if I'm just crazy. You're healing."

"Oh."

" 'Oh' is all he can say. Look, Ammo, you're not dying anymore. You're—" He stared up at me and narrowed his eyes. He looked as if he'd seen his mother in a cathouse.

"Your hair!"

My hands shot up by reflex. It felt the same. "What's wrong?" He'd gotten me all fidgety.

"Your roots are black!"

That might have angered a showgirl. I was stunned. I turned to see my reflection in his sink mirror. My mess of gray hair seemed to float a millimeter above my scalp. Peering closer, I saw black roots at the base of the dull, old fibers.

"What is this?" I didn't like surprises.

"Don't ask me, Dell. I never majored in miracles. Give me a million bucks and I might be able to find an answer for you. Or just pay me the fifty you owe me and we'll call it square."

I peeled off a few orange sawbucks and handed them over. He tossed them onto an instrument tray and shut off the plaque. "Thanks. Now get out before scientific curiosity overwhelms me and I decide to vivisect you."

Easing the door shut behind me, I walked down the silent, musty hallway toward the stairs. I decided to perform my own test. The stairs seemed less formidable. I ran up two at a time.

My legs and lungs hardly noticed.

Mystified, I walked toward my office door. It stood halfway open, throwing a trapezoid of light across the cracked linoleum of the corridor.

There are times when the answer to a burning question lurks just beyond a door such as that. This was one of those times. I quietly slid my automatic from its holster. Something clattered inside my waiting room. A pair of feet scuffled about.

I edged closer to the door, keeping an eye on the shadow that flitted about into the hall. One step brought me inside the doorway.

His athletic body neatly filled the light gray suit. His back turned to me, all I could see was a head of brown hair and gloved hands clasping a walking stick.

"Mr. Ammo," he said before turning to see me.

"Reverend Zack." I slipped my pistol away and leaned against the jamb, arms folded.

"I'm expected, then?"

"Like famine after flood." I stood my ground. "What do you want?"

"The project we discussed. You've had time to reconsider my offer."

"The answer's still no."

He looked me up and down. A smile spread across his smooth face. "Nice head of hair you might be getting there."

I knew what he was getting at. I played dumb. Inside, something began to quiver.

"Yeah. So what? Maybe I've read a book on life extension."

"And your aches. Gone?"

"Yeah. Gone. For a while. What of it?" I knew what of it. And I knew what he would say next.

"I told you I'd give you something to help you reconsider my offer. Shall I take it back?"

That was it, then. I'd never before met someone with an offer I couldn't refuse. I was staring at the ultimate Godfather. If that term could be applied. I wasn't going to give in that easily, though.

"Take what back?" I lit a cigarette and watched the smoke arch upward. I put on my best act of calm assurance. Inwardly, I quaked.

"Come on, Dell. We can play ridiculous head games for hours. The truth is you don't want to die, and I'm offering you a way out."

I moved behind my desk to sit down, dousing the cigarette in a coffee cup. "What's the deal, Zack?"

He sat in the easy chair next to the couch. When he lit a cigarette this time, I tried to see exactly how he did it. I wasn't too sure he used a lighter.

"The project involves a single killing. One being." Waving the smoke away from his face, he smiled calmly.

"Being?"

"He is known by many names. Jehovah. Allah. Brahma. The King of Kings. The First Cause. God."

"I see."

"The All-Powerful. The Creator."

"I get you."

"Yahveh. Adonai. El Elion."

"Check."

"The Lord. The Infinite Spirit. The—"

"All right!" I shouted. "I understand. *Kapish. Comprendo.* You want me to bump off the Big One!"

"Uh—no, not really," he said quickly. "Well, yes."

"Zack—I don't believe in God."

"You don't have to. Just assassinate Him."

"You *have* flipped out."

"I have not. He exists just as surely as I do.. He threatens my control of this spiritual plane. Kill Him."

I lit another coffin nail, whiffing the smoke carefully to make sure I hadn't been slipped anything funny. The chair creaked as I leaned back in it. "Okay. If I buy the premise, I buy the bit. Say He does exist. What happens if I kill Him?"

"You shall have eternal life. As long as you wish. Youth, health, vigor—"

"I've heard about your tricks. You'd welch somehow. Turn me into a young, healthy, vigorous grasshopper or something."

"No monkey's paws, Mr. Ammo. I promise you."

I had to laugh. "Why should I trust you? Aren't you called the Prince of Lies?"

It was his turn to laugh. "You listen too much to my detractors. Propaganda always paints the enemy as a hideous monster while whitewashing the favored side. I could tell you stories about the last few Creations that would make your hair sizzle."

I poured a final trickle of whiskey from the sack in the drawer, took a deep sip, and considered.

The whole thing stank. He could simply be an agent involved in some intricate scheme that included faked medical reports, mimetic drugs, spying, squealing—and a hell of a lot of gall.

"I doubt that there's anything you can do to convince me that any of this is real. But let's assume it is. What happens if I don't agree to kill Him?"

He stared at me coolly. "You'll be very painfully dead within three months."

"I could always kill myself before then."

"In the opinion of some theologians, that would send you right to me."

"Would it?"

He smiled and tapped his cane against the floor. "Far be it from me to disparage any religion. I'm the Prince of Lies, aren't I?"

I stood and rammed my fists against the desktop. "Listen, Zacharias, you're the one who doesn't want to play head games. Here it is straight. First you have a nervous breakdown on TV and declare yourself Earth's master. Then you come to me and tell me to kill God. You don't even *ask*. It's practically an order. You—or someone—is playing poison with my body. You know damn well that I want to live, so you threaten me with death. You want me to kill something I don't even believe exists. As far as I'm concerned, this is either some trick or you're psycho. But you're a rich psycho. I know what sort of bucks the evangelical racket brings in."

I paused for effect. I didn't have any. He just stared at me with a distant, aloof gaze.

"My fees on the case will be five hundred a day, plus expenses. And I mean five hundred grams of gold. To be deposited in the Casino Grande vault. I'm not taking chances with paper money again."

He calmly said, "Four hundred."

"You want me to kill God and we're haggling over the price?"

"Oh, all right. Five." He removed his glove and extended his hand. "Shake on it."

"Give it a rest."

His hand stayed up. "Really, Mr. Ammo. It's for your own protection."

I'd heard that from enough shysters in my life. We shook. His touch was hot, his grasp firm.

"No contract? No signing in blood?"

"Mr. Ammo." The corners of his mouth turned up like dead leaves curling. "If it is a sin merely to contemplate a venial or mortal sin, then I assure you that the spoken willing-ness to commit the one *immortal* sin is quite enough for my purpose."

"And what is that?"

"An end to sibling rivalry." He turned to leave the office—by ordinary means.

Before he had walked out of my waiting room, I called after him.

"Hey! Wait! Where do I find God?"

His voice trailed behind him as he spoke without turning. "That is a search many have conducted with much less reason than you, Dell Ammo. Good luck."

His footsteps resounded hollowly on the floor of the cor-ridor. The elevator whined into life.

I wondered whether it would stop at any floor or just keep going. . . .

"Jesus Christ," I said, sliding back in my chair. "Son of a bitch."

4
THE BAUTISTA CONNECTION

I had a contract to kill God. And I'd never reneged on a contract before. How hard would it be to kill someone who didn't exist? And how long could I draw pay and expenses before Zack noticed that I hadn't eliminated his imaginary competitor?

I began to understand how séance artists felt about their profession. It's great work while it lasts.

Zacharias intrigued me. He didn't act insane, but then neither did politicians. He just talked crazy. A famous TV evangelist who had preached the word of God for years to the nation via satellite now wanted Him out of the way.

It sounded as if it would be bad for business.

All right. I'd get a cut of it without firing a shot. I had a contract to kill God, and I was going to kill Him.

No matter that it might take years. At five hundred a day.

Plus expenses.

I took a brisk walk the next morning. Down Figueroa to Fifth Street, crossing piles of rubble and shattered glass that spread across the pavement like webbed hands reaching for the opposite sidewalks. The air smelled cleaner, and a smear of blue sky hovered at the zenith. It was a great day to begin my quest.

A couple of blocks down Fifth stood the library. Nearly everyone used the computer plaque for news, information, and entertainment. The same satellites that brought the Right Reverend Emil Zacharias and his Hallelujah House into people's living rooms permitted anyone owning a plaque access to the Smithsonian library computer. Except for the people who liked to collect first editions, or those addicted to the smell of paper and glue, libraries and books were obsolete.

And then there were the old dogs who are slow to change. Count me in. I wouldn't feel as if I were learning anything if I weren't in a library building toting around a stack of ungainly books. It felt cozy.

I had optimistically prepared to spend an afternoon discovering exactly what God was. When I reached the religion section, I realized that I'd underestimated by about three lifetimes.

After an hour of randomly walking about peering at titles, I had a stack of books under either arm that covered each major religion. I felt like a student cramming for finals. I suppose I was.

Hell, I was being paid for it.

The next several hours consisted of reading one definition after another, either totally contradictory or as clear as the La Brea tar pits. Apparently, God is self-surpassing, an unmoved mover, a standard of reality, the supreme reality, the sole reality, temporal, eternal, infinite, finite, infinite-finite, an object of direct experience (that would be just my luck), one with man, apart from man, apart from *everything*, part of everything, everything. The beginning, the beginningless . . .

By closing time, my head pounded as if it had been borrowed for a performance of the Anvil Chorus. I left the library knowing less than ever. Before, at least, I'd had some idea of God. He was this hairy thunderer that some people thought was necessary to keep them from bumping into telephone poles. I'd gotten along quite well without Him for fifty-two years. Now I suddenly had to know who He was and the only image I could conjure up was that of some blob of something out somewhere doing somesuch somehow.

Not much to work with. This contract had more false leads than a hooker's smile.

A cold wind from the west blew down Fifth Street, kicking up rubbish and dust. I kept my head down and watched the garbage eddy around my feet with each step.

Kill God.

The idea seemed even more absurd now, away from the calm confidence of Zacharias. Maybe I had been right all along, and this was some sort of plot. Entrapment. Psych warfare. Revenge.

It was all too complicated, though. In my profession, death moved at the speed of a roadster, a bullet, a beam of laser light. No assassin ever received the kindness of an elaborate death scheme, no matter how artistically he conducted his own kills.

No. I knew at the time what I was agreeing to. I hadn't merely sold my soul. Souls he handled like petty cash. I had contracted for the Supreme Patricide.

I should have asked for a thousand a day.

Kill God? What a joke. Do I make it look like an accident? Natural causes? Or just a bullet in His third eye?

I needed a professional opinion.

The wind died down as I walked over the Fourth Street Bridge, to be replaced by a thin autumnal fog. The overhead lamps glowed with the light of another age. My feet scuffed concrete, heels tapping against cracks, soles grinding over rubble. In the distance, traffic roared along the Hollywood Freeway. Only a whisper of engines reached me through the fog. A thin crescent moon rose in the east. It would be morning soon.

At the Fourth Street onramp to the southbound Hollywood Freeway stood the Church of St. Herman of Alaska. Actually, it was a run-down slum hotel that a priest friend of mine had converted into a mission. He usually kept the front door unlocked, so I let myself in.

Father Joey Moreno leaned forward in one of the church's two pews. His thick right hand grasped a bottle of Chianti that he snorted down lovingly. A pink stain colored most of his white collar.

"Hey, Joey. Too much sacrament."

He belched, twisting around to see me. His rust-hued locks blended into his beard to frame his dark face in a soft triangle of frizzy hair.

"Dell! How goes? Come to convert? Or converse?"

I smiled and sat next to him. "I'm looking for God, Joey."

The bottle slid from his fingers into the next pew. He twisted around. "Won't find Him, Dell. Been looking for Him for years."

He peered down at the floor, then stamped his foot. "God's a cockroach, hombre. Split Himself into myriad parts to keep an eye on us."

I could tell this would be a conversation at cross-purposes. "How's the congregation?"

"Sinners still sin. And bingo Saturdays."

"You can't give me a lead on God's whereabouts, though?"

He stood to his full six-foot-two and bellowed, "Go thee forth to the highest, for the highest shall become the lowest and the lowest shall become the highest!"

He dropped to his knees, begging St. Herman to eliminate the liquor tax, compulsory education, and foods fried in Crisco.

I stashed the bottle behind the card table altar and left. So much for the voice of authority.

Sunlight splashed the northern Arco Tower remains with smeared reds and oranges as I returned. Rosy-fingered Dawn had not yet touched the streets. I walked in a dreamy morning world where light filtered down indirectly from the sky, softening every shadow. An occasional spear of sunshine lanced into the street, reflected from a high window.

On the corner of Figueroa and Fourth stood a man in a dark suit. He held a bunch of magazines close to his chest like a shield. The covers faced outward. He spoke quietly to the bums that passed him, and he didn't seem to mind being ignored. He was portly, short-haired, and a little nervous. I didn't blame him, considering the locale.

I wandered over to him to check out the 'zine. Sure enough, it was one of those religious societies. Maybe it was worth a try.

"Say, pal. Know of a way I can find God?" I judged the direct approach to be best.

He wearily handed me a copy of the magazine. "Simply accept Jesus into your life. He is the path from sin to salvation."

Salvation wasn't exactly what I was looking for. "No. Thanks. I mean, I want to *see* God. In the flesh. Or whatever."

He sighed and answered without looking at me. "Give me a break, mac. I've got a long day ahead of me, and I don't need sarcasm."

I nodded. He was right. A breeze almost tugged the magazine out of my fingers. That was when I noticed it was a Hallelujah House publication.

"Say—this is Emil Zacharias's group, isn't it?"

"Yeah." He didn't seem too pleased by the association.

"Do *you* think we're in occupied territory?"

He shrugged. His gaze never crossed mine for more than an instant.

"You might say that Satan has a foothold in this world. C. S. Lewis thought so too, and you wouldn't call him nuts."

"I wasn't calling anyone nuts," I said. "Do you think God will accept his challenge?"

"Christ the Lord will return to implement the Kingdom of God. It's in the Book." He flinched once or twice while speaking. His gaze darted about to search for someone else to rescue him from the grilling.

I was just getting interested.

"Do you think Zacharias was trying to send an SOS to God? Trying to hasten the Second Coming?"

He slowly shifted from one foot to the other. "Look, brother. I don't know why you're so intrigued, but no man can hasten His return. Not even Emil Zacharias. He flipped

— 39 —

out. It happens sometimes. There was a guy twenty, twenty-five years back named Jim Jones. He flipped out lots worse. Everybody's entitled to crack a bit, especially in Southern California. That doesn't invalidate two thousand years of philosophy and prophecy."

He coughed. The eloquence may have been too much for him. "I gotta go now. Quotas and such."

He walked away from me with short, tired steps. It was going to be a long day for him.

I climbed the stairs to my office and spent the next hour pacing around, searching for a lead, some method of bringing me closer to the Supreme Recluse. None of my previous contacts would be of any help. And Zack was unwilling to offer any assistance.

While stretched out on my couch to catch a doze, an idea hit me during that moment between dreamy slumber and drowsy waking. After allowing a minute or two for my senses to catch up with my thoughts, I seized the phone and punched up information.

"City?" a raspy voder asked.

"L.A. I need the number of God Almighty."

The computer searched for a moment, then replied in mechanical deadpan. "Not listed, sir. Would you like an operator?"

"No, thanks. Connect me with the Bautista Corporation on Cordova."

The line rang for a couple times, and a soft voice on the other end answered.

"Bautista Development."

"Ann Perrine, please."

"May I ask who's calling?"

"Dell Ammo."

She put me on hold for a few minutes, then I heard a click.

"Dell?" Even over the phone, her voice reminded me of satin and soft lights.

"Yeah. Look, I know this is out of line, but you told me to call you if I ever needed help."

"Of course."

"Yeah. Well, this'll sound like a crazy old man talking. I need some . . . help in researching, uh, religious matters."

Her voice betrayed a sudden interest.

"I minored in philosophy at UCLA. What do you need?"

I tried to ease it to her. "It's sort of nuts, but there's this guy who's offered me lots of money to find God. He's convinced that God exists somewhere and can actually be— hunted down."

Silence shot back and forth over the line for a dozen heartbeats.

"You're looking for god," she said. "For real."

"In the flesh. Or whatever He uses."

"Why?"

"The money."

"And you want me to help you defraud this man?"

She asked the tough ones. She'd either think I was a crook or a psycho. I preferred the latter. I'd rather be thought of as insane than dishonest. I cleared my throat.

"I don't think it will be fraud. This guy seems convinced that I can find Him." I switched on a gizmo attached to my phone that checks for listeners. The lights flashed green—the line was secure.

"He gave me a contract to track down God and kill Him."

"Kill *god?*"

I gave her credit for not laughing out loud. When I didn't answer, she said nothing for a long time. Convinced that she had hung up, I softly muttered a "damn" and lowered the receiver.

"Dell," said a small voice in my hand.

I raised the horn to my ear. "Yeah?"

"I told you that if you ever needed help, I'd do all I could."

"You will?" It was my turn for incredulity.

"I can't stay on the phone much longer—"

"Meet me at Auberge tonight." My heart pounded faster than the old thing had a right to. "Cocktail lounge of the Hope and Anchor. At eight."

"Right." She hung up without a good-bye.

"I'll be damned." The realization that I might very well be seemed less painful now. Blasphemy loves company.

On the lower levels of Auberge, guards handled trouble from the riffraff. On the upper levels, the guards served the same approximate purpose. The riffraff, however, seldom hung around—the prices were too high. I was reminded of this as I gave the waitress several scraps of orange paper to ransom my drink.

My watch read 8:13. I was beginning to feel like a jerk. Maybe she was the sort who would say anything to get a crank off the line. Maybe I was still dying from the cancer and hallucinating everything.

And I was only on my second drink.

A short time later, Ann showed up carrying a fat gray attaché case. She saw me stand and came to the table.

"Sorry I'm late. I had to get this from Archives." She set the luggage against the side of her chair and sat down.

"What is it?"

"The corporation's library. In case you need to do research."

"I've got a plaque," I said.

"Do you want your information requests going through the library satellites? The airwaves aren't necessarily secure, you know."

The waitress drifted by again. Ann ordered tequila, Kahlúa, and milk—a Tall White Bull.

"You're taking this pretty seriously," I said.

"I'm an accountant—paranoia is an occupational requirement." She looked directly at me. "You want to find god. You might as well start by telling me what kind of god. Define him."

I hadn't considered that there might be more than one kind of God. "The usual run-of-the-mill God. Miracle maker. Controller of lives. Watcher over us all."

"Is this god—the one you've been hired to kill—is he different from man?" She frowned at her own question.

"Excuse me for sounding like a prosecutor. I'm just trying to help."

"Sure. No problem." I took a drink. "Sure He's different. More powerful. More knowledgeable."

"The difference, though—is it one of kind or degree?"

"Huh?" She'd just gone beyond the limits of my self-education.

"Is this god a more powerful and intelligent *man*, or is his power of a different *nature?* Is his knowledge a nonhuman variety?"

She had me there. "Just the typical sort of unfathomable God that most people believe in."

"Well, if you can't understand god, you'll never be able to find him. And to use the term to mean anything less than a difference in *kind* is a misuse of the term. A more powerful man or alien may be godlike, but he wouldn't be a god."

I slugged down the rest of my drink. "Why are you bringing all this up?"

"I just want you to know what you're getting involved in. I think you've already started on the wrong foot. Have you looked through any books?"

"A lot of theology texts."

"You can't go to the people who believe already. They've made up their minds and want to convince you of their own personal heresy. Most theologians have no idea of what constitutes rational proof. Go to the antitheists."

"Who?"

"The disbelievers. At least they'll give you an idea of what god is *not*."

The waitress reappeared to deliver Ann's drink. She accepted it and covered the tab—and tip—without even thinking about it. I was growing fond of her already.

"You notice that I haven't asked you who wants god killed. I won't. I think the world would be better off without a god. And I don't think you're a mental case for believing that gods can literally die. Zeus is dead, after all."

"I thought he was simply doing time for rape."

She smiled at that and took a sip of her drink. "His worshippers are gone. Where does a god go then?"

"I think that was dealt with on a *Star Trek* episode."

Her eyes twinkled with laughter like northern lights. "*Star Trek* and *The Twilight Zone* both had a sophisticated grasp of theology."

"Are you old enough to remember them?"

She smiled like a debutante. "I have them on disc."

"And what TV show had the worst theology?"

"*Father Knows Best*, of course."

We both laughed. Then I heard someone behind me. Maybe *heard* isn't the right word. I had the same sort of crowded feeling I'd had the other night in the upstairs corridor. I turned around.

Fifty pounds of brat wrapped in hot pink velvet approached. She noticed me and changed her course to pass by, smiling wickedly. She strode up to Ann and whispered loud enough for the next three tables to hear.

"Don't worry about him trying to get into your skirt, lady. It ain't the meat, it's the tumidity."

"Cute," I said.

Ann eyed me, smiling dryly. "Friend of yours?"

"In no way, shape, or form—most of which she lacks."

"Cute," said the tyke.

I tapped a cigarette out of my pack. "Couldn't you go find a Shriners' convention and leave us alone? We're discussing negative theology."

She smiled a girlish little grin and winked at me in an adorable, innocent manner that made me want to kick her. She turned quickly and, ladylike, sashayed to another table.

The balding man there smiled through fat lips and leaned forward to welcome her, speaking quietly.

"A pretty child," Ann said, suddenly stiff as a schoolteacher.

"Pretty screwed up. In more than one sense." I tossed down my drink and sat back to scan the bar.

The gazes of several men, young and old, drifted toward Ann, only to drift away as though they saw her and just as quickly forgot her. Ann ignored them without any effort. Her long fingers stroked the sides of her glass, picking up droplets of moisture. She parted her rowan-hued lips to say something. A voice behind me interrupted her.

"Call for Mr. Dell Ammo." The waiter had been walking up and down the lounge, his voice carrying just enough to reach the tables he passed.

I stood to catch his attention.

"Mr. Ammo?"

I nodded.

"A telephone call for you."

I followed him to the telephones and stepped into the booth that he indicated. I thanked him and crumpled a fiver into his hand. He looked at it, mentally converted it from last week's value to this week's, and smiled broadly.

I lifted the receiver to my ear.

"Ammo," I said.

The voice on the other end was as smooth as a mortician's slab.

"Ammo—get off this God caper of yours. Zacharias is one washed-up preacher. Get wise—you're up against people who mean business."

"Yeah?" I retorted suavely. I couldn't place his accent. This was getting so overblown that I didn't even care about playing dumb. "What's it to you? If He exists, I'm no match for Him. If He doesn't, I'm only wasting my own time."

The voice spoke with slow amusement.

"Let's just say that the stakes in this particular game are high enough that it wouldn't even be worth your while to play."

The line clicked, followed by the buzzing silence of a disconnection. I hung up the receiver.

I hadn't figured anyone would take this whole affair seriously, let alone catch on to me so quickly. Now I had to plan more than a "killing" that would bring me a steady income. I had to protect myself from a second nut or gang of nuts. Great.

I mulled the problem over while walking back to the table.

Ann was gone.

The attaché case lay open on her table setting, its output screen alight. Bright orange letters glowed against a black background.

THE WAY OF
TRANSGRESSORS IS HARD.
PROVERBS 13:15

I looked around and saw no clue.

I did see the kid, though. She was guiding her bloated sugar daddy toward the exit. I raced over to grab her arm.

"Where'd she go?"

The fat man bridled. "Let go of her, fellah," he said around the edge of his cigar.

I ignored him. The brat stared up at me defiantly. "You'd have been watching," I said with a genuinely angry growl. "Where'd she go?"

"You're hurting me!" She tried to twist away. "It was two men in black."

The fat man became bolder. "Let go of her, you drunken bastard!"

I tried a bluff. The wrong bluff.

"Vice squad, mister." I reached up toward my breast pocket.

The man looked worried for an instant. Then he smiled broadly.

"Guards!"

I realized where I was and how the law was welcome. A neural interruptor field switched on, knocking me to my knees. Through a tingle of dulled sensation, I watched four arms seize me. They dragged me to an access tunnel separate from the corridors used by customers.

I tried another bluff. Another winner.

"I'm her father." Drool passed over my numbed lips. "I was just trying to talk to her."

"You should've given her a better home life, rummy." The voice spoke from far away. "She's got her freedom here."

A hatch whined open.

"Wait," I babbled. "I was with a woman. I think she's been kidnapped. The girl saw—"

"Right, pal. Kidnapped by a couple of priests. Tell us another."

The four arms propelled me from the hatch of the under-hill city. Except that I was at the top of the hill.

The hatch slammed behind me, and I rolled. The field of insensitivity they'd hit me with still deadened my nerves. I was thankful for that.

Dry grass and dirt patches whisked past me. Something hard hit my waist. It stung. I bounced past it and slid face forward to a stop at the bottom of Bunker Hill.

It didn't take long for pain to overcome the effects of the neural interruptor beam. My body curled up in a convulsion of agony, then snapped back. Shoes scraped against grimy concrete. Hands slid over crumbling pavement. After long moments of struggle, I stood.

The world tilted like some crazy Disney ride. I clambered for a parking sign to lean against, grasping it like a long-lost brother.

Down the block, someone screamed. Someone familiar.

I looked up and down the dark street. My eyes had a little trouble focusing.

I saw her. Two men in dark clothing dragged her toward a car, an arm each around her shoulders. Behind them, the door of a lower level loading dock dropped shut slowly. She struggled, blond hair whipping about.

They were at the far end of the block. I started to run as fast as I could. Pain shot through my left leg up to the hip. I reached for my Colt to find an empty holster. It must have fallen out during the roll.

The car engine whined into life as they stuffed her inside. Tires squealed, and the car roared in my direction. I performed the usual stupid action of jumping in its path. Rubber shrieked again; the car swerved around me.

I jumped for the trunk, missed, and came up with bloody elbows and a scraped nose. Wiping the dust from my eyes, I watched the taillights recede into the night.

"Look out, mister!"

I turned around. On top of the hill—in the hatchway I'd been launched from—stood the kid. Light poured out of the tunnel. Her giant shadow splashed down the hillside.

"Behind you, asshole!"

I whirled about just in time to enjoy the view of a black-jack zeroing in on my right temple. I didn't see stars. Just a lot of black that got blacker.

5
PRE
MORTEM

I woke up with a Rushmore-size headache in a dark little cell that made San Quentin look like the Biltmore. My bruises had been bandaged, and I was dressed in a light blue hospital gown. The smooth white walls teetered a bit as I sat up.

I eased my mistreated body up to walk around the cell. My shoulder intuitively sought the wall for support.

The smell of Formalin and acetone in the air forced the sluggishness out of my head. The phrase that most readily came to what mind I had was, "What a sap." Ann and I both captured. They'd probably left one mug to cover their escape. And the call—a diversion.

I hadn't expected such a reaction to an insane proposition. Maybe the Big Man *was* worried.

Heavy footsteps approached, slow and ponderous. A series of latches clanked back. The door opened inward without so much as a Lugosian creak.

In the doorway stood the largest piece of beef I'd ever seen on less than four legs. He had to duck to pass under the doorframe, which hung a foot higher than my head. His ghost-sheet pallor brought out the tints of red in his thin, strawberry-blond hair. The whiteness also contrasted nicely with his black clerical frock.

"I'm not ready for last rites," I said.

"Shut yer trap, Ammo, and set down. You ain't going nowhere." He talked like a rock polisher.

"Sure, Demosthenes, sure." I sat. The bedsprings groaned.

"Watch yer language, geezer. It ain't reverent fer a man yer age."

He leaned against the doorframe, blocking my exit as well as most of the door.

I knew any punch that I could throw would only tickle him and would split my knuckles open. So we waited.

For ten minutes he stood there, staring at me with calm green eyes that conveyed intelligence greater than his words communicated. I met his gaze, striving not to reveal my intentions through any involuntary motions.

I broke the silence first.

"Look, Demosthenes, why don't you go bite open a few coconuts while I toddle along? Kidnapping isn't the best way to gain converts."

"Ammo," his cement-mixer voice rumbled. "Whyn't you close your mouth so Brother Bannister don't have to come in and wire it shut to keep it from danglin'?"

He turned upon hearing distant footsteps. The creak of bedsprings when I stood brought him spinning around.

"Siddown, brother. Father Beathan's coming."

I swallowed a crude rejoinder and stood as tall as I could, wishing I had a cigarette. My nose itched madly under its bandage.

The steps grew louder, echoing down the corridor.

Demosthenes crossed himself and genuflected quickly. Through the door entered a man about half the lummox's height and a quarter of his weight. Old and withered, he carried an equally aged doctor's satchel in one wrinkled hand. He eyed me with a pair of pale grays that seemed too large for his small head. His gaze darted around the cell.

A second man followed him in. He wore a black frock and

a white collar the same as the other two. He stared past the old man at me and scowled.

"This won't do at all," he said to no one in particular.

"What's wrong this time, Father?" The old man scratched at his ear with impatience.

"Brother Matheny, how many times must I repeat? *Setting*. Setting is as important as set and dosage. This is a science, not some crude torture."

From the way he used the word *science*, I might have preferred crude torture.

Brother Matheny parted his desiccated lips, looked at me as though it were my fault, and turned to the Hulk.

"Brother O'Rourke. Find out where Father Beathan wants the sinner taken and take him there. And this, too." The satchel landed on the marble floor with a clatter. The little man stormed past Beathan and the ox.

It was a pitiably small storm.

Demosthenes stared dully at the departing Brother Matheny. Beathan stooped over to pick up the bag. He had a couple of inches height on me, though I outweighed his trim, athletic form. Thinning hair the color of an old battleship lay straight back, close to his scalp. His gaunt face was that of a dedicated Jesuit scientist—strong features; a calm, inquiring gaze; thin, tight lips.

He produced a hypo from his bag, filled it partially from an ampule. Clean fingernails tapped the syringe to loosen a stray bubble that he subsequently squeezed out.

"If that's how I'm getting the holy water," I said, "I don't want to stick around for Communion."

"You won't *be* around, Mr. Ammo." Beathan smiled wearily. "I'm afraid we'll have to . . . *sedate* you for transportation. Brother O'Rourke." He turned to the walking sequoia.

Demosthenes cracked his knuckles and reached for me.

They wanted me alive for some reason, so I felt I could risk my next move. Sitting down on the bed, I braced against the wall and kicked both feet into O'Rourke's crotch.

He huffed like a bull and backed off to raise his fists.

"Easy, Frank!" Beathan reached out to calm the big man.

The fists unclenched. "I forgive you," the rumbling voice said, "as even Jesus forgives you." He moved in again.

I kicked him harder.

In an effort to gain my attention, Beathan tapped me on the side of the head with a double fist. This time I saw stars.

Through a minor galaxy of multicolored lights and throbbing noise, I saw Demosthenes rolling on the floor clutching his groin. A needle approached my neck. Voices faded in and out and buzzed a million miles away.

"JesusJesusJesus damn him to hell . . . "

"Shut up and get him to Dissection."

"Make 'im *burn* Godalmighty it *hurts!*"

"Get *up!*"

Something eventually reached through the fluffy cloud of fuzzed sensation that enveloped me. I was dragged from the bed. Something stung in my neck again, and the constellations collapsed into black holes.

The universe vanished like God waking up.

God started dreaming again, and I awoke in a dark place. I wasn't sure I was completely awake, though. Something felt very wrong.

For starters, the floor rumbled and wiggled beneath me. The single light bulb hanging over me grew and shrank, pulsating opalescent colors. The ceiling squirmed like boiling pudding in slow motion. I tried to stand.

And watched my feet melt into the floor.

At first, I thought I'd slipped and fallen. When I grabbed for a nearby table and watched it twist away from me, I knew something wasn't straight, and it was I.

Blotchy hands, horribly withered, hung from my wrists. Beneath the hospital robe my body swelled and contracted. So did everything else. The whole room behaved as if it were hideously alive.

What Beathan had said about set, setting, and dosage suddenly came back to me in a thousand tiny voices. Something black and red flickered the word *stoned*. I knew it then and there. And the most frightening realization was that there was nothing I could do about it. I had to ride it wherever it would take me.

Somewhere deep back in what was left of my mind, I guessed that they'd drugged me to imprint something on my consciousness. Psychedelics—such as the one currently making me see the skeleton under my skin—have the effect of opening the mind to suggestion. The thought slithered through my mind and vanished the instant I laid my hand on the table. And put my fingers into someone's liver.

The cold, hard liver nestled in the middle of a corpse. Its skin had been folded away in sheets of yellow-gray to reveal its cold, hard organs.

The trouble was, the body squirmed around on the table, looking at me with frosted eyes. A tongueless mouth lectured me from beneath gauze wrapping.

"It is logically impossible to find God," the corpse said. Its liver turned into a bloated, bloody worm that ate into its lungs. "The object of the search is the searcher forever beyond your grasp. He is that and that is you."

"Shut up," I said, flowers parachuting out of my mouth. My skeleton turned into Malto Meal, and I slid once more to the soft marble.

All the other tables crowded in on me. I was surrounded by death and the smell of science. The tables shrieked back in a blaze of scintillating yellow. My tongue burned just watching the smells.

I stood again to walk like a fly across an inverted floor. My feet puddled and dropped bits of electric-blue shadow behind them.

I could see in both directions at once. All around me lay the gutted remains of medical cadavers. They'd all endured a good deal of use over the years.

That didn't bother me. My concern was that some of them writhed. Some groaned and gurgled. One was tap dancing.

An idea dripped acid green. *They're trying to scare the shit out of me. That's the reason for the cadavers.*

"Profound conclusion," said a face that pushed itself up from my wrist. "But why?"

"God is why!" mimicked a truncated torso, giving off an angry taste of violet.

"God is wry!" blinked a skinless hand.

"God is rye rot, right?"

This was getting unruly. The deceptive part of it was that my mind seemed to be alert. It wasn't like being drunk. Yet I saw these *things*.

A door pulsated like a heart at the end of a row of carts. Rubbery feet carried me through a sluggish stream of pink noise. Gnarled hands pushed the tables aside. I approached a massive blockade.

The door had a thousand locks on it, all covered with spikes. They smelled black all over. I stared for hours at them in an instant. Not knowing what else to do, I heaved my body against the barricade.

My skin broke open and splattered against the door. Locks and spikes dissolved into pools of noisy, noisome vomit. The stinking, vibrating mass flowed up the walls and away to reveal an open door and blinding bright hallway.

The hallway became a hole stretching down into white oblivion. I gripped fervently at the doorjamb. My fingers crumbled and split. Crickets and silverfish crawled out of the joints to jump and crawl over my arms.

I wasn't making much progress.

I let go and slid down the hole in a scream of lilac and ammonia. I shrieked all the way until I hit bottom. Panic bars reached out to pound me in the gut. A clear, white light surrounded me. It burnt my flesh, dazzled my eyes. Flakes of skin sloughed off like snow. Everything roared.

"Too loud!" I screamed. *"Too loud!"*

A hundred black and scarlet hands gesticulated in the sunlight, casting their own twisted shadows. Snake-tongued fingers pointed the way.

I looked in their direction. A lion crouched there, lurking in the distance. With a shattering growl it pounced and ran toward me. My feet sank into yielding pavement, holding me fast.

Soft brown paws burrowed up from the ground. They grasped my ankles. The lion raced nearer. As it did, its paws metamorphosed into hooves, its mane transformed into antlers.

A stag rushed at me, blood streaming silver and smokey in its path. In its eyes glowed fury and pain.

I stood my ground bravely—the paws and pavement that gripped my feet defied escape. Dust howled about me. The stag swerved at the last instant, pelting my body with gravel. Each rock cried out with indignity as it hit home.

"Get in!" The voice was an astonished, blurring rainbow. A white hand beckoned out to me.

I crawled my focus along the arm until I reached a face. Ann Perrine gazed at me, as clear as unaltered reality.

My hands groped for the smooth metal siding of the car that filled my vision. Suddenly I hung from it, dangling over an infinite, empty space. I screamed.

"Quiet!" a voice hissed. "They'll hear you!"

Time flowed below me like a sewer. I tried to convince my rational, panicky mind that none of this was happening. It didn't do much good. I pulled myself up to her, never letting my million eyes lose sight of her. I clung. I inched.

I was inside.

"You're safe."

I tasted her words—they felt good.

"It's me," she said. "Ann. What've they done to you?"

My voice rebounded with irritating volume. "I've got more dope in my veins than half of Woodstock Nation." That was all I could get past the clog of mealworms in my mouth. I stared down at my hands. The skin was blotched red and blue. The muscles palpitated erratically.

"You're safe," she repeated. Her arms reached out to hold me.

All I saw were scorpion claws, sickles, razor-edged boomerangs. I pushed her away.

"No," my voice fuzzed from somewhere. "Fear imprint." My mumbling sounded like waves of mush.

She stomped the pedal to squeal us out of the driveway and away. That didn't sit too well with my current condition. The acceleration pushed me through the seat cushion until only a black, hazy smear of Dell Ammo remained.

6
UNBELIEVERS

The ride was as much of a nightmare as the dissecting room. Shapes jumped from corners, colors rammed against screaming odors. I tried balling myself up as much as I could and only succeeded in curling smaller and smaller like Igli until I disappeared and returned to the passenger seat.

By the time we reached her home, I had almost completely recovered. I shivered and yanked myself together. An arm here, a leg there. One last squid stuck a tentacle at us from the bushes around her driveway as we pulled in to park. The fear still sat with me.

"It was just a bad trip, Dell. The things you're scared of don't exist."

I pulled over to the far side of the car, leaned up against the door. "They do, though. They're in my mind. Waiting like some punk around a corner. Waiting to strike no matter what I believe."

She unlatched the door and got me out of the car. I noticed that it was a Porsche 964. Not bad.

I stood and took a step up the brick path. I walked well

enough. What made me unsteady was the urge to flinch at every wavering shadow, at every flitting insect and bird. The breeze blowing up the back of my hospital smock didn't help much, either.

"Those people programmed the fears in, and you can reprogram them right out just as easily. That's what psychotomimetic drugs are for. Programming and metaprogramming. Better than hypnosis."

She used some pretty long words for an accountant. My suspicions weren't exactly lying quiescent. . . .

The house was no mansion. It sat up on a hill overlooking Silver Lake, one of many. The construction looked mid-twenties, maybe early thirties. She kept it in good repair. Two stories, white paint. A garden ran from the driveway to the front door, split by a brick walk.

She offered me her arm. I accepted it for reasons perhaps ulterior. She looked beautiful despite the rough treatment she had obviously received.

"Where'd you rent the car?" My mind had regained enough of its fortitude to wonder how the hell Ann had escaped her kidnappers.

"It's registered to a Reverend Morris Beathan."

I grinned even though my legs were feeling like unvulcanized rubber.

"What did they do to you?"

"More or less what they did to you." She fumbled about in her purse for the house keys. "They took me to the monastery and grilled me about you, about the contract, about Emil Zacharias, the TV evangelist. They thought locking me in a stuffy confessional for hours would make me crack. I pretended to and gave them a bunch of creative nonsense to keep them paranoid."

"Uh . . . such as?"

She pulled out a key ring made of silver and turquoise and unlocked the door. "I told them that we were making a horror film. The rumors were designed to build interest in the movie."

I frowned. "They bought that?"

"No. That was when they took me out, shot me up with junk, and locked me in the rectory with a little guy for a guard. I guess that's all they figured I'd need." She rattled the key loose and pushed the door open. "When I was done with him, he couldn't have broken his celibacy vows if he'd tried."

"The drugs seem to have worn off faster for you than they have for me." I stepped inside and watched my head spin.

"Are you kidding?" she asked. "I'm sailing the stratosphere!" In the subdued light of the hallway, I saw that her pupils were the size of dimes.

"Less than a novelty to you, I presume?"

She grinned giddily. "When I was a young, sweet, impressionable child of sixteen I consumed a greater variety of drugs than most people are comfortable pronouncing. I was always the only person in my group who could drive wasted." She closed the door and set the deadbolt. "When they started the injections, I was sort of grateful for the free vacation. They didn't expect me to be able to function."

"Why weren't you so resourceful when they first grabbed you at the bar?"

She shrugged. "They had the drop on me with guns. They didn't seem to care whether they killed me or not. So I went along."

My drug-sensitized nose immediately bore an assault by a riot of scents. It smelled as if we were in a flower garden in spring. I felt safe, reassured, cozy.

"What is that smell?"

"Just some flowers and stuff. Come on."

She led me through a hallway done up with the sort of knickknacks a woman accumulates. She sat me in the living room on a high-backed wing chair. The place had a few bookshelves with a fair amount of books. That's the way I gauge people, I suppose. The fewer the books, the stupider and duller the person.

She wasn't dull. Her actions revealed that much.

"Anyway," she continued, clanking around in the kitchen,

"I snuck out of a window and into the courtyard and hot-wired the first car I could get to."

"You have good taste in cars."

"I was on my way to call the police when I saw you."

"Forget the cops—they're just priests with guns."

I heard her laugh lightly. In a moment she appeared with a cup of coffee.

"Black?" she asked.

"Black." I took the cup and let the hot liquid warm my insides.

"Feeling better?"

"Yeah." I stretched and slid back in the chair. "I saw a whole lot of bad things back there. In my mind. I've seen worse in real life. I'll get over it." I let out a breath, took another sip of brew. My hair may have been getting younger, but I wasn't. I felt old and rattled.

Ann went back into the kitchen and reappeared with her own cup. She pulled up a chair next to mine and sat. A shaft of morning sunlight hit the lower part of her dress, shot-gunning silver and gold pinpoints around the room. Her hair hung in straggles caused by drying sweat. She'd been through a lot and came out looking like an angel slumming it among mortals.

I felt a few degrees less than mortal. The house was too cheerful to reflect the way I felt.

"They mean business, Dell."

"If they meant business, babe, we'd be under the church-yard by now." I finished the cup and set it aside. "Here I thought I'd just draw some pay for a few weeks from a flush eccentric. Next thing I know, someone's taking it seriously!"

"You took it seriously enough to accept the offer."

"If God is worried about me, why doesn't He just hit me with a bolt of lightning?"

"They say he works in mysterious ways. Maybe he's softening you up first." She grinned. Her eyes were mostly pupil. I understood why women used to put belladonna drops in their eyes. She looked achingly beautiful.

"Or maybe," she suggested, "the reactions to you are taking place through a network of consciousness."

What she said didn't make much sense, but I was still stoned enough that her words carried a profound impact. I sensed that something important was trying to get through. I answered with appropriate awe.

"Huh?"

She leaned forward, suddenly emphatic.

"People such as those monks are acting on feelings that don't come from within them. They're operating on emotions impinging on them from *outside*—from a worldwide reaction to our activities."

It was as if she'd stuck another hypo of junk into me. I felt a swelling tide of alarm flow over me. This was *true*. I was really supposed to assassinate God! And there were forces out to stop me.

And then I realized what was happening.

"What're you up to, Blondie? You're laying a program on me as thick as the one Beathan tried."

She stared with those black saucers for a moment, then said, "Everything will seem more important right now. Don't pay any attention to it. We've got work to do."

"What do you mean 'we,' girlfriend?"

She stood to lean over me. "Do you think that after what happened to me I don't have a grudge?" She looked as though she'd volunteer to pull the trigger on Number One all by herself. "This sort of thing has gone on long enough. It's all gone on too long."

"I work alone."

"Have it your way. The offer's there. What's that on your fingers?"

I didn't want to know. I raised my hand and saw gray gunk under a few nails. Memories flashed back. My stomach tried to beat the high jump record. I pressed up under my solar plexus to lift my diaphragm off the lurching organ. The sick feeling passed.

It was a technique I used a lot in my occupation.

A corner of my light blue hospital robe served to wipe the

particles of dead flesh from beneath my fingernails. "Left-overs," I muttered.

She wasn't distracted. "I can help you on this. I *want* to help you. I know someone who can straighten you out on a few things about what god is."

I relented. "Do I have time to put on something less drafty?"

She showered and changed her outfit to a skintight peacock-blue Danskin top and a ruffled turquoise dress. After taking my measurements in a giggly stoned manner, she hopped into the stolen Porsche to head for Hollywood. She was gone until well after noon.

I took the opportunity during her absence to look around. After all, even if she hadn't actually told me to make myself at home, I was certain that such was her intent.

A quick glance through the medicine cabinet revealed nothing but the usual assortment of feminine colorants and perfumes. No medicine. Healthy sort.

One room contained an odd collection of metal and crystal sculptures. Copper and onyx and silver and amethyst glittered under the light from a ceiling lamp. The curtains were drawn. Bronze and quartz and gold and peridot scattered colors about.

Her bedroom barely enclosed a king-sized bed decorated with an Egyptian motif. Lots of silk-screened papyrus leaves and scarabs. Stylized cobras. Very sexy.

I cut my tour short since I didn't know how long she would be out. I spent the next hour waiting for her, looking through her library. Real books, not plaques. Only a few of them were fiction. A good number concerned religions around the world and in antiquity. She owned books on history, mathematics, physics. The usual computer manuals were stuck here and there. All in all, a good balance.

Ann returned a few minutes after I'd settled onto the living-room couch. She tossed a navy blue pinstripe business suit my way.

I held it up. A lovely wool blend, not like the reflective stuff I usually wore to merge with the crowd. It fit in with the current style—wide lapels and shoulders, baggy pants with cuffs. Nostalgia for a time even I didn't remember.

A light yellow oxford cloth shirt and a navy-hued silk tie with nearly invisible maroon polka dots completed the outfit.

"Tasteful," I said, draping the wardrobe over my arm.

"Don't forget these." She pulled a pair of black wingtips out of a box and handed them to me along with a pair of black socks.

"Over the calf," I said with appreciation. "You know all the tricks of the trade."

She smiled. "You didn't strike me as the baggy-socks type. And I'm the one with the garters." She pointed to the already-familiar bathroom. "Would you like a shower?"

"I suppose I should, if we're calling on the country's top atheist."

Theodore Golding lived in Hollywood near his Philosophical Forum on the Foundations of Theology. The Forum was located on Larchmont, right next to Thucydides, a bookstore that he also owned. He must have had money to situate his esoteric businesses near the Wilshire Country Club. I was determined not to be impressed.

Ann pulled the Porsche up to a modest house on the four hundred block of Van Ness.

"That's Golding's home. Feel well enough to go in?"

With a shower and a new set of threads, I was more than ready for anything. "Bring him on. I think I can survive the experience."

"He can help you understand god better than any preacher or shaman."

"Certainly better than Father Beathan could."

She smiled. "Well, don't be too sure about *that*."

Golding answered the door himself. For a man my age, he had all the exuberance of a teenager in heat.

"You must be Ann Perrine," he said, snapping his fingers and pointing at Blondie. The finger shifted to me. "Because *you* don't look as if you'd sound as sexy on the phone."

Deep blue eyes gazed sharply from beneath jet-framed glasses. The frames matched his longish hair. Dressed in a bright red silk kimono, he stood a few inches taller and about fifty pounds lighter than I did. His voice had the vague musical quality of impish good humor. I suppose he needed it in his business.

If a man could live in a library, he might live as Golding did. Bookshelves lined every available square foot of wall space. Locked glass cases thrust out to serve as room dividers. What framed artwork he owned hung perilously here and there in front of the shelves. To top it off, in the center of it all stood a computer table sporting a library console.

Golding glided between the cases and around stacks of books until he reached a break in the mess that I arbitrarily declared the living room.

He cleared off a heap of plaques from each of three folding chairs. "I presume that this is your friend with the theological crisis?" He extended his hand as an afterthought.

I shook it. "Dell Ammo."

His grip was firm, pleasant.

"Good name," he said. "Spanish?"

"Just American."

He sat, folded his hands over his slim torso, and smiled. "Ms. Perrine tells me that you're experiencing problems of a religious nature."

I rubbed the bruise on the back of my skull and nodded. "You might say that."

"I must admit that I sometimes feel like a priest, the way that people come to me with problems of faith. Except, of course, that I try to steer the doubters *away* from God."

"I, uh, don't exactly have a crisis of *faith*, actually." I tried to phrase things so that I didn't come off sounding like the consummate buffoon. "I simply would like to know which definitions of God are false—"

"They all are."

"Yes," I said hastily. "But why?"

"Because God doesn't exist. It's just a concept that people have an uncommon affection for."

"It's fine to assert that, but lots of people—lots of intelligent, sane people—believe in God. What sort of proof can you provide that God doesn't exist?"

He grinned and took a deep, satisfied breath. I had the uncomfortable feeling of talking myself right where he wanted me to.

"You can't demand proof of the nonexistence of something. It's logically impossible. The burden of proof is on those who assert that God exists."

"Why?"

"For the same reason that—up until a few years ago—an accused man didn't have to prove his innocence in court. Suppose you told me that there had been a murder. You demand that I prove I didn't do it. I ask you who was killed—how, when, where. You refuse to tell me and repeat that I must prove I didn't do it. How can I logically prove the nonexistence of something for which there is no evidence? The burden of proof must always be on the prosecution—on the one who asserts that something exists, whether it be a crime or a god. Only when I'm confronted with evidence purporting to prove that God exists can I do anything. Then it would involve demonstrating that the evidence is in error."

"Which," I said, "wouldn't prove the nonexistence of God, only the inadequacy of the evidence."

"Exactly." Golding peered at me. "Have you a philosophical background?"

"No. I've given extensive consideration, though, to what constitutes proof in, um—judicial situations."

"So why the interest in God?"

"My client wishes to lodge a complaint about the Big Bang." I wanted some sort of an answer from him. "Maybe you can begin by giving me a few definitions—"

"No," he said. "*You* begin. You define God."

"I can't."

"Come now." He used both his hands to brush back his

hair. "Any God will do. Greek, Christian, Moslem, Hindu, Hebrew, African. . . ."

"The only thing I've found," I began, stuffing my hands in my pockets and leaning back in the chair, "that is common to all the accounts I've read is that God is unknowable to varying degrees. That makes my search a bit difficult."

He peaked his fingers together like Basil Rathbone contemplating a crime. "Epistemological transcendence. Yes. Claiming to know that something cannot be known, ever. Claiming to possess the omniscience to know that something will never be known. Contradiction and conceit—the traits of a successful theologian. In my book, anyone stating that God is incomprehensible is merely confessing the specious nature of his own arguments."

Footsteps approached from the bedroom before I could respond, saving me from having to think of a snappy rejoinder.

A short, slender woman appeared, wrapped only in a large burgundy-hued bath towel. She gave Ann and me a quick glance with large, dark eyes. Her throat made pardon-me noises.

"Ted?" she said in a gentle voice.

"Raissa! Come in and meet Ann and Dell."

She entered the room with a fluid motion of her bare legs. From the silver-streaked raven hair that hung down to the nape of her neck, I guessed her to be somewhere in her early forties. That body told some fine lies, though. Her arms, legs, face, and hands displayed enough youth in them to say what needed to be said about the parts of her hidden beneath the towel.

Raissa smiled warmly at the two of us and maneuvered her way past to reach the study. A word processor whirred and clacked into life. Soft tapping of fingers against keys drifted into the living room.

Golding smiled.

"The greatest joy in my life and my highest value." From where he sat, he had a vantage on the study that we didn't.

He watched her for a moment. "She gives great perceptual reaffirmation of my self-concept."

He shifted his attention back to me. "*God* is one of those words that has been bandied about into the realm of the meaningless. You can't define *god* any more than you can define *love* or *freedom*. Everyone has his own definition, right or wrong. With so many different interpretations of a term, the intellectual noise generated turns the words into nothing more than floating abstractions—words meant to conjure up an emotional image that's not concrete or identifiable." He stopped to smile at Ann and wink. "How'm I doing?"

"The gods that existed before the advent of Judeo-Christianity were far more concrete," she said.

"Yes," he agreed. "And they were denounced by later theologians for being *too* concrete, *too* easy to conceptualize. Who needed to pay a priest to communicate with such deities when an idol in the living room was sufficient to invoke the spirit?" He looked over into the study. "Raissa! Make us some coffee!"

"Fuck off, love—I'm on a hot streak." The word processor buzzed and clattered.

Golding smiled. I wondered whether the man ever frowned. I sniffed the air to check for the aroma of burning hemp.

"I guess I'll make the coffee." Golding went to the kitchen, sidestepping books and plaques all the way. He spoke over his shoulder.

"As with any type of fiction, Dell, suspension of disbelief is an absolute necessity in religion. Faith is the tool used to undermine reason and circumvent proof. Faith supposedly operates where reason is deficient. *Shit!*"

A coffee cup clattered to the floor. He stopped to pick it up. "Religion, like politics, cannot be defended as rational."

Ann smiled gently. "You put in a qualifier back there, Mr. Golding. About the older gods."

"Yes I did, Ann. And I'm about to get to that."

I stretched my feet out and sighed. I wasn't getting anything that I figured would be of use. I stood and walked into the kitchen, pulling a cigarette from the pack in my coat pocket. I had to ask him the question. Directly.

"Look, Golding." I lit up the coffin nail. "I just want to know one thing." I paused for dramatic effect and took a deep drag. "Whether He exists or not, a lot of people act as if He does. With that in mind, how can I kill God?"

The canister of coffee slipped from Golding's hands to thud against the parquet linoleum, spilling its grounds like jewels from a chest. I had finally succeeded in getting him to frown.

It was actually more of a scowl.

"How, precisely, do you plan to kill God? Poison? Drowning? High explosives? Magic?"

"That's what Ann thought you could help me with. I—"

Anger gathered in his gaze like a burning L.A. smog. "Kill something that doesn't exist? Kill a mere idea floating around in people's minds? I'm sorry if I seem insulted by your intrusion here. I don't have much time for cranks. You may have the coffee I promised you, then I'd like you to leave."

"Dell is serious," Ann said. "I thought that your experience—"

"That's rather the point," he snapped. "My experience. I've been fighting a battle against antihuman, antirational, antijoy brutes for thirty years. The most I can show for it is a few thousand people who now aren't afraid to question their early conditioning. That's good, and I've made a living at it. Around the world, however, murder and plunder still thrive in the name of God. Look at what Ireland is doing to Ulster and vice versa. Look at what Israel and PanArabia are doing to one another. Look at the Church that gathers and hoards gold and art treasures while its adherents starve, that smugly states that 'the poor are with us always' without admitting that there's such a thing as *less* poor and *less*—" He looked at Ann for a moment. The muscles in his face relaxed, though what remained was less anger than weariness.

"Do you think that, because I'm an atheist, I don't take

God seriously? Do you think that a doctor doesn't take cancer seriously, simply because he thinks it has no place in human life?"

"Cancer exists," I said. "A doctor can find it. He can cut it away. He doesn't play word games to deny its existence."

Golding paused for a moment to consider my non sequitur. He smiled once more. Almost impishly.

"Many cancers are created by the mental attitudes of the victim. So it is with God." He tapped at the side of the coffee pot with fingernails immaculately maintained. "You want to know where the current God came from? The Judeo-Christian God evolved as a *construct*—as a political effort to accumulate church power and crush the followers of older, established religions by making the new God more powerful, more intrusive, more petulant, and more irrational than any previous god or goddess. The Levite priests of Israel brazenly copied religious concepts of the Aryans, the Sumerians, and dozens of other Indo-European races. The theft from the Romans and the Greeks was even more obvious—they just changed the names a bit. Jove became Je-ho-vah, Zeus became Ya-Zeus, the goddesses Ma and Rhea became Ma-ria."

That was too much. "Are you saying that the Jews adopted the religion of their enemies?"

"Can you think of a better way to co-opt your foes? Can you think of a better way to attract possible converts than to use their own symbols? How do you think the Christians co-opted the Jews and the pagans? Certainly not by offering a totally different religion to usurp its predecessors. They incorporated the old religions almost whole cloth while simultaneously stripping the symbols of their former meaning. The Babylonians still worship Ishtar? Substitute worship of the Virgin Mary. Egyptians believe that Osiris rose from the dead? Have Ya-Zeus do the same."

Golding seemed to be warming up again. He began to spit out snippets of historicity as if they were theological watermelon seeds. The outcome was about as intellectually tidy.

"Mount Sinai stood for centuries as a mountain holy to

the moon god Sinn, long before Moses went there to speak to Yahveh. And this new god's burning bush was nothing more than a psychedelic substance called loranthus growing on acacia—a bush sacred to the Sun." He prattled on while getting the cups and saucers. "The story of Christ is a slipshod retelling of the Mithras and Osiris legends grafted to the clumsy attempt of an aggressive rabbi to be crowned King of Israel.

"They made this composite God of theirs an incomprehensible mishmash of conflicting traits. He was as rational as Apollo and as murderous as Typhon. The priests kept everyone on His good side—for a price. The same group—the same philosophical movement that devised and later refined the Judeo-Christian God—outlawed the older religions and slandered the Old Gods as devils and demons."

Golding made motions as if he were coming to an important point. I had long before lost interest and was more mesmerized by the coffeepot in his hand. It floated and dipped with his every gesture. The dark brew inside sloshed and swirled, never quite reaching the rim. My vision of having a hot cup of java in the near future dimmed considerably.

"They reserved their greatest hate for witchcraft, though. They rightly recognized it as a primitive form of science, not merely a rival faith. Science—in any form—is anathema to faith. How much more skeptical is the one who experiments with herbs or symbols or rituals to pick what works best compared to the one who places absolute trust in a priest or rabbi or imam?"

"I suppose you could ask Uri Geller."

He wasn't about to be sidetracked. The coffeepot sloshed precariously with every jab of emphasis he made at me. "Why do you think chemists, astronomers, and mathematicians were branded as warlocks and sorcerers during the Dark Ages? Why were Galileo's discoveries slandered as the Devil's work? He and others were using the scientific method of observation, theorization, and experimentation that paralleled that of ancient forms of witchcraft!"

"Are you defending witchcraft, Mr. Golding?"

He looked at Ann as if she'd just stepped on his eyeglasses. Her question disconcerted him so much that he actually poured a cup of the coffee and handed it to her.

"No," he said. "Of course I'm not." He pointed to some jars on the counter. "Creamer and aspartame over there."

I raised an eyebrow. Aspartame had been banned shortly after the discovery that its use resulted in increased intelligence.

I took the cup he offered. It was lukewarm. One of the pitfalls of philosophy, I suppose.

Golding sounded almost defensive. "I'm merely saying that—historically—it's been downhill all the way, religion-wise. Besides, witchcraft per se is a craft, not a religion. It's a primitive form of science conducted by members of a religion. In much the way Lysenkoism was a crude science conducted by members of the Marxist faith."

Ann lowered her cup to say softly, "Lysenko didn't follow the scientific method. Witches do."

Golding raised an ebon-and-gray eyebrow in her direction. "Yes. And unlike Judeo-Christianity or Marxism, the Old Religions had quite understandable deities. Gods and goddesses who didn't take as great a delight in slaughtering their creations. Even as scandalous a god as Zeus was outmatched by the murdering war god of the Old Testament or the nearly identical Allah or the manic-depressive masochist of the New Testament. The old ones didn't issue as many commandments and contradictory orders.

"But, of course, I'd rather not have anything to do with them at all. Which is why I'm an atheist, not a Druid or something. All right?"

Ann nodded. She seemed vaguely troubled by his speech, though she hid it behind her cup of coffee.

I yawned. "I am serious," I said, "about killing God."

"Oh, sure."

"Look at me, Golding."

He lowered his gaze to stare down on me. The kimono

would have seemed ludicrous if it had been on anyone this side of Christopher Lee. It gave him an air of imperious superiority.

"Do I look like a kidder, Golding?"

"You look like a hood."

Ann opened her mouth to protest. A motion of his hand silenced her.

"An educated hood, perhaps, but a hood nonetheless. You are a man who thinks he can change things through violence, even if it's the civilized violence of mockery. It's ideas that change the world, Mr. Ammo—not force or ridicule."

"So you can't help me." I swirled the remaining coffee around in my cup.

"Help you to do what? Actually kill God? The idea is absurd! Changing the way people think is the only way to improve the world."

I stared into my cup. Perhaps improving the world was not my client's intention. I knew that achieving a promised immortality was mine. I doubted that the drive to better the human condition had much bearing on the contract.

"I know I'm on the right track," I said. "People would just brush me off otherwise." I gazed up at him to add, "People have been trying to stop me."

"Then I wish you luck. The only good God is a dead God."

From the study drifted warm laughter. Raissa said, "Remember Spencer on freedom, Ted?"

Golding smiled sardonically. "Yeah. Remember this, Dell—no god is dead so long as one person has faith. You'd have to convince *everyone* that God doesn't exist. That's the enormity of your mission."

"Enormousness," Raissa corrected, entering to pour some java in her unwashed cup.

Golding laughed. "The usage would be correct from the theist's point of view. Few people can countenance their gods getting snuffed."

I slugged down the rest of the tepid jo and set the cup on

the Formica countertop. An odd chill came over me that I attributed to the carbon-remover I'd just swallowed. When I chanced to glance up past Golding, my spine took a trip to the Antarctic.

Blood dripped slowly down the wall.

It began at the ceiling and spread down and across the eggshell-toned paint. It flowed fanlike down the wall, glistening wet. Something throbbed in my head with a sick rushing sound.

"What's the deal, Golding?"

"Hm?" He stared at me as if I'd had a stroke. He turned to follow my gaze, swallowed a mouthful of coffee with calm ease, and shrugged. "That? I'm afraid the upstairs bathroom leaks. I haven't gotten around to—"

"A tub that leaks blood?" My hand edged toward my empty waistband holster.

"Blood?" Raissa looked up, mystified. "That's a water stain."

No one said a word for a long moment. I looked at the wall again. A semicircular rust stain discolored the paint. It didn't move. It looked dry. Like an ordinary water stain.

Ann gasped in shock. The cup fell from her fingers to shatter loudly against the linoleum. Coffee splashed against her ankles, dripping down to her shoes.

"It was blood!" she cried. "In my cup!" She rushed to my side and held on, suddenly terrified. Perhaps Father Beathan's fear imprinting had had some effect after all.

"It looks disturbingly like coffee," Raissa said, deadpan.

Ann trembled like a moth inside a fist. "Blood. It was. Red and salty. Thick. Clotted."

Golding cleared his throat. "I think you'd better take her home."

I didn't feel so grand either. "Yeah" was all I could muster. I guided her out the front door to the car.

They must have thought we were insane. The idea had crossed my mind, too.

"I saw blood, Dell."

"So did I, sweetheart."

"They didn't."

I nodded and put her in the passenger's seat. Her hands shook when she gave me the keys.

"Drive over to Hollywood Boulevard. Quick."

I climbed in and tried to start the engine. It growled without catching.

The same cold feeling that I'd had in Golding's home overcame me again. I felt a tremble of fear—real fear—begin to grow.

Around the edges of the instrument panel welled droplets of red ichor. They grew and linked together to run down the sides of the dashboard.

The same thick, warm fluid pulsed out of the ignition switch, soaking my fingers.

Ann pushed away from the panel. Her hands wildly sought the door handle.

"He's on to us," she murmured. "Get awa—"

She touched the handle and shrieked.

Blood was trickling down from the roof in rivulets and streaks across the sideglass.

"Get me out!"

I flung my door open, ignoring the sheet of red that splashed over me. Blood squirted from around the edges of the passenger door as I yanked it open. Her shuddering form collapsed into my blood-soaked arms.

"Get me out!" she cried. "Get me away!" She clamped her eyes shut.

In an instant, the carnelian stains vanished from our clothing. It didn't dry up or fade or anything. It just wasn't there anymore. The Porsche's interior sparkled like new.

"It's gone," I said, standing her up carefully.

"It'll be back," she said with grim certainty. Nervous hands wiped at her eyes. Her heels clacked loudly against the sidewalk.

I strode up alongside her. "Where are you going?"

"I've got to get to Hollywood Boulevard. There's a place there . . . " Her golden mane fluttered in the breeze that blew from the north. Her skirt rippled, clinging and sliding around her legs and thighs. Not a bad sight, had I been in a more receptive mood.

I looked back at the car. Shadows flitted around it like an outtake from *Fantasia*. I didn't go back to find out if they could drive.

I fell in stride with Ann. She took long, leggy steps with a panicky determination.

"What's on Hollywood? More gremlins?"

The walk calmed her a bit. She inhaled the afternoon air deeply. After a moment's thought, she said, "It's a sort of shop. It's been there for years. The woman who currently runs it is . . . sensitive to these things."

"Splendid," I said. "Now we're dragging in fortune tellers."

She stopped to stare at me as straight and as pointedly as a spear. "Maybe *you* can explain the blood. And why the others didn't see it."

I tried to think of causes, reasons, rational explanations. "The drugs?"

She frowned. "I'm not having a flashback, if that's what you're getting at." She smiled stiffly. "A friend of mine once told me that practically no one is so lucky as to get a free trip that way." She increased her stride with even greater intent.

The hair on my arms prickled. The icy feeling spread across my shoulders and up the back of my head.

Something was happening. The air grew rank and stale. More so than usual for Hollywood, that is.

Ann pointed to the side of a building on Melrose Boulevard. With a tone of hysterical triumph, she said, "See?"

I squinted. The vague outline of something—it looked like a moosehead with drooping antlers—shimmered almost invisibly on the south side of the building.

Blood flowed down the building, staining brick and glass, turning brown where it dried.

We weren't the only ones to notice it this time. Scores of cars squealed to a halt at the intersection. Not all of them did, though. The traffic jam was almost instantaneous.

Dozens of people climbed out of their cars, pointing and staring. One man gestured wildly at the building. The woman with him shook her head in confusion. He pointed again. She shrugged as if nothing were wrong with the building but *plenty* was wrong with *him*. He looked one last time, gave up, and drove into the snarl of confusion at Melrose and Van Ness.

"See that?" Ann asked again, pointing to the crowd. Some people stared in shock at the building. Others stared in amazement at the people craning their necks. "Some see it. Some don't."

"Can't be holograms," I offered weakly.

"Holograms don't feel slick. Or taste salty."

We walked past the crowd on the south side of the street, moving through a whirlwind of chatter.

I glanced up again. The building appeared normal. Yet that chill was still with me.

A hand seized my shoulder. I whipped about to grab it.

My fingers clamped air.

The crowd had dissipated, and no one but Ann stood within a yard of me.

Another something stroked the side of my face.

"They're touching you, too?" Ann asked. She snapped her right arm sharply as if to free her wrist.

"Ann—what is this? Ghosts in broad daylight?" A bunch of wet fingers dragged over my face like snails. Voices hissed in my ears.

Ann gritted her teeth and broke into a run.

I ignored the invisible tentacles that clutched at my hair and raced after her. She ran wildly, trying to escape the phantasmal hands. The effort was pointless. They kept pace with us, tapping and stroking and grabbing and tugging. Shadows darted about at the edge of my vision, always vanishing at the turn of my head.

My longer strides brought me to Ann's side in a few frenzied paces. The Hollywood Cemetery blurred by to our left. I half-expected the graves to pop open and expel dead actors, looking as pale and gray as their fading images trapped in silver.

Despite my jitters, nothing arose from the graveyard. The trouble lay ahead on Santa Monica Boulevard.

Ann screamed, stopping suddenly to clutch at me. At first I thought hers was another invisible hand and ignored it. She nearly pulled me to the concrete.

"Look, Dell!"

A runny red fluid gurgled up out of the storm drains and sewers, filling the street with blood. Once again, some cars stopped, others honked angrily and sped about. Wheels splashed blood in crimson sheets across pedestrians. Dozens of people stopped in midstride to scream. Or vomit. Or faint. Others noticed nothing but their fellow-travelers' strange behavior.

"It's not real!" I shouted to Ann and the crowds. "We *know* it! How come it's still there?"

Ann looked as if she'd been worked over by a cop. She still flinched at the hands running over her, but she ignored them as much as she could, same as I.

She took shallow, long breaths to control her panic. "We're getting psychic impressions from an outside source. It'll affect us regardless of what we believe. Let's *go!*"

The light changed. She delicately lowered a petite foot into the flowing ichorous river. A couple of cars tried to run the light while swerving around the petrified rubberneckers. They skidded to a halt, splashing gore in all directions. Ann nodded at them and crossed.

I followed. Though our crossing produced a queasy sloshing sound, it didn't *feel* as if we were fighting a torrential stream. Even the slap of the blood against my ankles—a warm and sticky sensation—didn't feel like wetness.

We managed to make it across Santa Monica without serious consequences. The clamor of terrified pedestrians and motorists made the streets sound like an insane Shriners' convention. The air was drenched with the smell of blood, like a low, dank fog.

When we stepped out of the stream, blood stained our legs all the way up to midcalf. I felt as if we'd taken a stroll through a slaughterhouse.

I can't say when, but the stains vanished a few seconds after we were out. I looked down and they were gone.

So was the river.

My mind felt weak and dull. I was watching my nice, solid, normal world fragmenting about me.

"We're at the center of it, that's fairly certain." Ann removed her shoes when we reached Fernwood. She ran faster without them.

We got halfway past the Channel 11 building when she doubled over and stopped, one hand against the paint-scrawled wall. She looked like someone who'd been kicked in the guts.

"What's wrong?"

"Cramps." She clenched her teeth. "Worst I've ever had."

"From the running?" I reached out to support her.

She only groaned and bent further over.

Picking her up before she tumbled to the sidewalk, I held her to me as best I could. I'd handled drunks and saps and stiffs in my time but never a sick dame. I wasn't too sure what to do.

"Get to Hollywood," she murmured. "Let's get—" She spasmed in agony.

I lifted her up to carry in my arms. She clung to my neck gratefully. Her legs bounced up and down with each step I took.

We crossed Sunset that way. I doglegged over to Bronson and headed up toward Hollywood Boulevard. That same chill ran up and down my flesh. Ann shuddered.

The hazy L.A. sky dimmed. Dark clouds billowed up overhead, the color of clots and scabs.

Ann's jaw clamped her teeth together with grinding pressure. The pain pulled her into a fetal position. "Dell," she whimpered.

A gash tore across the cloud bank. My skin felt cold and clammy against my clothes as I watched. Ruby droplets fell in bands and sheets like a monochrome borealis. They seemed to drift slowly toward the ground.

I stopped to gape, hypnotized.

With sudden intensity, the blood hit the sidewalk and streets. Thick slapping sounds like spilling porridge drowned out the roar of cars and commerce.

All around us a vermilion haze hung like a curtain. Clothes stuck to skin. Ann's long blond hair fell in fat, dripping ropes to pull her head backward. I draped a handful over my arm. Brakes squealed somewhere in the bloody rain. Metal screamed. Glass shattered.

People cried out.

I ran toward an apartment complex on the left. Heavily overgrown with tropical plants in the finest Southern California tradition, it beckoned with the promise of protection from the storm. I splashed toward the courtyard.

It was as if we'd entered another climate. One with sane weather.

The ground was dry. Overhead, blue sky—as blue as it can get in L.A.—spread from horizon to zenith. The street was dry and clear. Only the people acted strangely. They covered their heads, huddled in doorways, looked fearfully at the sky.

They still saw it. Some of them. Once again the illusion seemed to affect only a portion of the population.

I lowered Ann to the driveway and took a step out onto Bronson. In the space of that step I left clear skies and dryness for buckets of blood drenching the earth from heavy black clouds.

I was soaked to the bone. I took one step back. The day returned to normal L.A. autumn.

Ann stood slowly. "My cramps are gone." She fussed with her hair. Perspiration dampened it a bit, but it flowed golden and free as though never touched by the blood outside.

She ventured a step past the property line, grabbed at her waist, and stumbled backwards to safety.

"It's like the corpse grinders out there, yet we're fine here."

I nodded and searched for a cigarette. "They could jack up the rents for that reason alone."

The apartment building possessed its own charm aside from the mysterious protection it offered. Christmas lights hung between the two parallel apartment blocks, imparting a festive mood to the surroundings. It sure looked more cheerful than Old Downtown.

"It's only two blocks to Hollywood," I said. "If we just concentrate on the fact that it's all imaginary, I think we'll make it easily."

Ann looked at me as if I'd asked her to jog up Everest. "Do you know what those cramps felt like?"

I shrugged. "I've been fondled with brass knuckles in the same locale a couple of times." I stepped out onto the sidewalk. "Besides, the rain's gone away. Come on."

Sirens whined somewhere east on Sunset.

She reluctantly followed me, keeping so close to my side that I could smell her perfume as well as when I was carrying her. The mysterious showers of blood had done nothing to wash it away.

We passed a small clump of tenement buildings on Carlton and reached Hollywood Boulevard in a few minutes. Traffic flowed at its normal slow pace. Old hulks and long sleek limos mixed together in automotive democracy. Too late in the day for bums to be sleeping on the sidewalks, yet still too early for most of the hookers, the street boasted a blend of tourists, business people, and shoppers.

Some still watched the sky, shrugging their shoulders and trying to explain what they'd seen to those who hadn't had the pleasure. We passed by a young couple trying to comfort an old woman who sat on the sidewalk tugging at her rosary.

"*Sanguinis Virgine*," she muttered over and over. Blood of the Virgin.

It was as reasonable an explanation as any.

"Another block," Ann said, walking carefully to avoid stepping barefoot into any of the trash and crud lining the Street of Dreams. We headed east until she nodded to her right.

"In there."

The building was a modest storefront, not connected to any of the other buildings by shared walls. On the plate glass—in large, ornate script—was the name

Trismegistos

and in smaller, less flowery letters,

CANDLES
INCENSE
OILS
SPELLS
AND OTHER
TOOLS

"Oh, no." I grimaced.

"It's all right, Dell. I know the woman who runs the place."

"How?"

She stopped, halfway opening the door, to put her shoes back on.

"Well, if you must know, Bautista Corporation owns the building. I drew up the lease." She went inside.

A bell tinkled merrily to summon a pretty young woman from the back room. She wore a full-length violet peasant dress of a style that might have been popular a generation ago. Black hair trailed down her back in one thick, intricate braid. She smiled at Ann.

Ann smiled back and sashayed over to her. They spoke quietly.

Since I wasn't invited in on the tête-à-tête, I took the opportunity to nose around.

The store didn't look spooky or witchy. Three aisles of glass display cases sat under two banks of fluorescent lights. They, and the shelves along three walls, composed the entire shopping area.

Candles and vials of colored stuff constituted the majority of the sale goods. The contents were typed on Avery labels. No pretense of the supernatural tainted the place. It was as straightforward and businesslike as a corner pharmacy. More so. It lacked the garish display ads that promised miraculous cures.

One case contained an assortment of knives labeled ATHAMES. They were the only really witchy items in the store. Some of the daggers were plain, in black wooden sheaths. Others bore intricate ornamentation. A bronze dragon formed the hilt of the fanciest. It grasped the blade to its belly, its tail twisting around to form the finger guards.

It was priced out of my reach.

"Dell."

I turned to see Ann swing her arm lightly in my direction. I walked over to the pair.

"Kasmira will take us to see Bridget," she said.

"Who's that?"

"The owner. Kasmira is her granddaughter."

I followed Ann and Kasmira through a bland, ordinary door in the back of the store. That's when things stopped being ordinary forever.

7
WITCHES

She might have been dead the way she stood so still. Dead and propped up against the door at the end of the narrow hallway.

Kasmira stepped up to the old woman and stopped. Ann and I waited a respectable distance away.

Thin, bony arms rested against her chest, folded. She wore a pale blue caftan robe, roped at the waist with a white cotton cord. She stared at us with the same clear jet eyes as her granddaughter. Her hair was long for an old woman's. It hung in gentle gray waves down to the small of her mildly curved back.

"Well?" she croaked. She wasn't unpleasant to look at. She carried her years with pride and dignity. She simply looked *old*.

Ann stepped forward. "I'm Ann Perrine. We met once, a few years ago. I work for Bautista Corporation."

"And *he?*" she asked with a disdainful glance. The emphasis she put on my gender was as sharp as her athames.

"Dell Ammo," I said. "Ann tells me you can explain what's been going on outside. Did you get a look at it?"

Bridget smiled faintly. "I felt some static. Something screwed up a spell of mine, so I asked Kasmira to check things out. She went sensitive and saw what the others were seeing."

"Blood," Kasmira said softly.

"Yes," said Ann. "She told me that much. Can you track down the source for us?"

The old woman unfolded her arms and stood away from the doorframe. Picking up a cane from behind a wall hanging, she leaned forward to say, "That's hard work. Why should I do it?"

Ann stepped very close to the woman and whispered in her left ear. Bridget shook her head, pointing to her right. Ann changed sides and whispered again. Bridget frowned for a moment.

Her eyes widened. "Others have tried," she said, "and failed miserably."

Ann smiled at me. "None of them were professionals." She seemed to be enjoying all this.

The crone narrowed her gaze and peered at me as if I were a bad joke. "That has little bearing on why you wish me to unravel a psychic incident."

I continued to search for my cigarettes. "We're apparently the center of the occurrences. Perhaps the focus of a"—I had to clear my throat before saying it—"a psychic attack." I gave her the rundown on our mile-and-a-half excursion. She grilled me all through it with the incisiveness of a district attorney.

"The image on the building. It looked like a moosehead?"

"Yeah," I said, "sort of. Like a lousy drawing. The antlers drooped and the eyes were under them, off the sides of the head."

"The break in the clouds—was it round, square, oval?"

"A rip. A long slit, like a cat's eye." I watched her for a clue. Her face was impassive. "And then," I said, "we ducked into that apartment complex and everything stopped as long as we stayed inside."

She nodded and smiled. It was a cagey, smug sort of smile. "That has nothing to do with your problem. A pair of quite powerful witches once lived there. They stayed long enough to create a zone of safety. Many circles such as that exist. You don't see any blood drizzling in here, do you?"

"Can you determine the source?" Ann asked.

Bridget shifted her position and sighed. "That would require some effort to discover."

The customer bell rang. Kasmira stepped out front to handle it. Paying trade, after all, came first.

The old woman stood her ground. "You still haven't given me a reason I consider sufficient. It's not as though I can rattle off a quick prayer and an angel pops in with the answer by special delivery. Results vary according to the time and energy invested. You're asking quite a lot of an old woman." She stared at us, waiting.

I figured that she wanted her palm crossed with a little silver. I was wrong.

Ann's lips tightened to a thin line, then parted. Her voice took on an edge I hadn't heard before. In a low, cool tone she spoke, gazing at Bridget with a chilling gaze.

"The lady requires your assistance."

The old crone stared back for a long moment, a silent communication ping-ponging between them. In that time, the lines from decades of frowns appeared as deep furrows above her eyes, only to fade when she broke into a warm, assured smile.

A wrinkled hand tightened and loosened around the cane's grip. Bridget nodded for a moment. Her eyes closed lightly, then opened. She turned to reach for the doorknob behind her.

"In." She pointed toward the darkened room.

Ann stepped in. Bridget followed, snapped on a light. I brought up the rear, wondering what sort of mystic nonsense would happen next. Only I wasn't too sure that the word *nonsense* worked as well for me as it used to.

The room enclosed an area not much larger than the waiting room of my office. Dark, heavy curtains bordered three walls, including the one with the door. Bridget closed the door and drew the drape across it.

The wall to the left was covered with a bookcase stuffed ceiling high with books—old and new—and rows of computer plaques, each hand-labeled with its contents. In front of the draped wall opposite the bookcase squatted what looked like a cluttered coffee table. It supported candles and wooden carvings of deer and crescent moons. The obligatory crystal ball sat in a bronze eagle's claw right next to a ceramic incense burner shaped like a dragon. Every so often, little puffs of smoke snorted from its nostrils.

The wall across from the door had a low, Japanese sort of table near it. Bridget sat down on her heels and beckoned us to follow.

Ann sat in the same fashion. I creaked down on my backside and folded my legs in front of me. The parquet floor hadn't been waxed in decades. It felt cold, but not chilly.

"I'll do this for you," the old woman said. "Just sit there and be quiet."

I finally found my pack of Camels—they had migrated into an inside coat pocket I'd forgotten existed on the newer styles. Before I'd even pulled one out of the package, Bridget eyed me.

"No smoking."

I nodded and returned the pack to its hiding place. It was a reasonable request.

A second later, she lit up enough incense to fumigate a flophouse.

Ann straightened up to take a deep breath of the stuff. She closed her eyes. The only indication that she'd been through any sort of ordeal was her kinked and tangled hair. The rest of her bespoke the outer calm of a resting feline.

Bridget slid a deck of cards from the table's edge to its center. Her fingers nimbly shuffled the deck.

I noticed that the cards were larger and thicker than the usual cards I'd played with. She mumbled to herself most of the time, her voice as soft as silk against satin. She began laying the cards out as if she were playing Solitaire.

I had some trouble figuring out the suits.

There were paintings of a man hanging by one leg, men and women with swords and cups, cards with fools, lovers, and buildings being struck by lightning. Each one seemed to have been drawn by a different artist.

I had no idea the Tarot fad had lasted this long.

She finished laying out the cards in a sloppy pattern. For a long time she just sat and stared at them. Her dark gaze flitted between scanning the cards and glancing at me and Ann. She said nothing.

"Well?" I asked after a few minutes. I was getting antsy.

She held up one hand and scooped up the cards with the other. Ann opened her eyes to look at me and smile, shaking her head a bit. She turned toward Bridget and closed her eyes again.

The old dame reshuffled the deck, murmuring in a low tone. I sighed and looked around the room.

The curtains—colored a rich, earthy hue of redwood soaked in burgundy—blocked almost all the noise from outside. The only sound in the room was the slide and slap of cards being redealt.

When she'd laid out the cards, only silence remained.

After a long wait, Ann cocked open one eye to look at Bridget. The old woman gazed from Ann to the cards, then back again to Ann. She appeared amply astonished.

"Blessed be," she muttered in a breathless old voice. "*Kasmira!*" The shout sounded like a gunshot.

The girl entered quickly.

"Fetch me two orange candles and the large purple one. Remember to mark them down as office use in the inventory."

Kasmira nodded and whirled about to leave. Even in her haste, she maintained an air of otherworldliness.

"Over here," the crone said, making her way to the altar. Her cane tapped against the wooden floor like a skeleton's heel. She eased down, took a moment to adjust her dress, then began to arrange things on the top of the low table. She made with small talk all the while.

"What do you do for a living, Mr. Ammo?"

I shrugged noncommittally. "Find missing movie stars, prevent world wars, calculate batting averages—the usual."

She set a couple of white candles on the table around a chalked-in star. The five-pointed variety. She harrumphed and continued.

"The aura of death that you radiate—is that the usual, too?"

That made me frown. I never thought of myself as a particularly transparent person.

"A living soul projects many aspects," I said. That ought to amuse her.

"So it does, Mr. Ammo. So it does. On this plane and others. I see death in Malkuth—the sphere of Earth. Higher in the Tree of Life I see—other manifestations."

"I see." I didn't see.

Kasmira stepped in with the three candles. Bridget took them and thanked her. "Now watch the store, dear, and don't let anyone—or anything—disturb us."

"Yes, Grandmother." The girl tipped her head and ducked out of the room. The door swung shut, closing with a muted whoosh.

"It would appear, Mr. Ammo," the old dame said, "that you have an impressive destiny awaiting you."

"Mom will be thrilled."

"Yes, Mr. Ammo," she said, putting an orange candle on one of the points of the star. "She will be."

The old sorceress threw more incense into the dragon's belly. The room faded in a microcosm of L.A. smog.

Ann took a deep breath, savored it with a smile, and let it out slowly. I tried not to choke.

The lights dimmed. She probably had a switch under the altar. A dull red glow from the censer illuminated our faces.

"I must ask silence now, until you are requested to speak."

Ann and I nodded.

She struck a long wooden match, flooding the room with a surprisingly bright light. The flame touched the purple candle to ignite the wick. She lit the two orange ones next and finally the white ones. Five bright flames flickered at the points of the star.

She mumbled phrases that sounded like the echoes of a dying race's last words—or like the whispers of a new race's first. Sweet smoke wafted and swirled around her to catch orange light and black shadow. Her age-ravaged face became a harsh, angular mask mouthing her chant.

She broke the cadence of her invocation to say, "Join your hands." She resumed her mumbo-jumbo. Ann reached out, and I took her hands in mine. They felt smooth and lusciously warm, like ivory left in the sun. Our fingers entwined into a kind of quadruple fist and remained tightly bound between us.

Bridget's right hand reached out to clutch our fist. Her skin felt feverishly hot where I'd expected the cool touch of old age. Fingers like talons gripped the mass of locked knuckles and held on tightly.

A cloud of smoke from the dragon blew into my face, stinging my eyes. I blinked and tried to stop the irritated tears from flowing.

Bridget took a sudden sharp breath. In a loud, trembling voice, she mispronounced Ann's name—calling her "Anna Perrenina," as if she were Russian or something. The old woman's face grew placid, though her hand retained its iron grasp. She spoke in English now.

"The blood you see is the blood of the Maiden. The first blood. Blood of the Virgin, the Moon's tide. The tail of the Dark One points the way out and down, running near full circle."

She paused, her eyebrows wrinkling above sealed lids.

"The paradoxical one is the gambit. A thousand men, yet none. The obsidian blade is poised, the blood to flow greater."

Her voice rose in pitch, sped up. "Beneath the Earth is the realm of monsters born of fire who shun both day and night. The time of the Number is nigh! Two great forces must join, and two great forces must clash!" Her hand snapped away from ours and pointed at me.

I felt that terrible cold envelope me again.

"The storm is in your center!"

She seemed to be staring at me right through her shut eyes. Her finger wavered, drifted away from its target. She moaned.

Without warning, the candles fell over—knocked by something unseen. In the sudden, chilling darkness, I yanked my hands away from Ann and struggled to rise, listening for intruders.

Bridget breathed wearily somewhere on the floor to my left. Ann held her breath in silence.

From outside the room came the sounds of shattering glass. Kasmira's screams drifted through the walls and curtains with muted intensity, like a dim, nightmarish memory.

I made it to my feet and felt my way toward the door. Even the glow from the embers of incense had died out. I heard more glass breaking.

Ann found the light switch and turned it on. The bright glare of the overhead fluorescent tubes nearly blinded me. I saw her turning to attend to the fallen crone.

"Thanks, angel," I said, rushing to the door.

The crowd busting up the store stopped the second I stomped in. They were a strange lot—mostly young, mostly well-dressed. Trim, shaven, shorn. The black, leatherbound books they used to swat at the merchandise were like badges on cops. The crosses they swung as swords to smash bottles and panes told me the whole story. Or so I thought.

"Knock it off, kids. Go show your religious tolerance somewhere else."

They stared at me. I felt colder than ever.

The cleanest, most upright-looking of the bunch—an auburn-haired boy in a blue serge suit—stepped to the front of the crowd and ogled me with the look of a rabid gopher.

"We know what you witches are up to." His voice trembled with rage. "God told us you're the one. You and these devil-worshippers have made a pact to—"

"Look, kid." I raised my voice to carry across the crowd. "I don't care what personal revelations you get in the bathtub, but I'm just a normal man doing normal things in a normal place of commerce. Scram before I call an atheist."

The kid held up his crucifix. The others followed his lead. I must have disappointed them when I didn't burst into flames or transmute into a bat. I made the mistake of letting loose with an appropriately derisive snort.

The youngsters took a collective step forward, broken glass crunching under their heels.

"Now you've done it," Kasmira said from behind the counter. "Jesus Chr—"

The ringleader's voice exploded. "A *witch* profanes our Lord's name!"

"Thanks, Kas," I said.

A cross spun through the air, whirring till it bounced off the steel edge of a shattered display.

I resorted to my parole officer image. "Can it, punks. You're not giving your faith much of a public relations boost."

"We're ready to die for our Lord," shouted a voice from the back.

"Right," I said, "and ready to kill for your Prince of Peace. You dopes give me a pain where I put chairs. For the second time—scram!"

The kids looked at one another nervously. The one with the loud mouth spoke in a voice that quavered with anger.

"There shall come a Rapture when all true Christians will rise unto Heaven, leaving you and your scum to the Earth and its Tribulation—"

"Well," I said, looking several of them in the eyes, " 'the dead in Christ shall rise first.' Anyone want to get at the head of the line?"

The loudmouth in front suddenly looked as if he'd been struck in the face with a brick. He stared at a point somewhere behind me. So did the others, with varying degrees of alarm.

"We turn our backs on you. 'Get thee behind me, Satan.' " He turned and spoke over his shoulder.

"Prepare yourself for Judgment, 'for the Lord shall descend from Heaven with a Shout!' "

"I'll buy earplugs. Beat it."

He pursed his lips in repressed fury. "A lake of burning brimstone is waiting for you and your kind." He walked toward the exit as if in a daze.

Without so much as a parting shot, the rest of the flock ambled out of the shop. They mumbled among one another like JD's dispersed by a cop.

I turned around to see Ann standing a couple of feet behind me. I'd almost smacked into her. She had her hands over her head, her fingers pointing forward. A smile of triumph spread across her lips.

"You can lower them now," I said. "This wasn't a stickup."

She smiled even wider until she took a look at the mess.

"Damned fishheads." Kasmira rose from behind the counter to start recovering the salvageable items. "It happens every year, right after Hallowmas," she quietly muttered.

"It looks like World War Three," Ann said, stooping to pick up a red candle molded in the shape of a woman. She gazed at it with a sad frown.

"Bridget's all right," she said to Kasmira. "She's just exhausted. Do you have insurance?"

A weary voice from the back said, "Of course we do—through Bautista. Oh, shit." Bridget stared at the devastation.

"It's not too bad, Grandmother." Kasmira used a dustpan to scoop up multihued piles of incense. "Just a couple of windows and the main counter. They didn't take anything, and the expensive stuff's OK."

"Damned Christian of 'em." The old woman paused to give me a twice-over. "You're a bright bit of luck that's stumbled into our lives. Beat it before I lose my womanly grace."

I glanced at Ann for a clue to my next action. She busied herself helping Kasmira.

"Go on," Bridget fumed. "You may not realize it, but you've got work to do!"

"Such as?" I asked.

"First, you've got to decipher what I relayed to you." She leaned against her cane, striving to look inscrutable.

"Why don't you save us all a good deal of time and tell me?"

"Because," she said with a sly smile, "I don't know what it means. I'm simply a vessel. I convey a message, using the best images I can. It's garbled by its transference through various spheres and planes of reality."

"I never cared for parlor games, lady."

"Mr. Ammo." Her voice was suddenly placating—almost friendly. "This game you've chosen to play involves far more than one mere parlor. This one is for the entire world and all it reflects."

I picked up a couple of bruised candles from the floor, dusted them off, and placed them by the cash register.

"The whole ball of wax. Right, lady?" I nodded to Ann and turned to leave. Blondie stayed put.

"Hang on, Dell. I've got a question." She turned to Bridget. "Is there a new moon coming up soon?"

"It's tonight. Tuesday morning, actually."

"That clinches it." Her demeanor changed to intense determination. She turned and beat me out the door. Her hair shone in the sunlight like ropes of gold chain. "Thanks for everything!" she called back to Bridget. "I owe you a million!"

She glanced back at me. "Let's go, Dell."

"Where?"

"Your office, for starters."

"It's a long walk downtown. Or would you prefer to go back for the Porsche?"

She blanched.

"Besides," I said, "the car's hot. It probably has a want out on it by now, and I know lots of old associates who'd love to see me put away for a minor felony. It'd be a great joke."

I shook my head. A Santa Ana wind had turned the day pleasantly warm outside. We strolled east on the boulevard. The Bible-thumpers had made themselves scarce.

We walked down to the freeway bus stop and waited for

the connection to Old Downtown to show up. Unlike the true believers in the store, passersby didn't pay us much notice. Quite a few of them still seemed to be wandering around in shock.

Ann sat down on the bench beneath the overpass. She seemed unconcerned about the dust and city grime. "The important thing to do now," she said as if continuing some other conversation, "is to decode what Bridget said."

I sat down, stretching my legs out. "She said that even *she* didn't know what she meant."

She stared up at the gray concrete overhead. "The blood was the blood of the Maiden, the Virgin. A girl's first menstrual period. She said that it was the First Blood and linked it to the cycles of the Moon. That was pretty explicit. The cramps I experienced confirms that. Severe menstrual cramps, and I'm nowhere near my own period."

I nodded politely and watched the traffic speed by. I wasn't too interested in women's medical problems.

"Dell," she said finally, "we're going to encounter a lot of things that seem strange or inconsequential on the surface. We have to be aware of *every little detail*. The phenomena that a lot of people call 'magic' consist of methods to unlock selected portions of the human mind. Once open, these parts of the mind can perform astonishing feats and induce power-ful changes in the outside world. After what happened to us, you can't deny that there are certain people who can see things that others can't."

I didn't like it. It sounded too self-consciously mystical. "I could still be tripping on the drugs," I said.

"Not many people see an RTD bus stop on acid."

"Could be a bum trip."

She sighed and stopped tugging at her locks. She'd only succeeded in making the mess worse.

"Dell—just because most people can't integrate a variable across an interval doesn't mean that a mathematician is a magician simply because he can."

"It would have a thousand years ago."

"Yes, but we see the difference now. The mathematician has merely been trained to use a part of his mind in a specific manner. A . . . whatever you want to call her—a witch—is trained to manipulate a different set of symbols for the same purpose: to understand and utilize nature."

The bus arrived. I flagged it down.

Ann stood and stretched like a gold and turquoise cat. She wasn't concerned with any reply I might have made. We were both tired.

The bus lumbered off the freeway and slowed. It was an aging thing, wary of its movements. It hissed and grumbled to a halt, its brakes creaking like old muscles.

Ann paid for both of us. I picked seats near the rear exit. The only other passengers were an old woman behind the driver and a young bum behind us. The old lady wore a rotting brown cloth coat and held a paper bag full of paper bags to her chest. She muttered quietly to the outside world, damning it for her grief.

The young man sat reading a trashy pornoplaque, the cleanest thing about him. Sweat stained his denim jacket in twin circles under his arms. He chewed on something that occasionally dripped past his lips into his ruddy beard, disappearing from sight.

After several minutes of uncomfortable silence, Ann asked, "Do you believe in god? Really believe?"

"No. It wasn't part of my upbringing."

"Do you believe in Satan?"

"It's a package deal, sister. I don't believe in either. If I need to see the devil, I only have to look as far as a local precinct house where a cop beats out confessions. Or a government office where nicely dressed agents take your money to line their pockets. Or the city streets where some punk would kick his grandmother's head in for a quarter."

"Humanity's not all that bad, Dell."

"Sure," I said, "I know—somewhere there glows the pure fire of truth, reason, justice, and hope." I drew a cigarette from my pack and lit it. "I'd like to find it someday."

The old lady at the front looked at me and pointed at the No Smoking sign. She coughed into her hand, looked at it, and wiped it on her coat.

Ann didn't notice. She smiled at me. "You may have your chance yet."

"Yeah. And pigs may fly." I gazed out the window. "Speaking of which, that police helicopter's been circling Van Ness for quite some time."

Ann looked and frowned. "Think they found the Porsche?"

"Money talks. Cops love to listen. The church can make lots of conversation." I smiled. "I wonder how Golding's going to explain it."

"Let's get back to the rest of the message." She chewed on her lip. "Do you think we should risk going to your office?"

I took a long drag on the cigarette while considering the question. Finally I said, "I think we'll have some time before any officer decides to brave the Arco itself. The story about the radiation dies hard. Beathan and his boys are more likely to conduct the search rather than bring in a third party."

"Gambit!" she said suddenly.

I ground out my cigarette butt under my heel and turned toward her. Her eyes had regained some of their life.

"A gambit is a move in chess where an unimportant piece is sacrificed near the beginning of the game as part of a greater strategy."

"And who's the pawn we're looking for?"

"Bridget said, 'The paradoxical one is the gambit.'" Ann mused for a moment. "'A thousand men yet none' is a paradox."

"It's a contradiction, actually. You think a thousand men are going to be sacrificed somewhere?" I watched the 'copter circle around south Hollywood a couple more times. They gave up and flew east.

"Maybe a thousand men. Maybe none." She leaned back to stare at the ceiling. "The paradox is linked to the gambit somehow. And what about the monsters beneath the earth born of fire and all that?"

I shrugged. "Hell, obviously. It's got to be all a metaphor."

"Yes! But for what?"

I spread my hands helplessly. "I'm no philosopher."

The bus rumbled over the Harbor Freeway junction, which was more pothole than pavement. It lumbered up the Third Street offramp. I pressed the bell strip to signal the driver. He turned around to look back at us with languid, pained eyes. Air brakes wheezed, coughed once, and growled us to a halt. The doors ached open.

"Metaphors are fine," I said, stepping off the bus and extending my hand to her like some scruffy Galahad. Like a tousled Guinevere, she took my arm and stepped to the pavement. "Except that a metaphor can be misconstrued. Look at the different ways the stories in the Bible are interpreted. That stuff she mumbled could have a hundred different meanings. If it means anything at all."

We crossed the freeway overpass to stroll down toward Figueroa and the Arco Towers. Ann grew moody.

"We'll just have to keep at it until we find the answer."

"Fine," I said. "My fee is five hundred grams a day. In the meantime, I'm involved in another project."

She stopped and turned toward me. The wind from the freeway blew through her hair, tugged at her dress. Her hair and shiny Danskin top shimmered in the descending sunlight like a dream of drifting gold dust on a distant blue horizon.

"This *is* part of your project. Those phenomena were no coincidence. Those priests didn't pick us randomly to kidnap. Those Nazarene Nazis didn't just happen to pass by the store and decide to smash it up. They recognized *you* as being a focal point of fundamental importance."

"So I've got someone running scared. So Ammo's setting up the crime of the millennium. The world trembles." I kept walking.

She fell in step with me after a moment. "It's more than that, Dell. Bridget said, 'The time of the Number is nigh.' I think you just hit on it. We're less than two months away from the millennium. A lot of people believe that the millennium will mark the return of the kingdom of god."

"Then they'll be off by a year. The millennium begins with the year two thousand *one*."

"People like large round numbers."

"Yeah," I said. "Especially on pieces of engraved paper. And that's just what all the professional prophets and doom-sayers have been getting in exchange for undelivered goods."

"Wouldn't it be nice to change that?"

We'd reached the bottom of the offramp. I turned right at Figueroa.

"Killing God wouldn't change that," I said. "If He even exists at all, He hasn't done much to prevent people from exploiting His name. Removing Him won't stop the con game."

"It might," she said, "if the victims saw through the sham."

The day was still clear, the sky about as brown as it usually is in fall. Most of the derelicts were somewhere else. A beautiful day. Not a drop of blood in the sky. Old Down-town lay quiet and still, the late afternoon shadows long and cool.

Ann stopped to point in shock at what was left of the sign advertising the underground Arco Plaza shops. The shops had been abandoned after the blast, of course, and the below-street mall sealed up.

"Dell—" She dropped her arm down and turned to me. "You know the traditional image of the Devil's tail, don't you?"

"Long. Black. A heart or spade shape on the end."

"Like an arrow."

I nodded. She nodded. We looked at the Plaza sign. A fat black arrow described a three-quarter circle to point down-ward.

" 'The tail of the Dark One points to the out and down, running near full-circle,' " she recited. *"He's down there!"*

It was as if someone had thrown a switch.

I tried to ask, "Who?" but the word froze in my throat as I stared at the sky. Without a cloud anywhere, the sky suddenly darkened. A wind whipped up behind us, icy and insistent. My ears rang from growing pressure, like an in-audible vibration that blanked out all sound. Above us, the jagged remains of the tower were transformed into a gleaming black dagger poised over the earth.

"We can't get down there," I said over the deafening silence. "The Plaza's been a ruin ever since the bombing. Abandoned. Most of the radioactive debris was washed into it during the decontamination."

Ann stared in horror at the phantasmal ebony blade suspended above us. Blood formed along its cutting edge, running down to fall in impossibly huge droplets to the rubble in the street.

Laughter echoed up from somewhere. A mocking, derisive obscenity that sounded uneasily familiar, like the voices that shout in nightmares.

We both stood our ground. Shadows reached down from the lightless sky to flit about us. They snaked and twisted about, always at the edge of perception, just at the far corner of sight.

"How dangerous is it down there?" Ann asked.

"You have to ask?" I swatted at the spooks even as the wind pushed us closer. "I lived two hundred feet above it for twelve years and got cancer for my trouble."

"If he's down there," she said, not even hearing my answer, "we've got to stop him." She glared unblinking at the dagger aimed at the heart of the world.

"If he's down there—whomever you mean—I need to get into my office. The church tithed my Colt when they sapped me."

"You want to go inside *that*?" The glittering, bloody image transfixed her.

I grabbed her arm. "Sure." I pulled her toward the mirage. "It's just like the blood before—an illusion. Fake. You want to burrow down into a radioactive swamp! Which is crazier?"

The cold wind had become a gale. It blew at our backs, urging us toward the glistening point of the blade. I didn't like that one bit. Maybe, I thought, just maybe some magical equivalent of judo was called for. Take the offensive. Turn the impetus against the attacker.

Running away seemed much more sensible.

Something small and hideously blue-black skittered past us, chattering like an angry monkey, to vanish into the false night. The shadows gained strength. They squeezed at our chests to keep us from breathing. My lungs labored like frantic animals in a giant's fist. I dragged Ann forward.

She snapped her wrist out of my grasp with a defiant tug. She didn't run away, though—she kept my pace. We clambered over crumbled steel and glass to reach the place where the tower's revolving doors should have been. A roiling pattern of black and gray enveloped everything. It looked like the surface of some horrid polluted sea. I reached out toward it, plunged into it up to my wrist. It felt like liquid nitrogen.

I screamed. The wind threatened to shove me completely into the swirling maelstrom. I curled my burning hand into a fist and rammed forward.

My knuckles cracked against glass. Cool, smooth, firm plate glass. The kind of glass you can see and feel on any building anywhere.

The shifting darkness raced away from where I hit to reveal the side of Arco North. Overhead, the knife and the blood unraveled into nothingness. The sky lightened to the intensity of approaching twilight—the west glowed red-orange. The wind died down to a gentle breeze. Everything lay in shadow, but at least these shadows stood still.

I had managed to come within a foot of the revolving door. We stepped through into the lobby and rushed toward the elevator. I didn't feel like climbing up and down stairs at the moment. I punched for the one operating car. It creaked to life like an old dog dutifully trudging down to its master.

"We've got to find a way down below." Ann looked at me. Her eyebrows arched with a gentle curve that straddled the thin line between an affectation of perpetual surprise and the impression of shrewd, shrewish cunning. They managed to frame her cool blue eyes with a deep warmth. When she wanted them to. Right now, the lines enclosed a look of tired persistence.

"I want to get this over with," she said. "I can't have this go on much longer."

"It'll be over soon enough, kid. Everything ends before we're ready for it."

The lift shuddered to a stop. The doors parted with the grind of metal that sees too little use.

I told her to hold the doors open while I trotted over to my office. She leaned against the electric eyes to cut off their light. She closed her own eyes, cutting off their light, too.

My office looked and smelled as it always did. Dead. Just like the promise of wealth and comfort I'd envisioned years ago.

Promises.

Life promised nothing except a pointless existence punctuated by an early death. Or so I'd heard.

My cheerful mood was not improved by the message on my answering machine. I rummaged through the desk for my other pistol.

"*Dell*"—the voice on the tape sounded worried—"*this is Joey Moreno. You gotta come over right away. Some priests from my archdiocese just left here, asking some really strange questions about you and that TV nut Zacharias. Something funny's going on. I'll be waiting.*"

The line clicked and buzzed. I found my other Colt Lightweight Commander, checked the magazine in the grip. Full. I slipped a second loaded magazine into my pocket. Feeling a tad more secure, I racked the action, snapped on the safety, and slid the gun into my waistband holster.

I dug up my Magna-Lite and flicked it on. The batteries still worked. Good.

I reset the answering machine and locked up. Ann was still standing in front of the doors when I reached the elevator. Her face had relaxed into a calm mask. Her purse lay loosely clutched in her hand. Somehow, her nylons had survived the ordeals and the barefoot walk unscathed. *Just like Hollywood,* I thought as I touched her shoulder lightly.

"Here's where we split up, Blondie."

She opened her eyes. "What?"

"Head over to Auberge. I'll meet you at the Cafe of the Angels when I'm finished downstairs. Get a room at the Hotel Libya if I'm late."

"No," she said, "I'm going with you."

"Look, sister, I happen to have a contractual immunity to radiation—I *think*. You're not so blessed."

"I—"

"You've got spunk. Just let a little common sense sink in." I let the doors close. When I sighed, it sounded just like the aging motor that lowered us slowly down.

"Angel, there's a time to flex your self-confidence and a time to play it wise. Assassins are some of the most cautious people around. Always cross at the green after looking both ways and overhead." I smiled. It didn't do any good.

"I'll guard your back." Her gaze was as cold as the polar wind. Her hand whipped something out of her purse. It glinted even in the diffused elevator light. She held it up to me.

The blade was as long as my hand, double-edged and vehemently sharp. The rainbow-tempered steel narrowed to a nasty point at the tip. The smooth black hilt was contoured and intricately carved to provide a sure grip. She held it as if she knew when to use it, and how.

"What did you say your job is at the Bautista Corporation?"

"Assistant comptroller," she said.

"Are your bookkeepers that difficult to keep in line?"

"The lady's got to protect herself. Lasers are too finicky, guns are too troublesome to maintain properly. Besides"— she lowered the knife—"there aren't many white knights around to save distressed damsels anymore." She laughed. Her face glowed with life again, like the moon coming out from behind an eclipse.

"The lady with a dagger, eh? Where were you thirty years ago? You'd have made a great comrade—or enemy." That did it. I was getting wistful. A sure sign of my dotage. I clammed up.

She looked embarrassed for a moment, then smiled as gently as a sea breeze at dawn. She slid the toadsticker back into its sheath in her handbag. It must have weighed half a kilo.

The elevator doors opened on the lobby—the farthest the car could descend. Some of Old Downtown's elite sprawled about the tattered chairs and piles of rags. The less drunken ones tried to argue about the recent inclement weather. Their conclusions were more elegant and metaphysical than mine, so I stopped listening and headed for the exit facing Flower. Ann followed.

"All right, sweetheart." I stepped through a hole in one of the glass panels that served as the doorway. "You're a free woman above the age of consent. I can see there's only one way to keep you from risking your neck—and I've never decked a woman before. Come on."

That sounded good. I nodded toward the subway-style stairs down to the Plaza. I looked tough. The image satisfied me. No need to let her know that I was as scared as a little kid caught in a war zone. The part that bothered me was that I hadn't been drafted—I'd volunteered.

There were two entrances to the Plaza on Flower. The one nearer Sixth Street was still buried under the rubble from the South Tower. The one by North was only marginally more accessible—years of neglect had not made the way any safer. Winds had pushed dirt and trash down the stairs to fill the bottom to thigh height.

I switched on the Magna-Lite. A white oval of illumination spilled across the quadruple doors. The glass panel of one had been smashed long ago. A mound of rubbish flowed through it to form an alluvial fan inside the Plaza.

I wrapped my fingers around the exposed edge of the glass. The butt of my flashlight tapped firmly against it. A large piece broke away on the second try with no more than a loud snap. A few extra swings cleared an opening wide enough for me to step through.

"Careful," I said in offering my hand to Ann. "Scars aren't fashionable this year."

She made it through easily. The steps beyond the door were cluttered with debris. Bits of broken masonry and pulverized tile covered the stairway in a rough, unstable blanket.

"I was here once," Ann whispered like a kid in church, "before they blew it up."

I nodded in the darkness and took a tentative step downward. It was like tiptoeing on castanets. I took the next step even slower.

"Why'd they do it?"

"Huh?" I tried to keep the torch beam steady for both of us. The steps were part of a broken escalator—we walked down it as slowly as debutantes at a coming-out party. I grasped the handrail just as the little sign on my left commanded. Gritty dust covered everything. A dank, sickening smell soaked the air, like the odor of dead lilacs in a forgotten tenement where someone lonely had died. Water dripped in a corner.

"The terrorists." She guided her feet carefully between mounds of rubble. "Why'd they blow up the towers?"

"Why ask me? I'm no expert." We'd made it halfway down the escalator. The air grew even thicker—a humid presence that clung like stale fog.

"Aren't you part of the whole terrorist scene?"

My foot jerked, sending a blue square of tile skittering down the steps. It ended its clattering descent with a weak splash.

Great—the Plaza's flooded. I wasn't considering that problem at the moment. I didn't want to be down there, with or without Ann, and she'd just hit a sore spot.

"What I do is the exact opposite of terrorism." If a whisperer can snarl, I almost snarled. "Terrorists kill innocents and noncombatants to create fear. They hope to use that fear to gain or keep power. They're always wrong. That's where I come in. Sure, I take pay from ruling class statists and secret conspiracies—yet I've managed to interrupt the careers of far more ambitious generals and would-be tyrants than anyone else in the business. I've never killed anyone who didn't clearly demonstrate that he'd had it coming. I've kept the world safe for . . . well, for whatever. I've stopped a dozen wars before they reached the shooting stage. And *yes*," I hissed, "I've assassinated *terrorists* of every political stripe. I've even taken the trouble to determine the consequences of my actions."

I paused to fume silently. At the bottom of the stairs, something splashed and slithered. Ann said nothing.

"I can say that I've consistently been on the right side, because killing tyrants for any reason is always a net good."

She smiled without mirth. "Is that why you took the contract on god?"

A shadow drifted at the base of the escalator. I wasn't sure whether it was the result of my wavering light beam or not. I stopped. My hand reached out to squeeze Ann's wrist for silence.

The shadow moved again, even though I held the beam as steady as a corpse's smile. Slowly I lifted it, playing the ellipse of white across the first level of the Plaza. A thin layer of water covered the floor. The blast years ago had imparted a distinct tilt to the mall, dropping it away from us in a gradual slope. I wondered how deep it might be a few hundred yards ahead.

I'd worry about that later. It was the thing a few feet in front of us that occupied my immediate concern.

The shadow stopped moving, even though my Magna-Lite hadn't. It took a deep, rattling breath as the pool of light approached. I flicked my wrist up—it didn't look as if it would scare easily. The thing stood in the clear white light.

A thing that had once been human.

8
RED MASS

It grasped a piece of metal as twisted and scarred as it was. I suppose it was a man.

He stared into the beam with squinting, dull eyes, his right hand clutching the contorted piece of steel as if it were a club.

I eased the Colt out of my waistband. I had the advantage, hiding behind the flashlight's glare.

We stood there, frozen, like a couple of mismatched gunslingers in some cheap gothic western. I waved the beam back and forth. The wet eyes in his deathly white face followed the movement. Perhaps *face* wasn't quite the right word. His head consisted of a lumpy mass of swollen pustules and ulcerated wounds. No hair grew anywhere on his naked body. One shoulder sloped lower than the other. Loose bits of flesh clung tenuously to his sunken chest.

A rat half-swam, half-scampered through the floating garbage. It bumped into the derelict's leg and angrily bit it. If he noticed at all, he owned a great face for poker. His pale eyes continued to watch the beam.

"Hypnotized by it," Ann whispered, pulling up so close behind me that I could almost smell her exhausted, womanly scent through the stench around us.

"Or crazy," I said, "from being down here since the blast."

"*Been up!*" The croak issued from beneath the fleshy lumps. He didn't seem to be addressing us in particular. "Been up when I get hungry. Lots of food if you know where to look. And I can catch it."

He lowered his club to lean on it, using it like a cane. A rheumy glaze coated his eyes, what I could see of them.

"Did we beat the Reds?"

I didn't know whether he referred to baseball or battlefields, so I kept quiet. I felt as embarrassed as anyone would feel, dropping in on Hell uninvited.

His free hand twisted around behind him as if to scratch at his back but fell feebly to his side. He took a tremulous step forward, sloshing water aside with his bare feet. The sorts of welts that covered his face were all over his body in small lumps and festering nodules. Here and there gray-white strips of dead skin hung like rags from a beggar.

I wasn't sure what to do next. Was he the one we were after? If not, did we have to get past him first?

He solved the problem conveniently.

"Fire down below," he murmured in a matter-of-fact way. His eyes glazed over sightlessly. They'd be sightless forever.

He fell forward, the steel strut slipping out under his weight. Slowly, as though savoring the moment, he slid along it. He didn't notice the jagged edges tearing chunks of bloodless tissue from under his arm.

The thin sheet of water parted to make way for him, flowing back an instant after impact to surround his body. At the base of his spine protruded the wavy blade of a flame dagger, placed there, no doubt, by someone who wanted privacy. Light bounced from it to a mirror on the wall, which reflected it to an unbroken piece of mirror on the opposite wall, and so on forever.

Nothing moved. Ann made the sound they usually make

in the movies—that sort of half-gasp that catches and holds in the throat like a butterfly waiting for a chance to escape.

I turned to face her. Sure enough, she had the back of her hand against her open mouth, her eyes wide with shock. The only difference between her and a thousand Hollywood corn-balls was the carving knife she grasped with a physician's steadiness. She lowered it slowly, her mouth still agape, nostrils flared as if to catch the scent of his departing soul.

I stepped over his inert form into ankle-deep water. "The answer to your next question is, 'He's dead, all right. As dead as a campaign promise.'" I extended my hand to her. "Let's go."

She took care to step over the corpse and avoid the area where some clumps of loose skin had splashed down. Once over, she did something that I'd only seen myself do. She crouched over the body to yank the flame dagger out of the dead man's back. She examined it for a moment, then let it dangle loosely in her grasp.

"Did the radiation turn him into that?" she asked, slipping the strap of her purse over her opposite shoulder to enable her to carry a knife in either hand.

She'd bounced back fast.

I shrugged noncommittally. "Whatever was killing him sure didn't work as fast as that blade."

I shined the Magna-Lite over the walls. Most of the colored tile had cracked and fallen away under the force of the blast years ago. A sign hung slantways on a single peg.

"Welcome to Bond Street," I said to the darkness. "Enjoy your walk. Watch for rats and mutants."

We sloshed past shops that had been hastily evacuated years ago. Their silent doors hung open, merchandise scattered. Not even looters wanted anything *that* hot.

We passed a travel agency. Mildewed, rotting posters exhorted us to visit faraway countries, some of which no longer existed.

My feet squished inside my shoes. The water level hadn't increased much. Most of it was probably waiting for us below.

"Down the stairs," I said when we reached the next

escalator. On either side of us, cracked mirrors reflected us to infinity.

My shoes crunched over broken glass and tile. The humidity increased with each descending step. I talked in an attempt to ignore the chill that crept up inside me.

"You're expecting some sort of sacrificial ritual down here, right?"

"All the psychic clues point to that." She fussed with the purse's narrow strap.

"What if *I'm* the sacrifice? We could be walking into a trap."

"Perhaps," Ann whispered. "The psychic images, though, seemed to come from the intended victim, not from the sacrificer. The blood symbols were feminine."

"So are you. You're not planning to play mumblety-peg on me with one of those toys, are you?"

She stopped at the third step from the bottom—the last step above the level of the stagnant, crusted water.

I took the extra step and slogged into the mess, shin-deep in the atomic sewer.

"What do you mean?" she demanded. In the overspill of the Magna-Lite, her eyes glowed savagely.

Hm. Maybe I *could* get her to leave, I thought, if I got her worked up enough.

"Sister, for all I know you could be leading me here for a little sacrifice of your own. *You* own a black blade—"

"The *hilt* is black—"

"You seemed a bit too eager to help a stranger do something as odd as hunt down God and kill Him. Either you're crazier than I am or you're not playing your full hand. Which is it?"

"We all have aces up our sleeves in this game, Dell, but I'm not the only player. Let's keep going."

I drew my automatic and held it at my side. The heat and the cloying atmosphere were getting to me. I wanted her to get the hell out.

"I've never plugged a dame," I said. "At least, not without a contract." I turned wearily, held the muzzle pointed ahead of me, and stepped further into the brackish, cool water. It sloshed against my thighs.

Ann made no sound following me in. She slid the flame dagger into her purse, leaving the black-hilted one in her right hand. She grasped it in the correct position for both gutting and pommeling.

The little hairs along the back of my neck stood nervously at attention.

Between the water and the floor rested a layer of scum-coated metal and masonry. I walked over the terrain as gingerly as a pickpocket stepping past a precinct house. Sometimes my toes or heel hit something soft or rolled across a formless, pulpy mass. I didn't want to know . . .

We veered off to the right. I stopped.

"Welcome to Fifth Avenue," she said, looking up at a peeling sign.

"Sh." Something buzzed in the silence. Rats cavorted off in the distance. How they could stand the smell was beyond me.

I flicked off the flashlight. We stood silently in a pitch darkness that—after a few moments—didn't seem so black. I must be getting old. Blondie was the first to see the light.

"Over there." She pointed.

I glanced squintily around until I saw a faint sliver of light illuminating a corner of the far wall.

"Could be light from the hole where South Tower stood," I whispered.

"Not at this hour. Come on." She slogged forward. "That's what we're looking for." At least we were heading toward shallower water.

Ann's foot stepped on something and slipped out from under her.

I was close enough to catch her just by reaching toward her sounds in the darkness. My arms tightened around her waist as though both had been built for that single purpose. I pulled her close. She smelled like summer would smell to someone who'd spent his entire life in winter.

Her arms wrapped around me—fists that clutched a purse

and a knife thumping lightly against my back. She pulled me even closer. Her hair brushed against my cheek, softly as a fawn's touch.

Somewhere, someone began to recite poetry. It didn't fit the mood. It wasn't particularly romantic.

"That's him," she whispered.

She untangled herself quickly to crouch low, listening.

Off in the dim glow ahead of us, a deep voice rumbled in loud, fearless tones. He must have surmised that no one would be around to hear him. He'd taken deadly enough precautions.

"In the name of the Ruler of Earth and the King of the World, I command the Forces of Darkness to gather and heed my call!"

Whoever was in there sounded insanely serious. And just a shade too familiar.

I thumbed on the flash and dripped forward as quietly as the first rays of dawn sneaking into a war zone. Ann kept by my side, holding her pigsticker with tight knuckles. We followed the buzzing noise and the light.

"The time of the Usurper is nigh!" the voice bellowed. "I call upon the Legions of the Night to rise up around me! Throw open the Gates of Hell! Come forward from the Abyss. Serve *me*, your brother and ally, your Father and Master!"

We rounded an oblique passage to wade through a small atrium. Twin open stairways cascaded into the slime pooled at their bases. The light from around a low corner at the far end of the corridor grew more intense.

The buzzing sound grew louder. An acrid aroma of some exotic incense filled the damp, oppressive atmosphere.

"Flies," Ann said, waving her knife around as if to slash them away.

The voice droned on, louder and more imperious. "By all the Gods of the Pit, I command these things to come to pass! Fire and Death! Blood and Victory!"

His voice cracked and boomed in a rich baritone, with all the force of a general marshaling his troops.

We splashed closer, wading through calf-deep water and

insects. The flickering light turned a shade more orange. I took another step forward and the swarm of flies closed behind me like a curtain. Ann followed me into the clearing and gasped as if she'd been stabbed in the stomach.

"Come on," I said. "We're almost out of the water."

The silt-smeared floor had bulged upward sometime in the past, leaving the part of the mall called Place de Bruxelles high and dry. We passed a jewelry store that some maniac had looted in spite of the radiation danger; I marveled at my *own* lunacy quotient.

I doused the torch again to concentrate on the harsh stream of light angling out of a wooden doorway ahead of us.

"In the names of the Princes of Hell; Satan, Lucifer, Belial, Leviathan! I summon forth the Powers of the Night! Crush the Enemy! Take this sacrifice, that His blood should drain as hers. Let His essence be cast to the eternal Winds as her life is thrown to the Void! As she dies, so dies my Enemy!"

I edged toward the doorway. My shoes had picked up an irritating squishy sound.

The place had been a chapel, years ago. Now, in the glow of a hundred black candles, a variation of Mass worthy of Disney County was in full swing.

A hooded figure in robes of unrefulgent black loomed over an altar draped in the same jet material. Atop the oblong slab lay the body of a girl, her face turned toward him, away from my view. I couldn't tell if she was alive or dead.

The chapel's decor had undergone a few minor modifications. The heavy wooden cross behind the altar had been inverted. From the cross hung a red and black image of an upside-down star. Inside the star was a stylized goat's head. Scores of black candles burned on the pews and railing. Their light flickered in the stifled atmosphere.

The robed figure continued to face the pentagram. I had a pretty good idea what was going on.

A long, thin dagger appeared from the folds of his outfit. He raised it high to the symbols above him. Its blade was as black as his intentions.

"In the name of Ahriman and Marduk," he thundered,

"of Coyote, Baphomet, and Sekhmet! Take this virgin blood and *drink!* I command thee to rise forth in beauteous terror to impale my accursed Enemy on the bifid barb of Hell!"

He whirled about with a rustle of fabric, raising the blade to drive it home.

I saw the man I most expected to see. I took aim with my pistol.

The girl turned her head away from the blade, screaming toward the door. And I saw who *she* was.

I almost burst out laughing. He had managed to pick an astoundingly inappropriate victim!

"Drop the sticker, Zack." I raced up to the railing and crouched to one knee, waggling my automatic as if I were a real threatening character.

Zack's soft eyes curled up from gazing at the kid. He snarled like a cornered animal. Knuckles tightened to glint like polished bone. Under his hood, his face ran through a spectrum of colors ending with purple.

"Get out of here!" he shrieked. "This doesn't concern you!"

I took one step up toward the altar. "Not that I like to kibitz or anything, but if you need virgin blood, you're in big trouble in L.A. That little tart you've got is about as pure as the whiskey in a skid-row bar."

The kid looked really scared. She stared up at Emil and the dagger. I figured I could shoot him on the downswing without her getting cut. The hilt looked heavy enough to upend if he dropped it.

The kid shouted, "It's not true, mister! He knows it's a trick. I never made it with anyone!" She looked straight at me.

The room faded away in a gray whirl. I felt abysmally cold and lost. Suddenly I saw the girl standing before me. She wore a leather outfit that on someone older would have been a federal offense. On her it looked silly.

"*I tricked them all,*" she shouted at me, so rapidly she stumbled over the words. "*We can talk here, a lot faster than in real time. I can do this with anyone. Or so I thought. I used it to get money. The old farts thought they'd got laid and I*

— 113 —

didn't even have to touch them. Honest. *That's why you caught me off guard. I couldn't grab your mind like that.*"

My voice came from somewhere else, as if I weren't talking. "*I got your distress call. You could have given us more explicit directions.*"

She looked terrified. "What *distress ca—*"

A scream shuddered around me. The gray fog vanished. I stood facing a screaming child. Zack still held his blade aloft, as if I'd only been gone an instant. I aimed with both hands and fired.

The pistol blasted, its report filling the chapel like a physical presence. Through the blinding flash and explosion, I saw Emil grab at his hand and howl.

"*Abbadon!*" he shrieked. "You'll pay for this, Ammo!"

"Deduct it from my tab," I said.

Ann glared at my client with a savage hatred. She made cutting motions in the air with her knife.

Emil stared at me, then at her. His lips curled back, and his voice reached straight up from the gutter.

"You! You fucking *mother!* I'll get you for this. Nobody betrays me!"

"I'm not betraying you," I said, stepping up to the altar to lift the kid's shuddering body off the black velvet. "I still intend to fulfill our contract. I'm getting new leads all the time. You've been an inspiration."

He never took his eyes off Ann.

"You'll regret this alliance," he said.

"I learned not to have any regrets," I said, stepping down from the altar with my small burden. "I've had a full life, and I don't give a damn what happens next. You're looking at the man who's going to pull the cosmic trigger and blow Number One into stardust."

"You talk a hard line, Ammo. Let's see some delivery."

He turned to storm out the side door of the chapel. I didn't want to imagine which direction he went from there. I'd glanced at the bullet wound through his hand.

It didn't bleed. Not a drop.

9
ISADORA

"A thousand men yet none," Ann said. She walked beside me, leading the way with the flashlight beam.

We departed the chapel, leaving the candles to flicker behind us. I wasn't worried about anything catching fire in this damp tomb. And if it did, the city fathers would probably applaud me for an act of urban renewal.

The flies were gone, the plaza silent.

I shifted the kid to piggyback when we reached the thigh-high water. "She put on a pretty swell act for a virgin."

"You have to nowadays," the kid said.

"What's your name?" Ann asked.

The kid squirmed a bit. "Isadora Volante. And it's no act. They got their money's worth. Weren't you convinced?"

I had to admit that she had a wild talent. Just how wild she didn't seem to know.

"Look, kid—"

"It's Isadora," she snapped, "when I've got my clothes off."

"Right. Listen, you acted as if you didn't know what led us to you."

"I don't. You weren't just passing by?"

"Ki—Isadora, you lit up L.A. with enough special effects to shame Cecil B. DeMille."

She snorted. "Well, I never noticed it. All I knew was, that freako tried to kill me and there wasn't any way I could even touch the son of a bitch. I've bounced some weird stuff back at guys, but whatever was inside *his* head . . . " She quivered and hugged my neck tighter.

"Go easy on him," I said. "He suffers from a massive inferiority complex."

A fluttering noise half-echoed from another part of the lower plaza. "Listen," I said. "More flies?"

"Too loud for that," Ann said.

"Let's change directions," I suggested. "We can try the northside escalators."

"Why?" Ann asked.

"Call it a hunch, call it intuition, call it a healthy cowardice. I don't think we should go back the way we came."

Ann nodded. "Lead the way."

I turned. The fluttering was behind us now. I jostled Isadora. "Hey," I asked softly, "you're not transmitting anything, are you?"

"Too tired." She leaned her chin on my shoulder.

The sound grew louder, like slabs of wet leather slapped lightly against one another. Ann and I waded as swiftly as we could.

I started to say, "Ann—."

And then they were on us.

10
THE DAMNED

The first one flew out of the darkness to strike my shoulder with sharp black talons fully extended. They ripped through cloth down into flesh. Blood welled up in droplets like dew on a beer mug.

No illusion. This was real. It hurt. The screaming grew louder.

Except that I thought bats couldn't scream.

Ann didn't make a sound, even when the other dozen or so swooped down the corridor, howling madly. Score one for her.

I dropped the kid into the drink to give me a little elbow room. I reached for my Colt, only to hesitate. The bats outnumbered my supply of rounds, and I wasn't such a fabulous shot that I could bring down small animals in this light.

My concentration was broken by one of the things slapping against my back and sinking its fangs into the nape of my neck. I reached up and behind to squeeze its little neck until it choked and let go.

Two of them had ganged up on Ann, and they weren't the storybook type that get tangled in hair. They went for her eyes. The others circled about, screeching.

I had problems of my own.

I pulled the struggling thing over my head. Bad idea. It tried to give me a Mohawk by raking its claws over my scalp.

I got him in front of me, though. We stared face-to-face. And what a face!

Where a bat's head reasonably should have been glared a contorted mockery of a human face, twisted in agony. Its lips curled back around huge, bloody fangs. Watching it as though I had nothing better to do at the time, I finally heard what it was screaming.

It screamed for forgiveness.

So did the others slashing at Ann in an unbatlike manner.

I thought about it long and hard for a second or so. But a generous nature is one of the virtues I lack.

Continuing to choke the tiny monster's throat with one hand, I twisted its body with the other. Its neck snapped like a hollow, rotted twig, and the thing fell limp. I dropped it from my hands into the sludge.

"Dell!" Ann grasped the flashlight in one hand, her steel in the other. She was cutting at the air again with the knife while swinging the torch like a club. Her purse slapped against her wet hip like a wrecking ball. It was a wonder she managed to remain standing in the middle of the fracas.

I splashed back up to the chapel gift shop. Inside the shattered window display were some shelves. I grabbed one, ignoring the crosses lying there. I figured they wouldn't help in my case.

I waded back into the fray. The plank worked fine. The first bat I hit flew halfway across the hall—though not under its own power.

I pulled off a bat that had plunged its teeth in the heel of Ann's left palm. Its face looked familiar, like that of a dead president or someone of that ilk.

I swung it around me like a chicken marked for dinner.

When its spine snapped, I threw it against the escalator steps for good measure.

The kid played it smart. She submerged as deep into the water as she could and ducked her head when one of them swooped by.

I grabbed my board and tried to improve my batting average.

Ann finally seemed to get the knack of keeping the bats away from her. Whenever she waggled her knife in a certain manner, they backed off.

I caromed another flying rodent off the walls in a banked shot. It splashed about angrily in the water before drowning. As creatures from Hell went, they were pretty tame.

One of the bats fluttered too close to Ann's blade. She managed to nick it.

Its shriek became a sickly moan. It didn't seem as if she'd done it much harm. It acted, though, as if she'd shot it full of hydrofluoric acid. The moan became a pitiful, rattling sigh, like air escaping from a bottle. It took one last wing-flap and performed a graceless nosedive into the water.

That made the others go crazy. Almost as one, they swept toward Ann. Her hair whipped about as she swung her dagger in wide angles and sharp turns. She must have had all the aces on her side. The bats almost looked as if they were diving into the blade's path. Within seconds, the rest of the bats fell sighing to the floor.

The place sounded like a tire-slasher's wet dream.

The room fell silent. Slowly, Isadora rose up from the water. Slowly, Ann regained her composure. Slowly, I grew aware of the throbbing pain and hot wetness at the back of my neck. I dabbed at the blood with a soggy handkerchief.

One of the bats that Ann had killed floated near me, face up. Its eyes were closed and—as much as possible around those vicious fangs—its human face smiled.

I felt that overall sort of shiver you feel when you touch something that's not supposed to be there.

"Come on," I said, trying to sound tough and cool. It came

out sounding hoarse and old. I took the light from Ann. Isadora followed on her own, to my aching back's relief.

I felt around for the base of the escalator. My toe found it, painfully. We rose up out of the slime toward the inside entrance to North Tower. Halfway up, I turned to shine the beam back past the kid. She was climbing up naked and dripping wet, looking like a severely misplaced water nymph. The light threw a circle of white on the lumpy surface of the water, where it shimmered and cast rippling reflections on the walls.

I noticed something missing in the water. The bats.

I didn't want to know whether they merely sank or vanished or danced out doing the cha-cha. All I knew was that I had blood coming out of various parts of me and that I ached like a second-place prizefighter.

Dell Ammo's a real hard man. He fights heaven and hell. Ammo's real tough. Ammo wants to lie down on dry sheets with an icepack and a heating pad. Dell Ammo wants life to ease the hell up on him.

I looked up to see a dark shape snarling at the top of the stairs.

Dell Ammo gets all the breaks.

I snapped the Magna-Lite up at it. The thing hissed and pulled back. I drew my automatic, whipped it a couple of times to get water out of the barrel, and waited. "Get behind me," I whispered.

"Right," Ann said. "I'll guard the rear." She wedged the kid between us.

The thing stepped into the light, crouching low. It looked like a wolf, but I wasn't calling any odds tonight. It had lost its fur sometime in the past, but had made up for it with thick scales of blackened, flaking skin. From the way it crouched, it gave no sign of being weak or sick. Tiny droplets of foam dripped from its slavering tongue when it opened its maw to snarl.

"Oh, shit," said a small voice behind me.

I took aim as it reared up to leap. The muzzle blast stung

my hand. The report rang in my head like the bells of St. Mary's.

The kick nearly threw me off balance on the slick steps. A firm hand at my back steadied me, pushing me upright.

"Thanks, sweetheart," I muttered through clenched teeth. I stared at the dog—or whatever it was. It had collapsed at the top of the escalator, dead before it could lunge toward us. The bullet had made a large, ugly crater in its crusted skin. This one bled, though, nice and normal from its mouth and nose. Its forequarters hung limply over the top step. Where there should have been paws, dirty, calloused hands twitched reflexively a few times and grew still. They looked as if they'd once been slender, graceful hands, perhaps those of a woman.

I said nothing. Ann said nothing. The kid said nothing. We all kept saying it until we'd edged past the limp, lifeless hulk.

Ann poked it with her steel.

"Are you sure it's dead?" Isadora asked.

"It won't bother us anymore," Ann replied. She poked it harder. It hissed slowly, languidly. Like an old woman recalling a pleasant memory. The sound stopped as abruptly as it began.

"Did you puncture it?" The kid looked at Blondie with a queer expression.

Ann looked back, her features calm. "It's dead, Isadora. Gone for good. I just wanted to be sure it wouldn't . . . revive."

I turned to face the next flight of steps. "If you're through playing coroner, angel, we can try making it to the top. This escalator heads right up into the lobby of North Tower. The fire doors were locked from the inside before they began decontamination."

Ann took the kid's hand to lead her past the corpse. "I suppose you've got the key?"

I flicked the safety on my Colt back and forth, smiling. "I have an Open Portal spell. Hasn't failed me yet."

I couldn't coax a smile out of either of them. I hadn't expected to. We were as raucous as a funeral home.

I beamed the Magna-Lite at the steel doors blocking the top of the escalator. Nothing there but some angular shadows and piles of rusty red dust. We started up the cluttered steps.

The stark shadows at the top shifted—with the bobbing of the light, I assumed, paying it no mind.

I felt that familiar shiver pass through me, though. Below us, I heard the scraping of tiny claws on steel. I froze.

The shadows above kept moving.

The footsteps below us slowed a few at a time. It sounded like rats.

"Just rats," I said out loud, more for my sake than the others. I took another step up and beamed the fire door.

The shadows looked even more solid in the direct light. Not good.

They continued to move and shift, keeping no particular shape for more than a few seconds. The wall behind them barely showed through.

A few high-pitched, thin voices at the bottom of the the stairs squealed, "Forgive us!" A few more whined in, adding, "It's not our fault!" to the chorus.

Tiny feet scampered to reach the first step.

The lady and the kid crowded up next to me.

I sweated what to do. Rats are more suited to shotguns than pistols.

I fired into the shadows ahead. They made bigger targets than whatever was closing in on us from behind. The round went through the one in the middle and spattered against the wall.

I should have expected as much.

I fired again. This one marked the wall with a silvery splash. The shadow continued its wavering motions, unbothered.

The things below us gained a couple more steps. They shrieked like a thousand fingernails on slate.

I was getting more than nervous. Just to have something to do while I thought things out, I aimed a third time.

"Out of the way!" shouted the blond and blue-green form

shimmering past me. She almost shoved me over the side of the escalator to charge up the stairs straight at the wraiths.

She screamed like bad opera and swung her arm.

The little beasts behind us gained a few more levels. I pulled Isadora in front of me, lifting her up from the steps with my free arm.

Ann's blade passed through the first shadow. It drew away from her, seeming to fold in on itself. The others pulled away toward the walls. She jabbed at each one. They vanished at the touch of her knife.

"*Let's go!*" she yelled, pointing to the padlocks on the doors. The screaming, pleading things behind me jumped up to my step a heartbeat after I'd started to run to the top of the stairs. It was a very quick heartbeat.

"Get behind me!" I shouted, handing the kid to Ann. I didn't know what good being behind me would do in the event of a ricochet, but it seemed the courteous thing to say.

The door's rusted hasps looked far weaker than the locks. I leaned the muzzle against the lower one, shielded my eyes, and squeezed the trigger.

The bullet tore through the hasp and ricocheted twice. Fragments of mirror exploded from the opposite wall to cascade down the escalator steps.

Loud animal cries rose up from below. They were even closer.

I reached up to shoot off the other hasp. The round went straight through the ceiling into the lobby. I hoped that no one was sitting right above us.

Blondie and I pulled at one door and managed to open it a crack. A sheet of light trickled in, along with a dozen or so years of accumulated trash.

Into that light swarmed the squealing terrors. Little rat heads and little rat paws. Attached to little human bodies.

I jammed my legs on one side of the opening and my back alongside the other. Old bones popped in surprise with the strain. The doors creaked and parted another foot or so. I shoved the kid through. My muscles felt like old rags stretching beyond their limit. I pushed Ann through just as she was getting ready to go at the little horrors with her knife. Enough is enough.

I squeezed past the opening. Debris clogged the fire-door channel, jamming the doors.

The three of us stood in a recess in the lobby at the base of another escalator. People rimmed the edge and stood at the top of the stairs, peering at us. They were the same old low-lifes I'd seen in the tower for years. I didn't even feel like warning them. I turned to take Ann's hand.

She held the flame dagger she'd pulled from the dead man. With her other hand, she struck her own blade against the bloodstained steel. After a half-dozen tries, an actinic spark flashed between the two weapons.

She'd have been a hit in Scouting.

A powerful toss of her arm flung the flame dagger through the doorway.

"Close it!" she cried, shoving at one side of the door.

I leaned against the other to push while the kid scooped paper and beer cans and cigarette butts out of the guiderails.

The rats began to howl and hiss in agony and release. The doors edged closer together. Through the shrinking crack sighed the tired sound of death.

The doors ground shut. I sat down in the rubble and felt my age.

Ann slipped her knife into its sheath and returned it to her purse. The things a woman hangs on to.

"Let's go," she said. "We can't stay around here."

I dabbed at the rips in my neck and scalp. The others didn't look too healthy either.

"There's a doctor on the fourth floor," I said wearily. "He can clean us up a bit."

Ann nodded and climbed up the escalator. I took off my jacket and offered it to the kid. She shook her head.

"No thanks. I'm used to it. I'm no traffic stopper, any-way."

We followed Ann up the moribund escalator to reach lobby level. Old drunken and drugged eyes watched us head toward the elevator. The excitement was too much for some of them—eyes began to unglaze and return to life. Luckily, the elevator waited for us at lobby level. We stepped inside before anyone had a stroke.

La Vecque's office door opened. A young, muscular man in a white tunic stepped out carrying a portable cryogenic container that hummed quietly. His gaze flicked toward us— suspiciously at first. Then his look grew mystified. He probably wondered why anyone would come to La Vecque with a medical problem.

I knew why *he* dealt with La Vecque.

"Just back from Disneyland," I said merrily.

He frowned and lugged the freeze unit quickly toward the stairs.

I pounded on the office door. Behind it clattered the sounds of frantic tidying. After a few moments, La Vecque piped frantically, "Who's there? I've got a shotgun!"

"Relax, Doc. It's me. Ammo."

The door creaked open, hesitated for an instant, then swung wider.

"Who're they?" the old bird asked, letting us in.

"Casualties, Doc. That's as deep as the inquiries get. I was hoping you'd fix us up."

"Sure, Dell, sure."

He had us shower one by one in the broom closet he had for a washroom. We put on paper gowns, and he checked each of us in turn.

The kid passed with not much more than a few questions and a quick glance-over. Ann had a nasty-looking rip on her arm plus scratches on her face and shoulders as if she'd been thrown head first through a plate-glass window. He tinkered with her while I rested.

By the time he got to me, I'd stopped bleeding. The first thing he did was to clean the wounds, which started the blood oozing again. He examined my scalp with an irritating lassitude.

"I'm going to have to shave some hair off."

"Go ahead," I said. "I was getting tired of the two-tone effect anyway. Take it all off."

"I'm not a barber." He rummaged in a drawer to find a razor. "Your preacher friend was looking for you a while ago. Moreno. He looked awful."

"Awful drunk?"

"Worse," he said. "Sober as a judge on election day."

I snorted. He'd copped that line from me.

"I told him you might be around somewhere, so he went up to wait for you."

That gave me a little bit of the chill I've been feeling only too often lately. Joey had been worried enough on the phone when he said he'd wait for me at the church. Could all this psychic pyrotechnics have reached him, too? Why else would he walk all the way over to my office at night? *Something* must have him scared.

I waited patiently for La Vecque to disinfect the wounds and lay down a bunch of tape sutures. He reached for a roll of gauze.

"That's good enough," I said, standing up. "I'm going to check in on the padre." I turned to Ann. "I'll rustle up something for the kid to wear. Wait for me here."

I picked up my gun and—paper robe fluttering—rushed out of the good doctor's office and hit the stairs like an aging greyhound after the iron rabbit. The concrete steps stung my bare feet with each bound. A few gasping strides brought me to my floor. I had energy that seemed to come strictly from panic. Events were closing in around me. Too much was happening at once.

I eased the stairway door open to listen.

Silence. As complete as snowflakes on cotton.

I held the automatic up and crept toward the office. My feet appreciated the carpeting.

The door stood slightly ajar, permitting a wedge of light to spread across the hall and climb up the side of the far wall.

I stood beside the doorway to hear the kind of total silence that an inhabited room cannot maintain. The air smelled of burnt gunpowder.

I kicked the door inward and dropped to one knee, scanning the room with eye and gat. Nothing moved.

Not even the body on my waiting-room couch.

11
PRIEST

Father Joey Moreno sat on the couch staring off into space. The bullet hole rested right between his eyes, just above the bridge of his nose. He looked surprised by it. They always do.

Some blood had trickled down the end of his nose to drip on the crotch of his black pants. It had dried. His face matched the color of his preacher's collar.

I didn't say anything, just looked around the room for clues. Joey hadn't left a dying clue—that's for the movies. This kill had been clean, quick, and professional. The torpedo had picked up the cartridge, or perhaps used a revolver.

Joey didn't care. He just stared in my general direction— two glazed eyes and a third dark, bloody one. The entire run of events had obviously alarmed him immensely.

Something smelled in the air, beyond the scent of cordite. I tried to identify it while I searched Joey's corpse. His bearish body resisted me no more than if it had been a couple of sacks of cement.

A bulge in his left rear pocket yielded a swollen wallet. I retrieved it and let Joey slump back while I perused it.

The cheap brown cowhide contained the usual accumulation of ID, credit cards—in the Church's name—and business cards of practically every other church in the area. Clannish sorts, I thought. I hardly ever kept tabs on my own colleagues.

Everything in the wallet suffered from varying degrees of wear. Most of the cards had smears of ink on them from the other cards.

All except one.

I pulled it out. Its edges were sharp enough to slice a porterhouse steak and the paper was as white as a dream about nurses. It hadn't even been filed with the rest of the cards but had been slipped into the money slot. The slot held a few hundred bucks worth of last week's folding paper. It wouldn't have bought a meal then—it couldn't buy a gumball today. Not that it mattered much to Joey now.

I fingered the card, turned it over. On the printed side—in small, dignified letters—was engraved

ST. JUDAS CHURCH
OF HOLY TRIBULATION
AND TAX EVASION

"TO FIND LOVE,
ONE MUST FIRST KILL GOD."
PHONE: 666–HWHY

"Was it the archdiocese that had you scared, Joey? Or was it this?"

Having delivered this annoyingly intriguing item, Joey continued to sit there, looking amazed. I reached over to close his eyelids. They resisted at first, then stickily slid shut. He looked less surprised, as though he'd overheard something interesting while dozing but thought it deserved nothing more than raised eyebrows.

I cased my inner office. Carefully. I picked up more cartridges for my automatic and scooped out what money the safe held. The stuff wound up in a briefcase, followed by a few personal items and a change of clothes. I thought a moment and added two extra shirts, a pair of slacks, and a belt.

I had a feeling I wouldn't be coming back for a while. The place didn't seem as secure against the riffraff anymore.

While pulling on some dry clothes, I made one phone call to a number I knew well. It was a number a lot of people knew, though you'd never find it in any phone book.

The line rang once, a receiver lifted somewhere in Los Angeles, and no voice answered.

"Disposal," I said to the silent other end. "Arco Tower North, room twelve hundred. Bury this one—he's a friend."

The party on the other end hung up without a word.

You can get anything you want in L.A.

I snapped the briefcase shut and locked my office up. On the way out, I stopped to look back at the bearish figure of Joey Moreno.

"So long, Father," I muttered. "Tell the head honcho I'm on His trail."

"Here." I tossed Ann a dark blue pair of pants and a white shirt. "You too." The kid got a red-checked Pendleton.

"It smells like fish," she said graciously. She swam around inside until her head and arms poked out of the appropriate holes.

"Was he up there?" Ann asked, stepping behind the office door to change.

"Mostly." I cadged a dry cigarette from La Vecque and lit up. The smoke cleared away some of the fuzziness upstairs. "I may have come across another lead. Let's go."

I handed our physician a wad of orange paper. "We weren't here."

"No one ever is, Dell." He paused. "How's your condition?"

"Aside from being sapped and doped and jumped on by little things that scratch, I've been fine. No more internal pains that haven't been externally caused."

"I'd like to schedule another body scan—"

I blew out a cloud of smoke. "Some other time, Doc. I'm taking a business trip."

"Where to now?" Blondie asked. Dressed in my old clothes that were baggy to begin with, she looked sufficiently out of vogue to beg on a Beverly Hills street corner as a fallen socialite.

The elevator creaked like a rattan chair. "Going back to my office is completely out," I said, running a few fingers over my lumpy scalp. "And since you're connected with me now, your place is probably under surveillance."

The elevator stopped, and the doors considered opening. Then they started working at it in earnest. They jammed partway, permitting us to squeeze our way out.

"Aside from an unpleasant experience at a dive called the Hope and Anchor, Auberge is a pretty safe place to hole up." I glared mildly at Isadora.

"Wasn't *my* fault," she said.

A couple of ordinary men with fat briefcases maneuvered past us toward the elevator. They looked as if they could be a couple of down-and-out businessmen out to collect on a debtor. I knew better. They had that edge to them.

I wondered how they would get the body out of the building. That was their problem.

"What do we do about Isadora?" Ann asked.

I hadn't given much thought to that. She walked beside us through the lobby, shirttails brushing at her knees. The old geezers had fallen back into their torpor—only a few watched her with empty, tired eyes.

The kid spoke without looking up. "Don't let any latent mothering urges overwhelm you. I've got my own place. I'll be heading back there to change into something that doesn't scratch. I'll sleep for a week, then get ready for more business." She acted as if she'd just escaped from an ice cream social. Maybe she'd seen so much hell in the minds of others that she found the real thing as easy to deal with.

We headed toward Bunker Hill and the entrance to Auberge. Ann put an arm around Isadora.

"Just stay away from strange men," she counseled.

"Lady," the kid sighed, "*all* the men I deal with are strange. This last one was just a bit stranger." She looked up at me. "You called him your client. What do you do? Pimp for him?" She suddenly got that nearsighted look a kid gets when she's suspicious.

"Nothing so simple," I said. "Besides, how did he get ahold of *you?*"

She shrugged. "He talked to me in Auberge, we went off to his house. By the time I'd discovered that I couldn't open his mind up to my suggestions, he'd hit me with a rag full of something that smelled awful. I woke up down there." She grinned. "I puked all over his altar. He got really pissed having to clean it up." She giggled like a drunken hyena.

"Someone should adopt you," I said. "You'd brighten up any household."

"It's best to forget about him," Ann said. "You're not involved in any of this."

"He seemed to think so. He grabbed me just a few hours after those other guys got you two."

"Just an unfortunate coincidence," I said, not liking the false sound it made coming out.

"Everything is coincident," Ann said. "It's the meaningful coincidences that are important."

We walked along the darkened street. I wasn't in the mood for deep philosophy at the moment. My senses were as sharp as a bowling ball.

Ann continued to talk the way one talks into a deep well.

"How coincidental were all those creatures in the Plaza?"

"Well, Zacharias wouldn't send them after *me*, would he? I told him I'd fulfill our contract."

Ann frowned for an instant. "Maybe he didn't like the way you interrupted his ritual. It may have altered his plans enough that he doesn't want you to proceed. Perhaps he's discovered something in the contract. Or something about you. Maybe he's scared. Whatever the reason, he wants you to stop."

"Look, Angel." I tossed my expired cig into the gutter. "If Zack wants to cancel, I say fine. He doesn't have to kill me to get me off this goose chase. But I'm not backing out."

"Maybe you know too much now just to cancel it and let it lie. Maybe you're a threat."

"Yeah. Dell Ammo. Fighting the forces of heaven and hell. One-man apocalypse. The bodies are dropping already."

"Has he flipped?" The kid looked me up and down.

"Forget it, doll baby. You've managed to land in the midst of a cosmic power struggle, and the poor joker in the middle of it all wants to get drunk and sleep the aching memories away."

When we reached Auberge and split up to go our separate ways, I did just that. In a nice, clean hotel room for a change.

12
ST. JUDAS

The nice clean sheets in the hotel room no longer looked nice or clean. Whatever I drank before falling into a stupor had sweated out again. I smelled as bad as I felt. Some memory from long ago slid away back where dreams come from, and I lay still, working at waking up.

After lolling about like that for a few minutes, I rolled out of bed and navigated toward the bathroom. One hot and cold shower and a shave later, I felt ready to make a phone call.

Pulling the business card out of my wallet, I set it next to the telephone and punched out the combination of numbers and letters. If the HWHY was some sort of mnemonic, I had no idea what it was for.

A female voice as pert and crisp as sunrise over the mountains said, "Forty-nine forty-nine. May I help you?"

"Is this the church?" I asked with a small degree of surprise. A church with an answering service?

"Church, sir?"

She must get darned few calls for them. "Uh . . . the St. Judas Church."

"Oh," she said with a pleasant tone. "One moment." The phone went silent.

I waited. A cigarette eventually found its way to my lips and got lit. Halfway through the smoke, a man's voice crackled onto the line. He had that sharp-edged bite that one would expect from a tough businessman, not from someone connected with a church. At least, not with a nonevangelical church.

"Who is this?" he demanded, as polite as a gunshot.

"A fellow believer," I said in a simpery voice. "A traveler on the path to understanding. A humble seeker after—"

"Cut the crap—I'm a busy man. Are you the guy that knows Joey Moreno?"

I stumbled over a thought. He'd caught me off guard with that one. "*Knew* Joey," I said. "He got iced last night."

It was his turn to pause. The silence on the other end was thick enough to lean against. After a moment, the voice spoke.

"How'd it happen?"

"Shot. In my office. I found him there."

"Did you by chance have anything to do with it?"

"Probably. He knew me too well."

Another pause. "That's a good answer. A very good one. Honest. I like that. Look, pal, I think I know what you're up to from what Joey told me. And I suspect that there's big trouble brewing because of it. And not just for Joey or you. This may have serious repercussions. Serious. I think we could both benefit from a talk."

He gave me an address on the eight hundred block of South Broadway. I told him I'd meet him in a couple of hours and rang off.

I ground out the cigarette and thought hard. It might be a setup. Whoever killed Joey could have planted the card on him. I loaded up my Colt and shoved it into my waistband holster.

The best way to find a trapper is to hang around His traps. . . .

In the middle of the east side of the block sat a squashed sort of building jammed between two other equally squashed buildings. A sign in the window hung at a careless angle.

CHECKS CASHED HERE
RUBBER STAMPS MADE TO ORDER
24 HOUR LEGAL FORMS
MAPS TO THE STARS'S HOMES

A three-by-five card—browned with time—was stuck to the window beneath the larger sign. The cellophane tape was likewise brown, curling away from the card and cracking in places. The card had two words and an arrow pointing upward at an angle.

CHURCH UPSTAIRS

I headed upstairs.

The steps looked as though they would creak as loud as bullfrogs in heat. I ascended slowly, touching only the outermost edge of every other step. It took awhile, but I reached the top of the staircase making as much noise as a foggy night.

The landing had been swept, at least, and the closed door had a small, engraved plastic sign.

ST. JUDAS CHURCH
OF HOLY TRIBULATION
AND TAX EVASION

I listened at the door. Voices beyond spoke casually. I liked that. I could hear every word. I liked that even more.

"If God is dead," asked a pleasant male voice, "what have people been getting at Communion?"

"A Guest Host." This voice was deep and gruff—the voice on the telephone. "Can we get back to work?"

"Okay. How's this one—'Bored with the Lord? Feast with the Beast!' "

"Catchy," the deeper voice replied, "but we need something that'll really inflame them. I want you to escape within three inches of your life."

The other man laughed. It was a warm, exuberant laugh. "You'd be happier if I were torn apart and martyred. *That* would give you some publicity."

"Don't think I might not prefer it. How about this—you could explain that all good Christians should actively support the Beast and the Antichrist because the Kingdom of God won't return until we've had a thousand years of tribulation. After all, if it's in the Bible, it's God's prophecy. And any good Christian can see the necessity of allowing God's prophecy to proceed. Hence, the most blessed Christians are the ones who put the Antichrist on the throne of the world."

There was a long pause. "Nah," said the higher voice, "too subtle."

I tickled my knuckles against the door. A couple of paint flakes stuck to my skin. I brushed them off as the door slid open.

I stood eye to eye with a beautiful man.

I couldn't call him handsome—his features weren't rugged enough. I couldn't call him pretty, because he looked in no way delicate. He was beautiful, that's all. And I'm not that kind of guy, either.

He looked at me with eyes the color of a morning sky near the ocean. They gazed intently, yet not disturbingly so. His hair was a mass of ringlety waves that curled down to his shirt collar. To call the curls blond would be to call gold a "yellowish metal." They shone, even in the dimly lit room, like the "yellowish metal" glows in bright sunlight. His face looked as though its expression could change from sardonic to dead serious with just a turn of his lips. At the moment, he was sardonic.

He scanned me with a grin. "Welcome to the holiest of holies—the church of He Who Would Turn the Last Supper Into a Friar's Roast." The grin was a beautiful grin—it didn't belong in this dump.

The room in which he stood was nothing more than a fifteen-by-twenty office. One dingy window looked out on a brick wall. What light the room had came from a pair of fly-specked bulbs overhead that burned uncovered. It gave the place all the hominess of a prison cell. Or maybe a prison library.

Shelves constructed of bricks and boards strained under the weight of books against every wall. There might have been fewer books in this room than in the home of Theodore Golding, though only because the sloppy, warped shelves could not reach all the way to the ceiling without danger of toppling. They looked as if a well-fed flea could have knocked them down.

In the center of the room—on a rug that had as much pile on it as a piece of burlap—sat a plain white altar with a man perched on top.

"Let the guy in," the man said in a tough, husky voice. "He doesn't need the spiel."

Adonis stepped aside. I stood in the doorway without moving. The man on the altar sat cross-legged, studying me. His thick, muscular body barely permitted the contortion.

He wore a suit that had been through three recessions, a depression, and maybe a panic or two. Someone such as he must have been around when they coined the word *burly*. Two beefy hands hung from his sleeves like chunks of rock laid across his lap. His face looked like a Teamsters' strike.

"You know Joey, right?" Bulldogs have barked more politely.

I pulled out a cigarette and made a big deal of lighting it.

"Knew," I said for the second time that day.

"I knew him, too." A little grief flickered in the man's eyes. Not much, but it seemed real enough. He unfolded his legs and got his arms in position to slide off the Formica cube. He stepped toward me, a much shorter man than I'd expected. He stared up at my eyes. Straight ahead, he'd have been gazing at my Adam's apple.

"Take the man's hat, Tom."

"That's not necessary," I said, blowing smoke in Tom's direction.

The beautiful face didn't wrinkle its nose or emit any prissy noises. His dreamlike blue eyes blinked twice, and a muted laugh snorted out of him with the sound of a distant drum.

I kept my hat on because I didn't want my current abstract hairdo to detract from my image.

"Your name's Dell Ammo," the short bear said. "Your business license lists you as a PI—which I don't suppose means Perfect Initiate—and I hope we've both proven we're tough and cool and can get down to brass tacks."

"You haven't proven much yet," I said. I was feeling wise. The smart guy. Dell Ammo—hard man.

Shortly after his fist connected with me, I was relocated to the hallway. He'd aimed for my solar plexus and hadn't missed. I made the sounds a drowning man makes and clutched at my guts. My right hand reached instinctively toward my waistband.

Seeing that, he turned to stroll back to his altar.

"Tough guy," he said through the thick buzz in my ears. "Has to pull heat at the first jab." He climbed up on the altar and folded his beefy legs with a yogi's agility.

I staggered back inside, feeling less the smart guy.

"Joey and I were friends in Berkeley," he said. "I was a right-wing conservative sort. Buckleyite. He was a Trotskyist. We met once when we both happened to be beating up some Larouchites. We found other interests in common and became friends, sort of. Over the years, he started reading a lot of Russian literature. I started reading Christian heretic and Gnostic writings. Joey got hooked on Tolstoy, started edging toward religious pacifism. One quarter, I see him come to class in a priest's getup. He'd quit the Trots to join the Russian Orthodox Church. Changed his major to religious studies. Same as Tom here."

Tom laughed. It wasn't quite the musical laughter of Apollo or whomever, but it had a note of carefree joy in it.

The grizzly voice continued. "Joey's folks were Mexican Catholic, so you know how they greeted him at home. When he came to L.A., he started working in the barrios. I don't know how he met you."

"We got drunk in a bar together once," I said. "He dragged me home."

"He was good conversation, Ammo. Same as Tom here. Good conversation is hard to find. Joey had a good mind—muddled sometimes, maybe a little naive . . ." He looked down at his hands.

I used the silence to scan the room for an ashtray. The butt ended up on the floor, ground beneath my heel.

Tom looked at me with a resigned smile.

"Joey apparently respected you." The fellow's voice had taken on a soft, far-off quality. That he knew me but didn't bother to give me *his* name was beginning to annoy me. His face, which looked as if it had been used to tenderize sides of beef, lost its tough, streetwise edge. "He was worried about you after a couple of big boys from his archdiocese paid him a visit." He shifted his weight around to take a grunting breath.

I closed the office door, though direct experience indicated that it wouldn't prevent eavesdropping.

"Anyway," he continued, "I suppose you'd like to know that they grilled him about you. That they asked rather pointed questions about your degree of faith, whether you believed in God or in Satan."

"So?" I asked. "Maybe they were checking the answers I gave on my application to Sunday school."

"You're like most people, Ammo. You think priests and bishops and rabbis and the like sit around praying and absolving people of the sins they've devised to instill guilt. Forget it. Religion is a con game like any other. It relies on efficient information gathering. You'd be surprised how well a confessional works for purposes of extortion."

"Even those they don't literally blackmail get shaken down," Tom said through a grin. "Who can resist throwing a few bucks toward someone who implies that you'll roast in hell for an eternity if you don't pay up? Certainly a far worse fate than any court or scandal sheet can threaten."

"Most people," I said, "seem willing to defer their punishment that long." I pulled up a dirty folding chair to sit on. "Get to the point. You knew Joey. Somehow he got dead in my office. What's that got to do with you and me?"

"Relax, Ammo," the guy on the altar said. "We're on the same side. I think." He pointed a thick index finger at me. "You're trying to find a way to expose religion as a hoax, and you're on some sort of a track that's got a certain group of powers-behind-the-throne scared out of their gowns. Enough for them to put a tail on Joey. Enough to kill him."

"So they kill him and don't wait around for me? As deduction, that stinks."

"Maybe something bigger scared them off. I was watching the news last night. Some fun happenings around Hollywood. More than usual, wouldn't you agree?"

He slid off the altar to walk over to where I was sitting. We were nearly eye-to-eye now. He looked me over, circling the chair. He peered at the scalp showing below my hat. He nodded approval at the wounds.

"Maybe you *are* a tough guy after all. Not many people go up against the Ecclesia and survive two warnings." He caught my frown of incomprehension. "*Ecclesia,*" he repeated, "with an impressively capital E. You won't find it in any reference book, even the ones that are fairly replete with information about Freemasons and the Bavarian Illuminati and other small-time conspiracies. Anyone you ask either won't know or will deny its existence. In religious circles, though, gossip circulates and leaks. They have their own unique conspiracy theories."

"Do they?" I asked, as raptly interested as I could be without stifling a yawn.

He poked at the still-swollen lump that served as a souvenir of my night escapades outside Auberge. Something dull throbbed through my body to ache against the newer bruises and slashes under my hat.

"The Ecclesia—" was about all he got out by the time my hand whipped around to sweep up under his chin. I had to crouch in the chair to reach that low. He sat with astonishing speed, landing on the floor with a thud that I thought would bring us crashing down into the shops below. He stared blankly forward, his hands useless by his sides.

I stood to look at Tom.

Adonis looked worried. It was an admirably beautiful worry. Michelangelo spent years trying to sculpt that kind of worry.

"Fine way to treat one another," I said to Tom. "We haven't even been formally introduced."

"Randolph Corbin," came a voice as thick as library paste. One hand massaged his jaw, the other extended upward, palm open. He leaned forward. I grasped his hand and pulled. My knuckles were sore from the punch, and his grip didn't help matters.

"Call me anything but Randy, and we won't cause each other trouble." He shuffled unsteadily to the white cube and leaned his bulk against it. It skidded a bit, dragging part of the rug with it. He shifted about to gaze up at me. I must have scored a hit on the button the way his round chin was getting rounder.

I felt bad about doing that. His face didn't need any more workouts.

"The Ecclesia," he continued, as though he'd just stopped for a breath, "is a loose association of high-level bishops, rabbis, imams, roshis, and various other shamans who have a vested interest in maintaining the power of religion. Organized religion. The kind that accumulates revenue. They consider any threat to the philosophical foundations of any faith to be a threat to all. They leave the lip service concerning holy wars to the lower echelons. In the same manner as the U.S. and the Soviet governments, they recognize that the pretense of being enemies is necessary to justify their mutual existences. Fear and hatred of the rival religion keeps the peons in line. The Ecclesia is securely entrenched. They've got the wealth of a dozen faiths to play with, and they're not interested in people who rock the boat."

He leaned toward me. "And you've got them worried, Ammo. Why?"

I smiled. Easing back in the chair, I pulled out another coffin nail and tapped it against the pack. Silently.

"They're sure as hell not concerned about me," Corbin said. "And look what I'm preaching." His arm swept about to encompass the room. "The Word of the Beast. The heretical absurdity that a true Christian should labor to bring the Antichrist to power so that God's prophecies can—finally—come to pass."

He frowned. "No one's ever so much as dropped me a nasty note. A couple of decades ago, when some researchers proved that Jesus had been rescued from the cross and lived to sire a child with Mary Magdalene, did the religious establishment even sniff? The book was a best-seller. Did the faith of millions come crashing?"

"Let me guess," I said. "No?"

"No. Even the revelation that the Death and Resurrection never happened bothered no one. Yet *you*—you they kill for." His fist pounded against the altar. "What's your angle, mister?"

I smiled. "Jovial old Jehovah is at the top of a hit list and I'm the torpedo."

Tom burst out laughing. Corbin stared at me. His chin was growing purplish. He didn't laugh.

"Don't get funny, Ammo."

"You seem to think I'm having a less than humorous effect."

"God's just one of a lot of ideas, Ammo. It's a metaphor for conscience—for the all-seeing eye that watches your actions and won't let you escape their consequences. God doesn't exist where you can track Him down and kill Him. You'd have to kill an *idea*."

"I'm hearing echoes," I said. "*Déjà vu*. I've heard all this before. Yet someone must think it's possible or I wouldn't be drawing a paycheck."

Corbin shook his head. Tom smiled again, saying, "Ghostbusters make a lot of money ridding homes of entities that don't exist. Someone wants you to exorcise the Holy Spirit. Better check your client's psychiatric record."

I didn't have to. I already knew it was pretty wobbly.

"Look, Ammo." Corbin spoke softly. "God is a concept

deep within most all of us that exists for a lot of reasons—fear, guilt, hatred. Sometimes even genuine worship and joy. It's other-directed, it's aimed outward from the self. When one is compelled to appease an all-powerful *thing* whose purpose is beyond human understanding, the stress causes severe psychological damage. In fact, the degree to which one achieves the good is the degree to which he or she *defies* the dictates of God. Or, I should say, what some *people* say are the dictates of God." He waved a hand about. "It's all just a way to keep people enslaved. To keep them from thinking, daring, or rebelling."

"Bravo," I muttered around my cigarette. "A brilliant new hypothesis."

"Not much of what I say is new," Corbin admitted, his face as pleasant as flat beer. "It just isn't repeated enough. The idea that one can live without God, or that He's a cruel hoax, or an age-old political tool is so alien to most people that they consider it a sin even to *think* about it."

"Perhaps," Tom cut in, "if you started grabbing people on the street, dragging them into alleys and hypnotizing them, you could get into their subconscious minds to pluck out the concept."

"Deprogramming?" It sounded like hard work.

Tom shrugged his suitably well-formed shoulders. "Well, not the sort that some church kidnappers practice. They simply reprogram in a traditional God to replace a socially unacceptable God. You'd have to leave them without *any* deep-seated theistic concepts."

"And there are as many concepts of God," Corbin added, "as there are human beings."

"*And*," Tom chirped, "you'd have to destroy the concept in everyone at once. Otherwise it might re-emerge and God would live again."

"Not only that"—Corbin strode around the room like a hyped-up fight promoter—"you'd have to provide enough intellectual ammunition to prevent people from backsliding. Something to battle their doubts with. Thought, after all, is the enemy of faith."

"You could use television. It's been used to hypnotize the masses for half a century." Tom was enjoying this as much as Corbin.

The stocky man ran his fingers along his chin. Touching the sore spot made him wince. He glowered at me. "TV's no good. Doesn't reach all the people. You've got to lower everyone's brain waves into a theta dream state all at once. As if they were dozing off. Yet leave in enough alpha wave state to enable them to alter their gestalts."

"Same as the ancient initiation rituals."

He smiled at Tom. "Hm. Isn't that so . . ." He nodded in my direction. "Know what we're talking about?"

"Alpha, theta—it's all Greek to me."

"Haw. Haw. Funny man. We're talking about brain wave frequencies." He looked at me with his small, buried eyes and shook his head. "A tough guy like you wouldn't care, would you?"

"I'm not tough. You said so yourself. I'm just a soft, sensitive guy who can't take rejection."

"Take a walk and never come back."

"I presume this concludes our audience?"

Corbin glared at me. "I've given you a warning and offered you my help—"

"Is that what it was? Sounded like a lecture to me." I headed toward the door.

"And you refused to come clean. Whatever you're trying, Ammo, you're up against stiff opposition. You can't do it alone."

"We all die alone," I said. "To kill, the only partner I need is my target."

"You're looking in all the wrong places."

I kept walking.

Tom stopped me with one lovely hand on my arm. "You can't leave without asking why he calls this the St. Judas Church."

"Watch me."

Tom was insistent. His fingers tightened with surprising strength around my arm. The friendly smile never left his lips.

"Because all the apostles betrayed their Lord, but only Judas felt bad enough about it to kill himself."

"Gee," I said, grasping Tom's wrist and squeezing until I felt cartilage grinding, "and all these years I thought Judas should be a saint because he was instrumental in granting God's greatest wish."

"Wish?" Corbin said.

"To feel what it's like to be human. To feel what it's like to die."

Corbin's jaw dropped as far is it could in its condition. Score one for me. Tom laughed.

I took one last look at that beautiful face and turned to go. His voice carried down the steps as I departed.

"How's that for meeting your theological match?"

"Forget him. We've got work to do."

The sound of Tom's laughter followed me onto the hot L.A. streets.

13
MORTIS OPERANDI

"Cancel the contract."

He sat on my hotel room bed, his black shoes on the bed-covers, his cane by his side. Even lying down, his evening clothes didn't show a wrinkle. He gazed at me with mild, friendly eyes. Their appearance was deceptive—the glance felt about as affable as a knife pointed at my throat.

I threw my jacket on the bed and closed the door behind me.

"What's wrong, Zack? Can't find any more virgins?" Ann had gone to her room with the kid for a moment. At least he'd caught me alone.

He folded his hands behind his head and lay back. "Let's not go into that. Let's just say that I've changed my mind."

I sidled up to the nightstand drawer to pull out a sack of bourbon. "Did I mess up your plans, Zack?"

"Thoroughly." He stopped trying to look amiable. "You don't have to go through with this. Just tell me you're canceling the contract."

I slugged down a good jolt of the sour mash. It warmed

me. "Zack," I said, "I've been thinking a lot about God lately, thanks to you. I was never a fan of Hallelujah House, but you've still managed to get my soul thinking about the Almighty. He seems to have screwed this world up fairly well, so I don't see any reason not to have Him deposed. I may even have the M.O. figured out. Everyone's been remarkably helpful."

"Keep the money. I'll even give you a termination bonus."

"Sorry," I said. "If I cancel the contract, I die."

"I guarantee that you won't."

"How do I know that isn't a Princely lie?"

He stiffened. "Cancel it, Ammo. Save yourself a lot of heartache."

"I'm no stranger to heartache, Zacharias." I eyed him from behind my glass of bourbon. "I take it you can't cancel the contract unilaterally." It was a wild guess, but from the way he tightened his jaw, I knew I'd hit home. "You can't even break your own promises. What a laugh!"

"The contract must be dissolved by mutual agreement, of course. You have nothing to gain by continuing this pointless endeavor."

"I'll have to think it over."

"There are powerful forces combining to stop you, Mr. Ammo. Do not add me to their legion."

I said nothing. For a long moment we stared at each other. He slowly moved a hand from behind his head.

"I sent a warning to you via an old man. Your lady left it behind." He quickly pulled something from behind the pillow and tossed it on the bed. He stood.

"I don't know how you two located each other," he said. "Suffice it to say that such treachery is unforgivable."

"I'll worry about forgiveness from the other guy, Zack." I glanced at the thing on the bed. It looked exactly like the flame dagger Ann had pulled out of the mutant. The hilt was still intact. The blade, though, had corroded as if it had lain under-water for a century. Rust flakes sprinkled the bedcovers in an oval around where it landed.

Zacharias opened the door.

"As I said once before, I do not tolerate betrayal."

The door slammed.

I picked up the dagger and looked it over for a few moments. Something had done a number on it. The blade very nearly crumbled in my hand. I filed it in the wastebasket.

So my client suddenly wants me off the case and needs my consent to do so. That put me in a predicament. I was moving on my own momentum now. I'd been sapped, drugged, kidnapped, and generally mishandled in the last few days, all in the name of God.

If He was anything like His followers, it wouldn't be murder. It would be pesticide. As far as I was concerned, this contract terminated with God.

Or me.

I withdrew what revalued money I had out of my various bank accounts and relocated to an office in the old Union Bank Building. It stood northwest of Arco Tower and had been protected from the bomb blast in South Tower by the bulk of North Tower's mass. I snuck back into my old office at night to remove everything I needed.

The next couple of days were spent in the new office overlooking the decaying ruin of Old Downtown. I sat by the window, thinking.

There had to be a way to kill God even if there were no *corpus Domini* before or after the act. If God didn't exist in some real, tangible way, then what was I up against? An idea, as Golding and Corbin both implied? Could an idea be so powerful as to rule the minds of men for a hundred centuries?

I shrugged. If people can believe in "just wars" and "honest politicians," they can believe in an all-powerful, all-seeing, totally benevolent God who permits suffering and evil to exist. When you begin with false premises, you can get any conclusion you want. True or false.

If God did exist, regardless of how He was perceived, perhaps He could be flushed out into the open by the same sort of tactics I'd use if He were only an idea. Maybe God isn't dead—but He's not at all well. How powerful is a God who—

in spite of Biblical warnings—is mocked, and mocked repeatedly with every disaster that's labeled an Act of God, our supposed protector?

How alive is a God that everyone laughs at? Or ignores? Or forgets?

This was giving me a headache. I switched on the TV plaque and flipped through the channels with the remote.

Channel 3 was running the fourteenth chapter of *Nixon: A Giant Betrayed*. I'd seen it. Channel 4 had a commercial for a licorice-flavored cereal called Krunchy Molas. Kids stuck black-stained tongues at the screen while a chorus sang the jingle.

I switched before I lost *my* breakfast cereal.

I flipped right past a rerun episode of *The Bold Bureaucrats* without stopping. Channel 7 was screening a double feature in its Appropriate Billing series. They were running this duo under their combined titles: *Conduct Unbecoming . . . An Officer and a Gentleman*. That was better than last week's coupling: *On the Beach . . . Where the Boys Are*.

I flipped to UHF. On Channel 23, piped in from Disney County, was one of the most odious talk shows on the air. It was also one of the most popular.

"Ladies and gentlemen," snarled a vicious announcer, "and all you welfare bums and draft-dodging slimeballs—it's time for"—a drum rolled, a flank of bugles sounded—"the most moral show on television, *Ad Hominem Attack*! With your host—a paragon of virtue who never lets a guest escape unscathed—'Beaver' Lenny!"

The audience cheered as if it were Superbowl Sunday. "Beaver" Lenny strode onscreen like a president on inauguration day. The camera angle was such that he looked taller than any mortal. He had silver hair, even though he was only thirty-five. The suit he wore was Wall Street Traditional. He smiled like a college kid and spoke with as much animated enthusiasm.

"All right!" he shouted, his dark eyes glaring at the camera with feral glee. "How do you feel tonight?"

"Morally outraged!" the studio audience cheered.

I was ready to find another station when he yelled back at them.

"Great! Stoke that rage, because tonight on *Ad Hominem Attack* we've got a real scumbucket for you. His name's Thomas Russell, and he's from a gang of degenerates called the St. Judas Church of Holy Tribulation and Tax Evasion."

My brain went numb with an odd panic. Was this another coincidence? Another *meaningful* coincidence? All my thoughts evaporated. This show might prove interesting.

Beaver Lenny stepped toward his audience, the camera pulling back to give a wide angle shot.

"St. Judas," he hollered. "I can understand the tax evasion part—that's as American as unregistered handguns. But *blasphemy?*" He grinned. "Well, fellow righteously idignant, how many bodyguards do I want for *this* creep?"

"Eight!" someone from the audience shouted.

"Come on," Lenny hollered. "You can do better than that!"

"Five!" a dozen or so shot back.

The host bounded around the stage like a teenager in heat. "C'mon, c'mon. He's a threat to our American values. He's trying to undermine our faith, our morals, and our *philosophical underpinnings!*"

"Three!" screamed half the audience.

"Two!" responded the other half.

"One!" they all cried.

"*None!*" The roar was unanimous.

"All *right!*" Lenny shouted back amidst the applause. "I face him alone! Man to worm! Let's welcome Thomas Russell!"

Tom wandered onstage, as smiling and as beautiful on TV as in real life. He stepped through a metal detector to reach his seat.

Lenny shook his hand and sat behind his desk. He looked delightfully ready to spill blood.

"Russell—you unmitigated scuzzpit—I understand you've written a book entitled *The God State*. I'll skip the obvious question of how one as morally bankrupt as you can even compose a coherent sentence. I'll even contain my amazement that

Taylor and Siegal published it—though it's typical of those corrupt East Coast culture-distorters."

The audience cheered.

"Let me start by asking you who in hell gave you the right to spout this drivel about the two greatest aspects of Western civilization—God and Government?"

The sardonic expression on Tom's face never even wavered. He seemed to be taking this about as seriously as his host.

"Well, Beaver, *The God State* is actually a sequel to my first book. In the first book—*My God, My Self*—I explained that God is an idea perpetuated as a means for the few to control the many. Initially, there was the priest class, who decided that all conversation with the forces of nature should be channeled through them. At a price, of course. In *The God State*, I deal with the rise of the Judeo-Christian cult of guilt worship and how religious ruling classes have—from the very start—been in control of every government in the history of mankind."

The audience booed. The microphones picked up someone hollering, "Sweeping generalization!"

"Many theocratic groups," Tom continued, "have been quite flagrant about their clandestine involvement, leaving their signs and symbols openly displayed as if daring someone to expose them."

"Come off it, you smirking heap of atheistic garbage." Lenny leaned forward at his desk. "Are you accusing the United States of violating its constitutional guarantee of separation of church and state?"

The audience cheered Beaver on.

Tom smiled even more broadly. "The Constitution isn't worth the parchment it's written on." Over the hissing, he added, "We're dealing with deeds, not words. Nearly every President of the United States has been a member of the Ancient and Accepted Order of Freemasons—a secret religious society—"

"That's old news. Disney County *perfected* conspiracy paranoia."

Tom leaned back in his chair. "Nearly everything in my book is old news. I display it from a new perspective. By the time you've finished reading it, you'll be more suspicious of the chaplains that roam the corridors of Congress, setting up prayer meetings. You'll notice the mystical symbols and sentiments expressed on our currency. Blatant theistic sentiments such as 'In God We Trust.' "

Lenny leaned on his fists. "I can't believe it! On my show, this pansy-haired wimp is attacking a tradition as old as our nation!"

"Not really, Beaver." Tom spread his arms out across the empty chairs flanking him. "The statement has only been on this government's money since 1864, when it was used as a rallying slogan for one side of a brutal, divisive war. It didn't even appear on all the coins until the twentieth century, when the five-cent piece finally received the Mark. And it wasn't until as late as 1954 that the slogan became the legal and official motto of the United States—during a flareup of patriotic witch-hunting."

Lenny turned to the audience with outstretched arms. "The phlegm-brained cretin is undercutting his own thesis!" he said with feigned amazement. "He's admitting that for nearly a century there was no religious control of government."

Tom waved his hand in dismissal. "They weren't as overt in their symbols primarily because most Americans still remembered the excesses of the God State back in England. The cults grew bolder, though. The Great Seal of the United States contains many mystical symbols. Significantly, they are all on the *reverse* side, which is never used to authenticate official documents. This is an astonishingly blatant depiction of the power of religion behind the throne of state."

"So what? If they're in control of every goverment, then the power is in balance and unimportant."

"*Yeah!*" screamed the crowd in unison. "*So what!*"

"The power is *not* in balance. That's why we have wars. The God State is *not* monolithic. Even in the United States there is evidence of an internal battle for control of this continent by at least two factions—a productive, isolationist sect of woman-worshipping pagans and atheists versus a brutal, interventionist patriarchic cult that worships the Hebrew and Christian god Yahveh."

"That's a pretty baldfaced mixture of blasphemy and treason, you feeble-minded, Bible-burning Satanist!" The color of Lenny's face verged on ultraviolet. He turned to the audience. "Do I throw this miserable sleazebag Antichrist out?"

"*Yeah!*" the studio thundered.

"You're gettting close, gutterbrain," he said to Tom. "One more bit of sacrilege, and you're finished."

Tom smiled, addressing the camera. "Consider this. At the outset, this country's coinage depicted symbols of liberty— goddesses offering gifts of bounty, eagles flying majestically free, native Indians still noble and unbowed." He put an ankle up on his knee and leaned comfortably back.

"Then in 1909, Victor Brenner designed the Lincoln cent. It was the first depiction on official U.S. coinage of a dead U.S. statist. It was a clear victory for the patriarchists, who'd had the generic term for a masculine deity on several coins for half a century—sometimes right next to Lady Liberty herself." Russell looked straight at Lenny. "I don't have to remind you that World War One began five years later, or that the United States was dragged in three years after that. Both five and three are numbers sacred to the Goddess."

"You're not only a syphilitic little jerkoff," Lenny shouted, "you're a shitbrained *mystic!*" He whipped his head about to stare into the camera. "Do I throw this godless son of a bitch out?"

"*Yeah!*" The audience was eating it up.

"I suppose this anti-American mystical babble will end with you describing how communism is a superior form of government because it's free of religious taint."

Russell smiled that beautiful smile. "Actually, Beaver, despite their professed and official atheism, the Communist bloc nations were seized and are still controlled by an ancient hierarchy of renegade druids. Holy men who betrayed their Goddess to seek power and conquest through magick."

"Druids?" Lenny didn't even try to contain his shock.

"Tree-worshippers? A bunch of looney-tunes with leaves in their hair in control of the most brutal and powerful nations on earth?"

Tom looked as pleased as a first-year chemistry student showing off the smoking ruins of his lab.

"Look at the flag of the Soviet Union. The symbols are right there."

Beaver Lenny buried his face in his hands, shaking his head from side to side.

"It consists of a golden sickle and hammer surmounted by a star, all on a field of red. The standard explanation of its proletarian, revolutionary derivation is nothing more than a smokescreen—much the same as the explanation of the Great Seal of the United States. There is a second, hidden derivation."

Russell looked toward the camera and raised fingers to count his points.

"One—the golden sickle was used by druids to lop mistletoe off oak trees in a symbolic recreation of the castration of Cronos by his son Zeus. Mistletoe is a phallic symbol, so watch out next Christmas—or Yule. Two—the hammer is suggestively phallic and crossing the blade of the sickle as if about to be cut."

He held up a third finger. "Three—red is the druidic color of death and life; it is the color of the food offered up to the dead during Hallowmas. And four—above it all is the five-pointed star—the pentagram, symbol of the Goddess, whom they still feel required to acknowledge. It is the single universal symbol of all magic, good or evil. You see it on scores of flags, even that of the U.S. And by the way, Beaver—red, white, and blue are the traditional colors of the Triple Goddess."

Before he could begin to use the fingers on his other hand, Lenny rose up to holler, "Are you implying that the Cold War has been nothing but a power struggle between bricklayers and tree-trimmers?"

"Not at all." Tom's smile remained just as broad. "While there have been minor skirmishes in which the leaders of one God State threw their slaves into battle against the slaves of another God State, *all the governments of the world are partners in crime.* They are allied to maintain their power and privilege. They're part of the same club. Have you ever seen the leader of one government personally jump for the throat of the leader of an 'enemy' government?"

"That's not how affairs of state are handled." Lenny sat again. He hadn't incited the audience enough.

"Indeed not," Tom replied. "Affairs of the God State are handled by forcing some eighteen-year-old to kill another eighteen-year-old while those who planned the slaughter call each other on hotlines to talk about the weather."

"That does it!" Lenny jumped up from his desk, advancing on Russell. "This is *my* show, and *nobody* says the U.S. of A. is in cahoots with the Commies!" He seized Tom's shirt and pulled him up to shout, *"Get off my show!"*

The audience went wild. They cheered, hooted, stomped. Someone threw confetti. They started to chant.

"Beaver, Beaver, Beaver, Beaver . . ."

Tom smiled, flashed his fingers in an "okay" sign.

The cameras barely registered the friendly grin that appeared and vanished from Lenny's face in the course of an instant. There was nothing "Beaver" Lenny enjoyed more than someone who understood the joke.

I switched the screen off to think for a bit.

I'd heard all the conspiracy theories before, probably even caused a few of them by the nature of my activities. I knew enough to figure out that any particular conspiracy must allocate its resources and confine its activities to areas that present either the greatest opportunity or the greatest threat.

If the "God States" were on my trail, I might have a difficult time surviving one breath to the next.

I needed a drink. Something to numb my mind. Reaching toward the desk drawer, I hesitated.

I had someone to drink with! I punched up the number of Ann's room over at Auberge.

"Sure," she said. "Give me ten minutes."

I poured two drinks. Getting drunk together was better than getting drunk alone. Even though the alcohol blocked the

world out, it permitted me to concentrate more closely, however fuzzily, on my own thoughts and on my partner's.

She arrived in a little over ten minutes. A sleek red dress
that had been poured on made her look like a pillar of fire
topped by golden sunlight.

I handed her a glass and said, "Here's to open government
and numb minds."

"Been watching Congress on satellite again?"

"Close—*Ad Hominem Attack*."

Ann snorted. "Those twits in his audience have their minds
set on getting hypnotized by that insulting creep."

"Hypnotized," I muttered. The bourbon trickled into my
brain. I took another slug. Something started to click.

Minds set.

Hypnosis.

Mindset.

Subliminal ads.

TV sets.

Satellite TV.

Set.

Setting.

Dosage.

"*Jesus H. Christ and his bastard son Harry!*"

Ann looked at me with a puzzled frown.

"Ann!" I shouted, jumping up from the chair. "I've got it
figured!"

She took a sip of the liquor and continued to frown. "Got
what figured?"

"How to kill God!" I felt a surge of excitement rush
through me. All doubts about my intentions fled—this was
what I wanted to do. Reaching for a notepad and pen, I
scrawled a list of anything that came to mind.

She nearly snorted in a delicate sort of way. "That easily?"

I kept scribbling. "Easy to conceive, difficult to execute.
That's how God's managed to survive this long." I took her
drink and slapped the note in her hand. "Let's get back to
Auberge."

She followed me out of the office, reading the list as intently as a tax auditor. "Mescaline, psilocybin, LSD-25, THC, fentanyl, STP, BZ, DMT, MDMA—are you singlehandedly trying to bring back the Sixties?"

"That's when the first step toward mass deicide began." We zoomed down to ground level in a blissfully operative elevator. The evening sky was dark and clear.

"Tryptophan," she continued, "Vasopressin, B-12, phenylalanine? Getting a bit health-conscious, aren't you?"

"I'm going to need it."

We passed through the old Bonaventure Hotel, striding past the dozing night clerk. One couldn't call the tenants in this high-rise anything but marginally wealthier bums than those who inhabited Arco North.

She read the remainder of the list. "What's all this other stuff for?"

"I'm not sure yet," I said, reaching for a cigarette. We entered Auberge at the hatch on Fourth and Hope. "I'm certain, though, that there's something still lack—"

"Oh no," piped the squeaking voice of Isadora Volante. "Who let you two in?"

I looked down at the telepathic runt, tapped the cigarette on the back of my hand, and raised it to my lips, smiling.

14
EYECATCHER

I wasn't too specific when I asked Isadora for her help in a little plan of mine. She agreed to help me after I pointed out that we'd saved her from Zacharias and after she determined that my credit was good. That left me free to concentrate on the setup.

The next day I canvassed advertising agencies from Capistrano Beach to Oxnard. By noon my ears begged for relief from the avalanche of garrulous pitches. Only a few of the alleged people with whom I spoke sounded more original than sandwich boards and handbills.

The handful of impressive ones I invited up to the Union Bank Building for a final decision in my office. Getting them to come to Old Downtown required that I reveal how much I was willing to spend on the campaign. After finding that out, none of them had any qualms about the campaign's contents, either.

Two days later, a dozen advertising types gathered in my office to win my business. They scuttled, strode, or swished in with their presentations in hand. I seated them around the room in a rough semicircle.

Ann watched the exhibition from the far corner. Her makeup valiantly attempted to disguise the dark half-moons of exhaustion under her eyes. She had offered to raise funds for the ads I'd proposed by playing poker at the no-limit tables in Auberge casinos. Her mood dripped from her like weak acid, cutting when it had the strength.

The first pitchman pulled some illustration board from a fake leather portfolio. You could have attached his face to an ax handle and used it to split logs.

"This is a preliminary concept," he said in a nasal voice, deeper than I'd expected, "of our visualization of the ideation you related to us over the phone."

Ann winced.

I lit up a Camel and leaned back to gaze at the small sign he held. In cheerful, pink-hued lettering, it read

YOU WON'T FEEL GUILTY
OR FULL OF SIN
ON THE FIRST OF THE YEAR
WHEN GOD'S DONE IN!

"Too wordy," Ann said, looking out the window over the L.A. basin.

The hack protested weakly. "It's a unified conceptualization that encapsulates the elements you requested—God's death and the date of it."

"It's a damned ad for Burma Shave," she countered, "not for a specific philosophical point. The date is vague, and *done in* is a colloquialism"—she turned to stare the man directly in the eyes—"and I could write better jingles on a Scrabble board."

The man harrumphed, retrieved his portfolio, and departed. Back to shaving cream, I suppose.

"Next," I said to the crowd.

One nervous young man gulped and rose. "I can see you're no match for me."

He left without giving us a show.

"Next."

A heavyset, ruddy man turned a sketch pad my way. Tasteful blue letters on a gray background read

GOD IS NOT DEAD . . .
YET!

"Not bad," I said.

"It's a negative," Ann said through a barely stifled yawn. "We need a positive statement that god will die. And the date."

"Is she with you?" the huckster asked.

"Next."

A short, plump, woman aged a few years older than I volunteered next. She peered at me cheerfully through thick eyeglasses set in a black pair of men's frames.

"So," she said, smiling, "you want to tell everyone that God's dead." She spoke with a mild Russian accent. Her hands made dramatic flourishes as she pulled a poster from a thick cardboard tube.

"Here's what's going to catch their eyes!"

The poster unrolled to reveal a carefully watercolored image of a crucified skeleton. It looked hauntingly lonely. On its shoulder perched the tiny skeleton of a dove. Beneath the scene—in lurid yellow letters—shouted the logo

THE YEAR OF OUR LORD 2000
WON'T BE!

The woman smiled with pride. She seemed to be the sort who probably had a lovely garden in her front yard and made cookies for all the neighborhood kids.

Ann cleared her throat as gently as she could. She looked in my direction, imploring.

"Uh—it's very nice," I said, "but it's, um . . . a bit obscure. It'll go right over most people's heads."

The woman nodded with a resigned smile. The watercolor disappeared into the brown tube. She shouldered her purse, headed for the door.

"Oh, well," she said, "win a few, lose a few—so it goes."

She waved at everyone remaining in the office. "Ta!" she said, sparkling merrily.

At least she had a good attitude.

I gazed over the remaining faces. Judging by expressions alone, there wasn't much hope left. Except for one.

A tall, chestnut-haired woman sat bent over a sketch pad, making quick motions with a colored pencil. She glanced up at me, then at Ann.

"I'll go next," she said in a voice as low, cool, and sharp-edged as chilled dry wine. "It'll save you time, and you can send the others home before they embarrass themselves."

The rest of the candidates muttered like discouraged coyotes.

"Over whose heads in particular do you not want to go?" she asked us.

"Over anyone's," I said.

Ann gave her the once-over about five times. "It's an idea-saturation campaign. We want to reach *everyone*. People who aren't open to rational arguments. People who only respond to emotional assaults, such as the illiterate—or the intellectuals."

The woman nodded and resumed her sketching. The other contenders watched in agitation. Her dark hair caught bits of light from here and there in the room to reflect a rich red-brown hue. As she scribbled, she spoke.

"If you want maximum impact, stick to simple symbols and wording. Now, what exactly are you trying to convey?"

I watched her long fingers at work. "We want as many people as possible to get the impression that God will die on the first day of the year two thousand A.D."

She wrote something at the top of the pad with swift, precise strokes. Several of the advertising hacks leaned over to see what she'd drawn.

One of them sighed, picked up his belongings, and made tracks.

After a moment of considering the finished product, she turned the sketch pad over to show Ann.

"I think that's it," Ann said with a smile. "Dell?"

The woman turned it toward me. Large letters blazed in sharp angles of crimson.

ON THE FIRST DAY OF THE YEAR 2000
GOD WILL DIE . . . .

I nodded. She knew what to give the customer. Then I looked at the drawing below the slogan.

It was a fair likeness of God from the Michelangelo painting on the Sistine Chapel. A good choice. Most everyone in the Judeo-Christian world and a good deal of people outside it have seen that image in one form or another.

A black circle surrounded the Godhead. Rifle crosshairs intersected at a point directly over His left temple.

"That says it." I stubbed out my cigarette. "Thank you all for showing up," I said to the others.

As they wandered out, Ann and I walked over to the woman. She stood. She was taller than I was.

"That symbol is going to be plastered all over the world," I said. "Who do you work for, sister?"

"Nobody," she said. "I own an agency called McGuinne-Corp. And my name's Kathleen, not 'sister.' "

I could see it would be the beginning of a beautiful relationship.

15
PROMOTION

"That's outrageous!"

Emil Zacharias glared at me with such utter, raging hatred that I had to clench my teeth in order to remain smiling.

He sat behind his desk at the Culver City office of Hallelujah House. I hadn't figured on finding him there—I'd only wanted to leave a note about what I was planning. His secretary, though, apparently had been expecting me. I was ushered into a munificently well-appointed office about the size of a small cathedral. There he lounged, as calm and pouty as a pampered cat.

He didn't stay that way for long.

"I refuse!" he screamed. "You can't force my hand on this one, Ammo!"

"I think I can." I lit a cigarette slowly, letting him stew for a moment. "The contract, as I recall it, was for five hundred a day plus expenses. All the bills I'm running up are legitimately involved in the fulfillment of that contract."

Zack leaned forward, palms flat on the desktop.

"I urge you once more, Ammo, to cancel the contract and quit this game. Give it up. I can't guarantee your safety otherwise."

"I'm not here to debate," I said. "I just want you to know that there may be a drain on your finances that I'm certain you'll find a way to replace. Hand over your checkbook."

He stared at me as if I'd asked for certain portions of his anatomy that (rumor had it) he already lacked.

"Don't bother signing them. I'm sure your bank will make good." I held out my hand.

With a feral growl, he pulled a large leather check register from the top drawer of the desk. It slid across the mahogany to my side.

"Thanks, Zack," I said, hefting it under my arm as I rose. "You'll be seeing the results over the next few weeks." I turned back at the door to nod toward him. "If I don't see you again, have a happy New Year."

"Drop dead."

"That," I said perhaps a bit too cockily, "is contractually excluded."

The billboard faced west on the Sunset Strip, visible all the way from King's Road to the top floors of the buildings lining the intersection at La Cienega.

A man in smudged white overalls applied paint to the last letter of the slogan. He lowered the scaffolding and stepped off, taking his brushes and paints with him. One last glance at a proof of the ad confirmed to him that he'd made a perfect copy.

He probably thought it was a promotional teaser for a new film or rock album. Had he known that there were thousands of people such as he painting or pasting up the same message around the world (on Hallelujah House's tab), he might have thought otherwise.

Ann looked at the sign, arms folded. Her golden hair streamed glowingly over the dark blue business outfit hugging her form. She gazed silently at the billboard.

In the lower right-hand corner, a faithful rendition of Michelangelo's God pointed His finger toward Sunset Boulevard. The rifle crosshairs painted over Him intersected at His left temple. The official slogan blazed in crimson above Him.

ON THE FIRST DAY OF THE YEAR 2000
GOD WILL DIE . . . .

"You think that no one will take it seriously," Ann said, running one long, earth-toned nail along her jawline.

"Nobody takes advertising seriously except advertisers."

We stood near the Roxy Theater. The day was only beginning to grow warm. Nearly everywhere else in the United States, mid-November brought an unusual cold. Predictions of a severe winter circulated alongside prognostications of far worse.

The tiny painter had disappeared behind the billboard. A moment later, the scaffolding slowly lowered to the ground out of our view. The word DIE. . . . glistened in the afternoon sun like fresh blood slowly drying. We turned to head back to where my car was parked, over on Olive.

"Though no one will take the ads seriously, it gets the idea of God's death into people's heads. That's part of the set Father Beathan said was necessary for his sort of method."

"I just hope we're not tipping our hand." She didn't look too pleased.

I shrugged. "No one will believe in a conspiracy that operates out in the open. It goes against human nature. Martin Luther King and Gandhi both unsettled their nation's rulers by openly announcing every move they were going to make. The tactic confused the enemy into looking for secret maneuvers where there were none. It drove them crazy."

Ann nodded with a distracted air. She seemed lost in thought. "Hitler," she said, "announced his intentions, too."

"And," I added, "nobody took him seriously, either."

"Yes, but look what happened to him."

"He was a politician," I said with a shrug. "They all fall, sooner or later."

"Primarily," a voice behind me interjected, "because they misuse magickal symbols." It was a beautiful voice.

Ann and I turned around.

"In Hitler's case," said Thomas Russell, "he made the fatal mistake of reversing the swastika—an ancient symbol of the sun—as a mark of earthly state power. His downfall was guaranteed from that point." He sighed. "I sometimes wonder whether all those pentagrams on the U.S. flag are going to save us."

He looked up at me. "I like your sign. Trying to cash in on millennial fever?"

"Fever?" Ann asked.

"Round numbers," he said, "bring out the mystic in people."

"Yeah," I said. "I'm starting my own end-of-the-world cult. Five grand gets you the privilege of taking orders from me and including me in your will. We'll be in the Mojave watching for the saucers. If it doesn't rain." We reached my car—one of the last Chryslers built. I leaned against the side to stare at him.

"So you're really planning to go through with it," he said. "You really plan to kill Him."

Ann gave me a sour look. "No one will believe an open conspiracy," she muttered, as biting as bathtub gin. Her gaze turned to the young man. "I don't think we've been introduced."

"Ann Perrine, meet Thomas Russell—religious studies student, author, and survivor of the *Ad Hominem Attack* show. Tom—meet Ann, my financial manager."

They made courteous sounds at each other. He looked at Ann to ask, "You've figured out a method?"

She merely smiled at him.

I did, too.

"Fine," he said. "Play the sphinx. It doesn't matter what you do to God. People will still act like bastards or not, depending on their perception of their own self-interest. It's just that without God, they'll have one fewer light to guide their actions."

"Or one fewer excuse for their evils." I opened the passenger door for Ann. "In any case, they'll have one fewer leader to obey."

"When did they ever obey Him?" Tom muttered. He turned to leave.

I stepped around to my side of the car. Ann had unlocked the door. I nodded a farewell to Tom and reached for the handle.

That's when the first bullet hit.

The side window shattered, the safety glass grasping the fragments like a spiderweb holding dew.

I ducked behind the door and grabbed for my .45.

"Down, Ann!" I shouted.

Tom hit the pavement and rolled between my car and a blue Subaru. Three more shots made their points against the maroon paint job.

I tried to use the sideview mirror as a periscope. No good. I coaxed the engine into life.

"Hey!" a voice screamed from behind. "You're taking my cover!"

"Sorry pal," I muttered. The car coughed and sputtered. "Come on, Fritz," I pleaded, "catch."

The engine turned and whined. It sounded like a Cuisinart.

The four shots were all that had been fired. That didn't encourage me to poke my head up. The Chrysler backed out and pulled into traffic without much benefit of navigation. I put our lives into the hands of the other commuters, hoping that their aversion to the cost of auto repairs would keep them from plowing into us. Ann said something under her breath that I didn't catch. If she was praying, I didn't want to know about what—or to whom.

At the summit of Olive, I peeked up to look in the rearview.

Tom raced away from Sunset, crouched low behind parked cars. A white, late model DeLorean Vendetta sedan squealed around a corner.

"Here comes the chase scene!" I hit the accelerator. The car raced to catch up. Other drivers blared their horns.

Pedestrians jumped out of the way. Bystanders grinned. They were probably looking for the movie cameras.

"Brace yourself!"

Ann wedged herself farther down into the space under the dashboard.

I tested the other driver's reaction time by ramming the brake pedal into the floorboard. The Chrysler skidded.

The other driver failed the test. The DeLorean's tires screamed in unison. I fought to stay loose and resilient. Then they hit us.

The roll down the hill outside Auberge had been worse. The sedan slammed into us while it was still braking. I took my foot off the brake and let the impact shove us forward. I floored it while the other car skidded sideways. A couple of sharp turns deposited us downhill on La Cienega. Ann sat up and looked around. After a couple miles, I checked for the DeLorean. No sign.

"Ecclesia?" she asked.

I shrugged. "Lead is lead. I don't care who fired it—it's impolite."

"What now?"

I cut over to Crescent Heights and turned toward the Valley. "Let's go shopping."

"This," the man in the lab coat said, "is the Theta Wave Amplifier." He rubbed one pudgy hand against the light blue enameling of the device. His body described the general outline of a small mountain. Or perhaps a large beachball topped by red hair and a beard that framed a ruddy face.

"We've been working on it here at Peripherals for the past ten years."

I wasn't interested in a history lesson. Ann was off talking to the owner.

He reacted to my lack of response by clearing his throat just enough to stuff a Twinkie into it. His extremely off-white smock served as his napkin.

"The Theta Wave Amplifier increases the activity of the

brain in the four-to-eight Hertz region—the frequency associated with dreaming and creativity. At the same time, it maintains a corresponding balance in the Delta and Alpha regions. We use it mostly to intensify dreams in thought-mapping of test subj—"

"Sold."

"Huh?" he said.

"I said, sold. I'll give you the delivery instructions and a check. If you have no objections."

"Uh . . . why, no." It was probably the quickest deal he'd ever made. Staring at me from under puffy eyelids, he asked, "What sort of research will you be using it in?"

"Something involving a twelve-year-old telepathic hooker."

He blinked a couple of times and reached for another Twinkie. The plate fell to the floor without his noticing.

We took a trip down to the trading floor of Auberge. Even though it was well after midnight, all the shops were open. Our destination was Selene Pharmaceuticals.

An alluring sky-blue dress enwrapped Ann in a disturbingly sexy manner, yet no one on the trading floor noticed her. I asked her about it. She shrugged, though her coolly flip reply contained a good deal of caution.

"I must have applied the wrong makeup."

We wandered through the drugstore, picking up the necessary contraband. As long as we were in Auberge, we could buy and do pretty much what we wished.

Once we left the complex, we were subject to the drearier laws of the City and the County of Los Angeles, State of California, United States of America. Which would mean we'd be about as safe as we were in Auberge, but we'd have to handle our own bribes.

Ann placed the drugs in an attaché case while I forked over some gold to the proprietor of Selene Pharmaceuticals, whose paisley shirt sported a patch embroidered with the name Tom. He hardly raised an eyebrow at the way in which we cleaned out his inventory of psychoactive drugs. His mind was quite probably elsewhere.

I lugged the attaché out of the store. "All we need now is a spaceship."

"I've been checking into that," Ann said. "Commercial Phoenix flights are all booked for the next five months, and no one is willing to sublet us some room. I even went as far as finding out about the two old NASA shuttles. It turns out that they're such rusty hulks, they'd cost billions to get working again."

"Well, we can't do it from the ground. The direct broadcast satellites can only be modified in orbit."

She smiled. "There is a way. A company called StratoDyne has filed Chapter Eleven bankruptcy."

I snorted. "I don't think even Zacharias has enough dough to buy a shuttle manufacturer."

"He won't have to. The owner will give us the company and its one working shuttle for practically nothing."

That puzzled me a tad. "Why do you think that?"

She smiled wickedly. "He draws to inside straights."

It was all she had to say.

16
POKER

The first blast of autumn cold blew through Old Downtown the next night. Twilight colored the sky a deep, somber red as Ann and I made our way from my office to Auberge. Wind eddied around the little hill and headed toward Westwood and Santa Monica. The frigid breeze transformed street dust and paper trash into dancing spirits, whirling like drunken show-girls down the avenues and alleys.

We passed through the security entrance to head for the Casino of the Angels. I wore a tux for one of the rare times in my life. Basic black with a light blue shirt that lacked all the effeminate ruffles that seemed currently in fashion. If I was a sore thumb, I was proud of it.

Ann had somehow managed to adhere an emerald evening gown to her skin. No detail of her allure could hide beneath the clinging fabric. She found some way to breathe, though. Did she ever. . . .

A slit in the dress traveled up her left thigh to where it had no business being. A slender blue garter peeked out with every graceful step she took.

I expected half the casino to suffer myocardial infarction when she entered. No one gave her as much as a mild glance.

Eunuchs. Or worse.

She took a seat at the no-limit poker table. Familiar faces haunted that patch of green felt. Big time gamblers. She was ready to slaughter them in her own lovely way.

"The one in the gray sharkskin suit with the pink shirt is George," she whispered back to me without turning her eyes from the action.

I made a noncommittal sound and left the table. It might take a while for her to up the stakes. I sauntered over to the dining area.

I returned an hour or so later. The first words I heard from the table were, "Jesus Fucking Christ!"

The skinny, dark-haired man in the sharkskin suit and pink shirt threw down his cards in disgust. He made a motion as if standing to leave, then plopped back in his seat again.

"One more," he muttered, "one more."

George was a born target.

Ann smiled at him. She didn't have to breathe a word. Her expression said it all quite plainly: *Sucker*.

The other five gentlemen at the table held divided opinions. Two of them looked as happy as Shriners at a hookers' convention, while the other three exuded all the warmth and personality of stale cigar smoke. One of the happy ones—a chubby old man with a prominent nose—dealt the next hand of five-card draw.

Ann tossed her head to one side, sending a cascade of gold over her shoulder. She drew her cards to play them close to her chest—which the lechers in the crowd finally appeared to notice.

The betting proceeded calmly, except in the case of George. He bet nervously and thoughtlessly. He was a plunger, all right, and a desperate one at that.

The pile of chips near Ann's elbow stood in shoulder-high stacks. Dozens of stacks. Had it been piles of paper money, there wouldn't have been as much of a mystique about it. Something in the way poker chips look and sound instills an almost religious reverence in people.

I lit a cigarette and stepped toward the table to kibitz.

Ann drew two cards and raised when her turn came about. The three grumblers—who looked as if they'd all come off the same boat from Sicily—folded immediately afterward. The fat man and a smiling, gaunt old gentleman remained in, hoping the odds would shift against her.

George stayed in, tossing his chips in angrily. His dark, tousled hair hung down in his eyes—eyes as furious as a cat cornered in an alley.

"Call," he said after the second round of raises. The chips skittered across the table to land in the center with the rest.

Ann laid down her cards. Three queens.

The plunger ground his teeth together and threw down his hand. Two pair with an ace kicker.

The other two players shook their heads at him and laid their cards face down.

"Lady Luck is certainly with you tonight, my dear." The fat man leaned back in his chair.

Ann smiled. It was George's turn to deal.

The skinny young man picked up the cards to shuffle them. He slammed the two halves of the deck together as though trying to hammer luck into it.

Ann gazed around the smokey room to find me. She smiled again and winked. Her eyes turned toward George, then back toward me.

The owner of StratoDyne dealt a round of five-card draw. Ann took three cards after the first round of bets, then immediately folded. This did little to endear her to several of the players, who would have forced her to stay in the game if the rules had permitted it.

One of the three little guys at the far end brightened visibly when he won the round.

George nearly bent the remainder of the deck in his fist. His right hand slid back toward the edge of the table, stayed there just long enough to tremble hesitantly, and safely returned to shuffle the cards.

I didn't like the looks of that particular motion.

"Stud," George muttered through thinned lips. He knocked a curl of black hair out of his eyes before dealing the hole cards.

Ann scanned the first round of face cards. Her gaze lighted on the fat man's card—a king.

"Fold," she said, sliding her cards forward.

George's knuckles popped.

Her face card had been a jack. To me, that meant that her hole card had been a king or lower. She didn't gamble—she played *poker*.

The kibitzers muttered among themselves as the rest of the hand played through. No one could help noticing that, while she wasn't winning anything at the moment, she also wasn't losing much. By the last round of betting, the fat man had squeezed out everyone but George. The younger man called.

He shouldn't have.

The fat man had four diamonds showing. Possible flush. The young man had a pair of black queens.

The fat man grinned, touched a hand to his thinning reddish-blond hair, and turned over his hole card. A king. Of clubs. He laughed, leaning back in his chair.

"Looks like I couldn't fool you, my boy! You won!"

The plunger flipped his hole card over to expose a third queen. "Three of a kind!" he shouted with sudden exuberance. His hands trembled toward the pile of chips.

"Hold it," I said, leaning over the fat man's shoulder. My voice sounded like Robert Stack's Elliot Ness. Even so, it had as much stopping power to George as tissue paper had to a rhino. I looked down at the fat man. "Take a look at your cards. That's no busted flush."

He leaned forward. One of the foreign guys laid a restraining hand on George.

The fat man sorted the cards out. "King, ace, jack, ten, and . . . queen." He looked up at me, then across to George. The other players developed an obsessive interest in the patterns on the casino ceiling.

"You were so anxious to bluff him out," I said quietly, "you overlooked an ace-high straight." The old man stared at his cards and nodded, dazed beyond speech.

I gazed noncommittally at George and cleared my throat. "Ace-high straight beats three queens." I said it in as friendly a manner as possible. Just a helpful bystander. I could predict what was probably coming next.

George looked at me with eyes the color of muddy water. "He didn't call his cards."

"He doesn't have to," I said. "The cards speak for themselves."

We shared one of those instants frozen in time that last forever and end in a heartbeat. His right hand fidgeted again. He shoved the chips away.

"Take 'em," he muttered. He said nothing while shuffling for the next deal. Stud again.

This time, Ann was ace-high on the first round. "The pair of aces opens," she said with a sweet smile. Maybe they believed her, maybe they didn't. Poker was as much an art of lying as was politics. Any dame that could handle something as cutthroat as a table full of men ready to rip out and devour one another's livers was a dame worth knowing.

On the second round of face cards, two of the Sicilians raised. The gaunt old man folded, stood gracefully, and headed for the bar. The fat man scratched at his nose, frowned, and threw in some chips to see the bets.

George looked at his cards. After pondering for all of a few seconds, he raised. I almost felt sorry for him.

Ann called, saying, "Okay, so I lied." She looked so troubled, I wondered what cards she did have.

The third round revealed no pairs among the exposed cards.

"Check," Ann said.

The three foreigners folded and began talking to each other.

The fat man checked, too.

George gritted his teeth and made his bet. High.

The courtly old gent returned from the bar, shaking his head at the younger man's desperation.

Ann raised him. Higher. "Maybe I don't have aces, gentlemen"—her voice drawled lazily—"but I've got something just as nice." She just let the sentence hang there, like lingerie on a breezeless clothesline.

The fat man scanned the cards displayed. He pursed his lips to blow through them like a horse. His cards slid toward the center of the table.

"I believe prudence forces me to fold." He inclined his head to the gold and emerald figure to his right. "You may have him, my dear. I think I've taken enough out of him, as you have out of me."

Ann politely acknowledged his words, then turned back to the game.

George dabbed at droplets of sweat gathering on his chin. I sidled over to him, reaching around him to snuff my cigarette in an overflowing ashtray at his elbow.

"I'd suggest folding," I offered softly. "It'll fool her into thinking you know what you're doing."

"I don't need—I can't. It's—" He breathed the stuffy air in short, frantic gasps.

Some people shouldn't play poker.

He raised his opponent by an idiotically astronomical amount. The crowd gasped.

"What a *mark*," somebody whispered.

Ann languidly threw in her chips. "Call." She had nothing to do but wait for the kill.

George dealt the final two cards. A deuce of clubs slid over to her side to join the ace of hearts, five of spades, and nine of diamonds.

He dealt himself a queen of spades next to his king, ten, and five of diamonds.

Ann's lips pouted in disappointment. She looked again at her hole card, letting her shoulders drop. "Check," she said, listless as wet newsprint.

Lights seemed to flick on in George's eyes. He looked at the chips between them—enough to purchase several Central American countries. He calculated madly. Nervous hands shoved the remaining pile of chips forward.

Ann stared emptily until George had withdrawn his hands. A grin spread across her face. She added the last of her own chips to the stunningly huge mound between them.

"And I raise you." The words didn't come out as a slap in the face, but the young man reacted as if he'd been socked. She had him pegged from the start.

I was pretty sure what their hole cards were now. Ann must have figured his out a few moves back.

George bowed his head to stare at the table.

"I can write you a check."

The gaunt old man bent over him to say, "You know the rules, my friend. No checks or notes. No lending."

It saved me from having to say it.

Ann straightened in her chair, making no sound. Her face had become as rigid as a stone carving. She gazed at George with wintry eyes and waited.

"I—" He glanced pleadingly around to the crowd. His gaze fell on Ann. "I have some shares. In my name. A controlling interest." He pulled some papers from inside his jacket.

I frowned. Had he been expecting to need them? Make that a *reckless* plunger—doubled and squared.

"A third of it should meet the raise."

Ann glanced at the shares with a disdainful look. "Oh, all right. You'll probably win them back anyway."

That, I thought, was unnecessarily cruel. The young man's eyes blazed like oil burning on a polluted lake. He threw in five of the folded blue sheets.

"I call." He reached to turn over his hole card.

"See you and raise."

Their gazes locked like handcuffs. The crowd stood like a statue garden, their only similarity their stillness. Their expressions ranged from disapproval to glee to shock.

The only one not frozen was George. He began to shake. His gaze fell to the remaining papers in his fist. He tossed them in.

I pitied him. Pity, though, has no place in poker. Then again, neither do fools.

She called. He turned over his hole card. He didn't have a

flush. Just a pair of kings, as she must have suspected. His right hand edged off the table to drop limply onto his lap.

All eyes stared at Ann's hole card, as if their combined hopes could lift it from the felt. It resisted. It lay there until Ann reached over to invert it.

An ace. A diamond for the heart already exposed.

The fat man laughed, looking at the loser. The tall old man gazed with sympathy at the pitiable figure. Ann motioned for a security man to retrieve her winnings. The shares she recovered personally, tucking them away in her purse.

The fat man's laughter faded like a good memory when he saw the pistol in George's hand. A maddened finger jerked against the trigger.

I tried to outrace the bullet. My arms rose up in a double fist to come smashing down on his right shoulder. Too late. The gun lunged backward in his hand. He dropped under my blow like a bag of wet garbage, the pistol falling onto his lap.

The chair Ann sat in had a hole in it. High up, at chest level.

Ann was gone.

While guards jumped on George's unconscious frame, I looked for Ann. I saw no sign until I noticed a mound of chips slide off the table. I had to concentrate in some odd fashion in order to see her. Staring more intently, I saw her shoveling the chips into a Mylar bag. Not even the guards seemed to notice her. Whenever someone stared directly at her, it was as if his gaze just kept moving.

I stepped over to her and knelt down.

"Congratulations," she said, handing me the shares. "You now own controlling interest in a failed spacecraft company."

Across the field of green, George stirred as if waking from a deep sleep. One of the guards lifted him up while the other deftly retrieved the pistol.

"Let's go." Ann shook her hair back and crammed the last few chips into the bag. She turned to go, only to bump up against the arm of a slender black man. He reacted as though nothing more than a breeze had wafted by.

A few men and women glanced at Ann as we waded

through the crowds toward the casino exit. Their gaze would light on her, then wander, their expressions growing blank.

My last view of George was of him being escorted to the security office by three gentlemen in nicely tailored black tuxes. He looked as if he'd been deflated and hung on a coathook.

"You rolled him like a drunk," I said.

She shrugged. "Poker is a lot like assassination, Dell. Sometimes someone gets wiped out."

"And assassination is a lot like poker—you've got to understand the minds of all the players." I spoke quietly, waiting for her to convert her winnings at the cashier. "What I've been trying to figure out all along is your part in this. A little roughing up by a priest wouldn't drive most people to such efforts."

She said nothing. The cashier calmly wrote out a chit. He might have been playing with the money all by himself for all the notice he gave Ann. You'd think they had women shot at every night.

She deposited the chit in her handbag. When she looked at me, it was with a flush of excitement. The light in her eyes warmed, like fire seen dimly through ice.

"I've got a lot more than that to get even with, Dell. A lot more than a little pushing around."

I stepped out of the casino with her at my side. "Let me guess," I said. "Your parents were Bible-beating fundamentalists, right?"

She grimaced. "Hardly."

"Then you possess the ultimate Electra complex, which you try to sublimate by helping to murder your heavenly Father."

She laughed. Her laughter grew louder and higher until it cracked.

"Not exactly," she said after a moment. All humor had drained from her face, as if someone had slugged her. She said nothing more until we separated to go to our hotel rooms.

The next day we visited my rocket factory.

17
STARFINDER

STRATODYNE CORPORATION

ALTERNATIVE TRANSPORTATION SYSTEMS

NO TRESPASSING!

"They don't encourage much walk-in trade, do they?" I stared at the peeling sign on the rust-stained gate. The cyclone fencing could have been torn apart with a buttonhook. A formidable padlock connected the two ends of a chain that could have been cut in half with a pair of scissors.

Ann reached over to the steering wheel to honk the horn.

"Not much need for security out here," she said. "But they try."

A faded guardhouse stood beyond the gate. A bent old black man in a gray uniform stepped out, unlocked the gate, and stepped over to my side of the Chrysler.

"We called," Ann said. "This is Mr. Ammo."

The old man nodded. "That's right. That's right." He walked back to the gate to open it all the way.

"Sort of lonely out here, isn't it?" I said.

The old man pointed at his guard shack. "That thing's full of a mess of books. Time to read's what I got. I'm seein' the world." He waved us through as if in a dream. "Seein' the world."

The path to the factory was unpaved. We kicked up enough dirt to signal our movement for miles. We wouldn't have to worry about that, though. Clouds darkened the sky overhead. The streets in Claremont a few miles back had been slick from morning rain.

A drop of water spattered against the windshield like an angry bug. A few more droplets descended from the sky to hit the car or make little dust explosions on the road. A starling hopped out of our way, cursing the twin intrusions of car and rain.

We drove into a narrow canyon that widened around a bend, revealing the vast StratoDyne manufacturing empire. A decaying assembly building covered an acre or so of real estate. Another acre of unpaved parking lot abutted its south side. A sloping concrete wall about a mile away separated the building from a circular concrete launching pad.

One lone thirty-year-old Buick, wearing more rust than paint, snuggled up close to the building. A crow cawed wearily, circling about the facility dodging raindrops. It landed on the roof of the building to seek sanctuary under a girder.

I drove down an incline toward the Buick. The rain had already begun to drag the road dust down the shoulders in little rivulets.

I parked in front of the other car. After a quick sprint, we reached a door marked GENERAL OFFICE, standing halfway open. A fluorescent lamp flickered inside. The rain fell around the building like a collapsing world.

Ann pulled the door shut. Her khaki jumpsuit looked like a leopard's spotted hide. The brass buttons and buckles that served as functional accents glinted in the unsteady pulsations of the indoor light.

The office was empty. The intermittent buzz of the lamp could not compete with the sound of the rain outside.

I looked around. Vacant chairs faced naked typewriters. Paper trays squatted on desks like starving animals, waiting to be filled. The wall clock was an hour and a half slow. Someone had once tossed sharpened pencils at a poster of a NASA space shuttle, where they still remained stuck. The words *Good Riddance* had been scrawled across the poster. I wondered whether they referred to the abortive NASA fiasco or whether a disgruntled employee had fired a parting shot. I suppose it didn't matter in either case.

Somewhere amidst the noise of the downpour, the sound of a radio faintly drifted into the room. It played a forgotten tune by an obscure rock band.

I glanced at Ann.

She shrugged. "Follow the music?"

I nodded.

The wet bottoms of my gum-soled shoes made annoying squeaking sounds against the cement floor. Ann's boot heels clicked in pleasant contrast. Neither of us could have sneaked up on anyone.

I felt like an explorer in a haunted tomb.

I preceded Blondie through the rear door of the office. It led directly to the main assembly room. Almost an acre of open space spread before us under a vaulted roof. It would have made an impressive indoor tennis court, though I'd seen larger ones.

Partitions hung here and there, obstructing our forward view. Looking up at the ceiling was the only way to see the entire span of the place. We weaved past several of the barriers. Then we saw it.

It lay there on its landing gear—white and gleaming and smooth and graceful. Like a giant dove, its wings were swept back in anticipation of flight. The cockpit stood twenty feet above us—a multifaceted gem inlaid against sleek pearl.

"It's beautiful," Ann whispered.

A deep voice behind us said, "It's a piece of junk."

We turned to see a tall man in a pair of greasy red coveralls. He was young, with the usual vague tan that typified nearly everyone from L.A. He sat next to the radio, legs outstretched, leaning against a pile of titanium struts. His fingers were interlaced behind his head.

"Junk?" My shoes squeaked with my turn.

He stood. "Old man Geislinger had a good idea, building low-cost space shuttles. Only problem was, NASA didn't want anyone competing with their overpriced jalopies."

I put a foot up on a crate. "They didn't like that, I suppose."

"No, sir! The Federal Trade Commission nearly drove the old man to ruin. The only money he made was in the counter-economy. When he finally *ad astra*ed, the company went up for grabs, and George Turner tried greenmailing a leveraged buy-out to drive the stock price up."

"Doesn't seem to have worked," Ann said, surveying the remains of the factory.

"No, ma'am. George was never much of a businessman. The greenmail blew up in his face. The management revolted and unfurled their golden parachutes. He wound up stuck with a gutted company and no one to run it. Then the Hudson Phoenix shot the cost of spaceflight right through the floor."

He stood to stretch, sticking his hand out to me. "The name's Canfield. I piloted some of the old man's shuttles until Georgie boy took over and I got put back in electronics."

He gave me a firm, friendly grip and an open, unpretentious smile. His prematurely gray hair was short and neat.

I introduced Ann and myself, then asked, "Can you fly this thing?"

He gazed up at the shuttle. "If I were suicidal. The old man had us building good, solid spacecraft. None of that multiple redundancy crap you find on most ships. He built them cheap and sturdy, and they worked just fine. Then Turner comes in and decides to comply with FTC regulations. It was downhill after that."

I didn't want to hear the entire history of StratoDyne. "What would it take to get you to fly this thing?"

"Modifications."

"Such as?" Ann asked.

He eyed her up and down, then let his gaze drift to the spacecraft. "I call her *Starfinder*. I like that better than *S–D/X–93A*." He stepped over to pat the underside of the hulk. "Yeah, a lot of mod—"

One of the glossy black tiles fell to the floor.

He picked the piece up. "George thought it would be wiser to copy the NASA way of doing things. Junked the old man's spray-on ablation that worked so well. I'd want to go back to that."

"Fine," I said. "How much will it all cost?"

"I'll do most of the electrical work myself, if you're really serious about this. The rest will probably run about a million or so. That's in Panpacific dollars, mind you." He tossed the tile into an oil drum filled with trash. "Where'll you be sending her?"

"To crash the gates of heaven and kill God."

He laughed, then said in a wistful tone, "I'd pay that price to get into space again."

I frowned. Was I getting another kook in on this? "We'll be taking her up to synchronous orbit. A satellite repair flight."

Canfield rubbed his jaw thoughtfully. "Lot of junk up there. Which one do you plan to retrieve?"

I smiled. "I don't plan to retrieve anything. It'll be an in-orbit modification, which we'll discuss nearer our launch date." I took a moment to eyeball the shuttle again. "I'm putting you in charge of hiring the right people as of now."

"Okay. Everyone's files are still in the office. I'll call the good ones back." He jerked a thumb toward *Starfinder*. "Her lifting tanks are still in Guatemala. Turner refused to bribe the local bureaucrats after the last flight. Other than that, we'll probably need a lead time of five month—"

"Can't," I said. "Five weeks max. We launch on New Year's Eve."

He gulped audibly. "Okay. Um . . . five weeks." He withdrew a small, bent notebook and a pen from his flight suit. "December thirty-one, nineteen ninety-nine. Hour to be determined." He looked up from the notepad. "Say—you're not involved with those ads I've been hearing on the radio, are you?"

"Open conspiracy," Ann muttered, looking away.

"Something about God dying on January first?"

I kept my mouth shut.

"Are they serious about killing God?" he asked.

"Were you?" I said.

We left him staring at us, his face a puzzled field of thought.

18
MAGICK

I spent more and more time either accessing information on plaques or sitting in the library in Old Downtown. I preferred being at the library. Sitting there in bad lighting, wedged between stacks of real books and old drunks, I absorbed all I could about religion, psychology, ESP, drugs. . . .

Each previous assassination had required extensive research and planning. This one turned out to be no different. The preliminaries usually consisted of surveillance—watching the victim to gain knowledge of his routines.

In this case, the Victim was well hidden. When it came time for the confrontation, I'd have to be ready for any possibility.

I had just finished scanning a book—the umpteenth by yet another illiterate who claimed he was able "to intimately contact" the Holy Spirit that was sending UFOs to tell us to eat wheat germ and bean sprouts and refrain from sex, profit, and other base urges.

I threw the book against a stack to my left. Nut literature toppled, spilling across the worn table. Another library patron, using a sack of plain-wrap gin for a pillow, roused a bit to eye me blearily.

I realized that I still didn't believe the crap.

The thought hit me like a set of knucks. Here I was up against God Almighty—encountering portents in the sky, priests bent on mayhem, and satanic rites amidst nuclear rubble.

And I still didn't believe that God was anywhere to be found.

"It's just fear," Ann said when I told her about it that night. We sat in the bar of Casino Grande.

"Fear of failure?"

"No. I mean that believing in god is just fear. Fear of the unknown. And no matter how much anyone professes *not* to believe in god, deep down there is that trace of fear of the unknown that impels the belief in an unknowable power beyond man. It's the existence of that fear that you must believe in. That is what you must attack."

Even though she'd been meeting with promotional people all day, she still maintained a glow of freshness and energy about her. She toyed with her champagne glass and smiled.

"In fact," she said, "rather than conjuring up a belief, perhaps you merely ought to suspend your *dis*belief temporarily." Her smile faded into seriousness. "Magical ceremonies and rituals are designed to create the sort of atmosphere you'd need."

I snorted. "Magic? You mean the sort of theatrical drivel Zack performs? Whom shall I cut open?"

She stopped fingering her glass to shake her head emphatically. "No. What he engaged in was a black mass—a Christian heresy. It *is* a magical ritual, but one hopelessly ineffective and crude."

She leaned over the table toward me. She seemed a touch drunk.

"I'm speaking of the Old Ways. The craft that Bridget preserves and practices."

I stared at her. "Witches?" This was getting to be too much. "Broomsticks and black cats and cauldrons?"

"We needn't take the cauldron, Dell." Having broached the subject, she took another sip of her drink, allowing her cool gaze to warm a bit. "You've read enough by now to realize that the legends of witchcraft consist of a lot of misinterpreted myth. I suspect the only broom Bridget owns is used to sweep out the store."

I polished off my bourbon and spent a moment surveying the patrons of the bar. No one appeared to be eavesdropping, though the wonders of electronics could easily have had me fooled.

"I had planned to do away with Him scientifically."

"Remember what Bridget said. 'Two great forces must join and two great forces must clash.' "

"Is that the final piece of the puzzle? If it is, *I'm* supposed to produce it with a flourish, and *you're* supposed to say, 'Astounding, Holmes.' "

She gazed at me with searching eyes for a long moment. She looked disappointed.

"Final piece or not," she said, "the answer to the puzzle is this. The two great forces that must clash are good and evil."

"I suppose I'm on the side of good? Look who hired me." I ordered another drink.

"Sometimes evil aims can unwittingly set good actions into motion," she said. "Besides, Zacharias changed his mind after thinking about the consequences." She plowed on, undeterred. "The two great forces that must unite are science and magic. The roots of god reach deep into magic and myth. Without magic, no amount of science can affect him."

I shrugged my weary shoulders. Her theory was no more ridiculous than anything else I'd considered.

"All right, angel. I'll give it a whirl. What have I got to lose?"

Ann stared gloomily into her drink and didn't answer.

19
CRONE

"Out, out, *out* of my store!"

Bridget appeared less than thrilled to see us again. Kasmira, dressed in a black, full-length peasant dress, watched silently from behind the cash register.

Plywood boards still covered the broken windows of Trismegistos. Wide strips of masking tape held gray chipboard in place over holes in the glass counters.

"Things have been rough, haven't they?" Ann said.

A pile of damaged merchandise lay on a card table. A sign hung from it, reading,

THE
"WE DIDN'T EXPECT THE SPANISH INQUISITION"
SALE—
ALL RED-TAGGED ITEMS HALF PRICE!

Bridget looked at me with poorly veiled unease. "I gave you your damned message," she said. "What more do you want?"

"Your help."

"Help in what? Your wild-gander chase? That insane advertising of yours?"

I bit the inside of my cheek, glancing over at Ann. She merely rolled her icy blues. *Yeah,* I thought—*I know.*

"We need a spell," Ann said. "A powerful spell. You have the knowledge. You have the power. Please help us." She reached out to touch the old woman's arm. Her frigid eyes warmed to pools of imploring dewiness. The angel really knew how to lay it on.

Bridget sighed miserably. "It's useless to fight. He has the whole world in His grip. Our influence is dying, crumbling." She shook her aged head. "Those few of us who have held on for so long have seen the light grow dimmer year by year, age by age. Perhaps this millennium *is* the Equinox of the Gods."

"No," Ann said, "I refuse to let that happen." Ann clasped the crone's arm tightly, her eyes narrowing with fierce intensity. "There comes a time to strike back with all the force we can raise. Six thousand years is enough time to spend enduring the whip and the rope and the flame. It's enough time spent hiding in the shadows, afraid to speak our truths. It's too much time lost in forgetting that *our* love is greater than *his* hate."

Ann released her grip. Bridget turned away.

"It *is* the Equinox of the Gods," Ann said. "His solstice is long past. Do you want to see him enthroned again for another twenty centuries?"

"I'm too old," she said as softly as a vanquished warrior.

"That is *he* speaking. He and his hatred of change through time." Ann touched the old woman again. "Your age is your wisdom. Your lifetime is your strength."

"Words," Bridget said, leaning weakly against the counter behind her.

"Words of truth. Words of magic. *Your* words."

Bridget merely lowered her head, shaking it.

Ann looked helplessly in my direction.

I let out an impatient sigh. "Bridget," I said, "can't you see that the lady is asking you to help us?"

She nodded, avoiding either of our gazes. Something stiffened in her spine.

"That a man should ask—" She looked up at me. Color returned to her face. "That a man should even *think* to reject his patriarchal God." She straightened.

In the corner of my vision, I saw Kasmira smiling, holding back tears.

"Mighty Isis, I'll *do* it! I won't refuse a request when it comes in such a manner." The fire of life seemed to flow back into her veins as she looked heavenward. "I've got nothing to fear from the likes of Him! My karma's safe. I love this life, and I'm ready for the next." She looked me in the eye.

"All right, God-killer—just tell me when and where and what restaurant we'll go to afterward."

"Blessed be," I muttered, lighting up a cigarette and tossing the match into a cracked incense burner. I took a long drag and let it out. "How do you like space flight?"

On December fifteenth, we threw the ad campaign into high gear. Kathleen had produced a slick, tight ten-second TV spot —short and to the point: blank screen for a couple of silent seconds, just to get everyone's attention. Then the familiar Crosshairs Over Jehovah would swell up on the screen, accompanied by an ominous drum roll and the announcer's voice-over.

"On the first day of the year two thousand, God will die."

We had it translated into scores of languages for worldwide transmission over the VideoSat network. That cost a bundle.

Hallelujah House, of course, was paying for everything. I was seriously beginning to think that the bank account was bottomless. Also, due to a stroke of genius on Kathleen's part, money was also pouring back into our coffers.

She showed up at my office one day with a paper bag (from some exclusive Rodeo Drive joint) filled with goodies.

"These," she said, "are selling like crazy."

Every one of them had either our symbol or slogan or both on them. There were GodKiller baseball caps, pen sets, tote-bags, buttons. Bookcovers, backpacks, headbands, armbands, and decoder rings. She unrolled a length of adhesive logo stickers.

"They're Scratch-and-Sniff," she said. "Smells like rosemary."

"Rosemary?"

"Well, I thought about blood, but we're trying to keep this upbeat, right?"

"Right," I agreed.

She'd paid an up-and-coming band called TransUranic Metal to compose a tune called "Nearer My God to Death." Our symbol was depicted on the album sleeve and on the laserdisc itself. She played the cut for me. It sounded like hogs being vivisected during a nuclear war.

"The kids love it," she shouted over the noise. "It hit *Billboard* at seven with a bullet."

They should have used the bullet on the band.

In the jarring silence that followed, she exhibited the remainder of the bag. Key chains, roach clips, rubber stamps, holograms, bubblegum, coffee mugs, posters. Pendants, embroidered patches, postcards.

"They're the hottest things on the market. Especially in the twelve-to-twenty-four bracket. Having your parents impound your cache of GodKiller Candy is a real status symbol."

"So it's popular. What about backlash?"

Kathleen shrugged, her long chestnut hair flowing around the shoulders of her rust-hued tunic. "Nothing to worry about. Evangelists such as Emil Zacharias and the like rail against the ads and hint at Armageddon. But they've been doing that for years. They just use it to get money."

I smiled. Zacharias must be burning mad if the money coming in to fight us went straight out again to help us.

"Maybe we can turn that to our favor," I mused.

I congratulated Kathleen on the campaign as she left. Everything was going marvelously well.

That same day, unfortunately, The Cardinal and his boys came to town.

20
CONVERSATION

Ann, Isadora, and I sat at a table in The Prisoner of Zelda eating a very late breakfast. The Great Gatsby atmosphere of the place grated on my nerves, but the kid seemed to enjoy it. She acted surprised when she discovered that the decor came from a period even before my time.

"Gee, this stuff must really be *old*."

Ann was outfitted in a breathtaking violet dress cut in a style that revealed everything yet displayed nothing. By rights, our table should have been surrounded by wolves.

No one even glanced at her.

Isadora wore a scarlet body shirt that displayed everything and revealed nothing. The color of her nail polish and eye shadow matched, making her look like a stunted neon sign. Her black picoskirt ended where her thighs began. I couldn't even look at her black fishnet stockings. I was still eating breakfast.

Her only nod to good taste was a GodKiller button pinned to her shirt.

The waitress returned, looking like a flapper who'd spent one night too many taxi-dancing.

"There's a gentleman who'd like to speak with you," she said, highlighting her speech with snappings of GodKiller bubblegum.

I started to rise, then cautiously sat. "Send him to our table." I was still smarting from what had happened the last time.

He walked toward us. Had we been in less civilized surroundings, I would have taken the opportunity to smear him into the ground.

Father Beathan smiled, pulled a chair up next to me, and sat with folded, calm hands.

"The first day of the year two thousand? How melodramatic."

"It makes its point," I said. I lit a cigarette and eyed him, awaiting his next move.

He looked past Ann at Isadora. "There are some people who would like to see you now. Immediately. If both of you will please follow me—"

"Both of us?" the kid asked, looking at Ann and me.

Beathan nodded, looking from Isadora to me, his gaze never lighting on Ann.

Ann made a silent hushing sign with her left index finger.

"Well?" the priest asked.

Isadora peered at me, concentrating. Suddenly, the restaurant seemed to tumble and fracture and crumble away.

The kid stood in a blank room wearing a diaphanous bit of nothing. Spectral winds blew dreamlike through her hair. I seemed to be watching her, but I couldn't see my own body.

"*All right, Dell—what's going on? Why can't he see Ann?*"

I shrugged invisible shoulders. "*It's some kind of trick she does. Or some kind of defect in her personality. You should ask questions, being able to drag me into Never-Never Land for a quick chat.*"

"*Get stuffed!*" The room dissolved like cotton candy in a rainstorm to be replaced by The Prisoner of Zelda.

"Quit looking like a brain case, Ammo. Come on." The kindly father drew something from beneath his frock. A blunt, rounded rod pointed unobtrusively from the end of a cylindrical grip. I faced the business end of a neural interruptor.

"Why, Father," I said in my friendliest fashion, "you could go to prison for ten years if you get caught carrying that."

He smirked. "You're one to care for laws. Do you know what you'll get for attempted deicide?" He gestured again with the paralyzer.

"Go ahead," I said. "Try explaining two unconscious people to the management."

"Good try, Ammo. This one's modified, though. Its power is set just low enough to make you open to persuasion."

I blew some smoke in his face.

"Come on, kid," I said. "Let's go whither the good Father taketh us."

Isadora, Beathan, and I stood. So did Ann. I left a wad of orange paper to cover the bill. As we headed toward the exit, I leaned close enough to Ann to whisper, "How long do you think you can keep this up?"

She whispered back, "As long as I'm around people who believe the lies that others tell them—or believe the lies they tell themselves."

I was hoping for something a bit more concrete.

I kept abreast of Beathan, staying between him and the kid. His constant glances toward her betrayed an inordinate amount of interest on his part. He wet his lips with the narrow tip of his tongue before speaking.

"So this is the way in which you choose to mock God." His lips pressed back together like those of a schoolteacher about to deliver a caning. "Defiling a mere child to appease your dark, animalistic master."

Isadora bristled at that. "Who're you calling *mere*, you bastard!" She darted around me to swing her foot at his left shin. Her pointed gold pump drove into his flesh.

I've got to give Beathan credit for not putting the NI field on us right there. He waved the thing at Isadora.

"Daughter of Eve," he said through gritted teeth, "your language is as filthy as your soul."

I restrained her this time. No sense pushing our luck. "Chill the rhetoric, pop. You want her to ruin her shoes?"

I could hear Ann's soft footsteps behind me. My mind did a sprint through Panic City. Did she have to follow so closely? What if her shield or whatever it was should lose potency? I knew other men to have at least *seen* her. She wasn't invisible. What if the others weren't fooled?

Beathan led us down a corridor toward the Auberge Hilton. He appeared unfazed by the wanton atmosphere and easygoing morality of Auberge, despite his wisecracks.

Two transvestites of the high-class variety strolled by us. One of them—a ringer for Veronica Lake—winked teasingly at the priest.

He ignored the gesture with a calm, disinterested expression.

His nudges directed us through the hotel lobby toward the elevator. He punched for the bottom floor—penthouse level in the crazy layout of Auberge. The penthouse suites were situated directly over a branch of the never-completed Los Angeles Municipal Subway. Only customers paying the highest fees could afford a suite near such a convenient escape route.

Beathan slipped the key card into the lock. The door eased open. He prodded me in with the muzzle of his NI. The kid followed between us.

Ann quietly slipped in last to hide in the cloakroom. Beathan still hadn't detected her presence.

The joint was big, by Auberge standards. Three steps led to a sunken living room that contained several couches, a gaming table, and a functional fireplace. I had no idea where the smoke went.

Three of the couches were arranged in a U-shape around the fireplace. Upon them sat the strangest collection of clothes this side of a Rocky Horror revival. There were a dozen old men in all, comprising a fairly thorough ethnic spread.

"Ah," I said casually, tapping the ash off what was left of my cigarette, "you must be the Ecclesia."

None of them said anything, yet somehow the room grew even quieter. The men stared coldly at Isadora and me.

"We are of dubious pleasure," said a shaven-headed man in a saffron robe, "to discover that you know of us." He looked as if he should be handing out incense at the airport.

"Relax," I said. "I read about you in the papers all the time. 'Ecclesia' this, 'Ecclesia' that—"

"Enough," said The Cardinal. He was dressed all in red, right up to his little beanie.

They were all old men. Some were fatter, some were skinnier. Some darker, some lighter. None of them smiled, nor did any look as if he'd smiled much since 1954.

"Let us get down to business." The Cardinal stood with a jangling of sacred hardware. "We have been informed by the Reverend Emil Zacharias that you are the mastermind behind this GodKiller campaign."

I smiled a calculated smile. "We're totally open in our operations. You could have come to our business office—"

He interrupted me. I didn't like that. "We want to know what you mean when you say that God will die."

"I mean what I say, fatso."

"Which God do you intend to kill?" he asked, as calmly as if he were asking about my vacation plans.

"All of Him," I said.

"Allah?" Some guy in a caftan jumped up as if to reach for his sword, only to discover that he wasn't wearing one. The Rabbi beside him tugged at the fellow's khaffia. They exchanged whispers for a moment before The Ayatollah grudgingly sat back down.

"A vast undertaking," The Cardinal said. His elocution was as full and round as Anthony Quinn with a sock in his mouth. "How do you propose to do this?"

"Trade secret." Let them sweat it.

The fellow in red fiddled with an ostentatious gold ring on his index finger. A crucifix hung heavily around the thick folds of his neck, as tasteful and as dainty as a solid gold hockey stick.

"Mr. Ammo, your effort to kill God will fail because God does not exist."

"Then why treat me any differently from any other Southern California nut? You could have saved a lot in airfare."

He smiled and reached up to touch his scarlet beanie. "Mr. Ammo. It is one thing to defy God, to set up a competing religion, or even to declare oneself to *be* God. None of these actions robs God of His primal position in people's minds." He peered at me straight in the eye with a gaze that emerged from two narrowed, murderous slits. "To imply, on the other hand, that God is a being that can be killed is to unleash an anarchistic impulse not seen since the time of the Corn Kings."

He stepped up to me closer than even most Europeans stand when talking to one another. His breath smelled of fish and Binaca.

"The desire to murder God is an almost universal emotion in human beings. If you succeed in destroying their God for them, if you show them it can be done, you will create two disastrous consequences.

"First, you will destroy man's desire to achieve, which is his only metaphorical means of killing God and maintaining his self-respect. Every man wants to be God, and every man labors in his own way to unseat Him. Second, you will eliminate guilt. More accurately, you will remove the means by which we are able to instill guilt in man—our only means to channel the God-killing urge toward productive ends."

He concluded, dramatically ponderous: "Killing God would destroy civilization."

I grunted unsympathetically. "Killing God would put you jokers out of business. That's all."

"Quite so." The Cardinal smiled. "Where would man go to be absolved of his sins if we weren't around to define what was sin? We would descend into violence and corruption."

"I see. In other words, we wouldn't be in our current state of peace and bliss."

"Things would be far worse, I assure you."

I rubbed an itch on my nose. "I'd like to see the results and judge for myself. If things go from bad to worse, we can always resurrect Him, right?"

"Bah!" The Mahatma pounded a fist against the arm of the couch. "None of you make a living absolving the sins of those who truly harm others, such as murderers and thieves. There are too few of them." He looked at me with black eyes buried in glossy olive-hued skin. "The religions you see represented by the Ecclesia—"

"As you call it," The Cardinal took care to interject.

"—have succeeded in transforming the act of *living* into a sin!"

Ah, I thought, *dissension in the ranks. Good.*

The Rabbi smiled conspiratorially at The Ayatollah. "We tell them they are evil for wanting too much. We tell them it is wrong to eat what they want, we tell them it is wrong to make love to whom they wish when they wish. They cannot question, for we say that the orders come from *gee-dash-dee*. Some of us here"—he glanced at the guy in red—"have even accomplished the laudable feat of damning everyone merely for being born."

The Cardinal smiled with pride.

I leaned over Isadora to whisper in her ear.

"Think you can handle the whole gang at once?"

She looked at me as if I'd asked her to jump over the moon.

"All of them?" She thought about it. "The only time I tried more than one was these Siamese twins who—"

"No details, kid. Did it work?"

She nodded. "Sort of. I don't know about this many."

The Cardinal cleared his throat. "We are prepared to be either generous or brutal, Mr. Ammo. Please consider wisely, since, in the event of a negative answer, we cannot permit you to leave this room ali—"

Fatso's face went slack, his gaze focused on some distant realm. The others mimicked him a second or so later.

Beathan fell back against the wall to slide down to the floor. They went as limp as rag dolls all over.

Well, almost all over.

I retrieved Beathan's neural interruptor and pointed it at him. His glassy eyes registered no emotion.

"Ann," I whispered loudly, "I think she's got them."

Ann emerged from the closet to gaze at Isadora. The kid sat on the edge of the fireplace, staring as blankly as the men she held entranced.

"Might as well sit down," I said. "We can't leave without her, so we've got to wait till she's finished."

"That could take hours."

"Time passes faster in her little world." I nodded toward the Ecclesia. "See?"

Several of the holy men began squirming about. Their dull, low moans were the sounds you'd hear from the depths of any mental hospital. Their pelvic motions increased in speed. The Mahatma and The Ayatollah slid jerkily to the carpet, their sight turned inward.

Isadora shook with fury or pain or terror. Tears started to run. She cried out once and fell to the hearthstones, trembling. When I knelt at her side, she reached up to grasp my neck.

"Let's get out. Please." Her words barely made it from her to me.

I picked her up. I had no experience in calming a wounded child, so I did the only thing I knew how to do—I let her cry.

"It was awful. Awful. They hated me for being a girl and they told me they wouldn't fuck me because I was a girl and unclean and I had filthy thoughts and I wasn't a virgin in my heart so they—they c-cut me up—"

She buried her face in the nook of my arm just as before and sobbed. The wet heat of her breath and tears soaked right through my jacket.

Ann fumbled in her purse. She stepped over to the esteemed members of the Ecclesia, who lay there with closed eyes and twisted, peaceful smiles.

"Let's go," I said. The place felt like a charnel house. A musky stench ambushed my nostrils.

She ignored me and the thirty kilos of kid I was trying to keep from dropping. She drew her pigsticker from its sheath and advanced on the man in red.

"In this sign," she said, "be conquered." She carved a five-pointed star in his forehead. Deep. The knife edged down to cut off the tip of his nose.

I hadn't thought her the vengeful sort. I really would have stopped her if I hadn't had my hands full. I resorted to the sternest form of moral persuasion.

"Why not just shoot them in the crotch and be done with it?"

She reached up under The Rabbi's curly hair to nick off a slice of his ear. "For your *Abodah Zarah*," she said to his sleeping visage. A trickle of blood snaked through his dark locks.

On The Ayatollah's cheekbone she inscribed something in swirling Arabic. "In the name of *Al Lat!*" She nearly hissed the words.

"Let's *go!*" I wasn't interested in skin decoration.

She turned to join me at the door. Her gaze was as blank and distant as theirs had been. She wiped her blade on Beathan's frock and returned it to her bag without looking. Her hand reached out to touch Isadora's head.

I waited for her to say something symbolic and important. Maybe even something comforting.

Her hand slid away silently, wearily, to drop at her side. She followed me out without a word.

21
YULETIDE

The promotional campaign was causing a riot among the press. Speculative articles spread through the tabloids like mold through roquefort. Editorials canted about the decaying morality that could culminate in such a mockery of All Things Sacred. Some of the more apocalyptic magazines and TV programs nailed our plan dead on. Hallelujah House was particularly unkind in its characterization of whoever was behind it all.

All of which only helped circulate awareness of the plan. The new zeitgeist spread almost without our help.

Kathleen intensified the program to include computerized telephone spotcalls, bulk-rate mailings, and skytyped messages over football games. The one above Notre Dame nearly instigated a riot.

Christmas approached with all the pleasantness of a funeral procession. Priests and ministers implicated our campaign with the international Satanist/Communist/Corporate/Secular Humanist conspiracy. Rabbis, imams, and assorted shamans hinted that only the Christian God would die on the Christian New Year. The brahmans sat quietly knowing—or pretending to. The nut cults came farther out of the woodwork.

I asked Kathleen to stick an ad in newspapers and magazines soliciting funds "to halt the God-killer's campaign of lies and deceit." The money it brought in went right out again for ads for both sides.

I spent most of my time in the library. If I could have injected the books into a vein, I would have been mainlining religious philosophy. The current stack of books included Kant, Spinoza, Nietzsche, C. S. Lewis, Ayn Rand, and Thomas Paine. I had Paine's *Age of Reason* in hand. He detested organized religions on the grounds that revelation could not be received secondhand. On that basis, he denounced the Bible as mere hearsay. That he promoted his own deistic, disorganized religion didn't prevent me from unearthing information that I found generally useful.

Ann wandered into the library at close to midnight. The official closing time was nine, but nobody really cared about books or libraries anymore. It was more of an underfunded warehouse than anything else.

She looked as if someone had crumpled her up, put her in a back pocket, and gone horseback riding. She plopped down into the chair next to mine and dropped her head upon a pile of notes.

"Happy Birthday," she muttered, looking down at the papers touching her cheek, staring blearily through the desk to the floor.

"Thanks, doll, but you're off by nearly half a year."

"Mm," she groaned, gazing through the papers to the other side of the planet. "I just finished speaking to Canfield. The crew's installed the Theta Wave Amplifier onboard *Starfinder*. Canfield's personally integrating the neural interruptors into the amplifier. And Bridget has submitted her altar design for the payload section. It looks good. It can work. Dr. La Vecque says that her heart's in prime condition—no circulatory problems. He thinks she can survive the flight." She sighed.

"What's wrong?"

She shrugged. "I thought that keeping the books at Bautista Corporation was a chore. This campaign of yours is so diversified that I'm shotgunning all over the place just trying to keep the finances straight." She raised her head from the table and rested it on one arm. "Working with Zacharias's money doesn't simplify things. He's being audited, so I've got to save his ass to cover ours."

I ran my hand gently through her golden hair. "He should be thankful for all the work you're doing for him."

She laughed in a peculiarly weak fashion. "One thing alone is keeping all of this from blowing us up into the public eye." She rolled her head to one side in order to gaze up at me. "Whenever I have to deal with people who might have an interest in tracking us down, they barely notice me and don't remember me five minutes after I'm gone."

"You make a great front man," I said.

She didn't take the comment well. "It's tough," she said. "It's tough knowing that you're moving through life like a phantom. Knowing that you drift through the memories of the people you meet like a faint breeze. Feeling that sometime— late at night—they'll remember you in a dream and wake with a shudder or a scream, only to forget again." She turned her face back down. "It's like not really being alive at all."

"How long have you been like this?"

She sat up and sighed. "All my life. There were times when even my . . . *parents* couldn't see me." She stared at the bookcases in silence.

I sat there watching her. Even though tired, she radiated a glow of life that warmed me to my soul—assuming that I still possessed one.

I quit dreaming and returned to my book.

After a moment, Ann said, "Dell?"

"Yeah?"

"I guess my point is that—with every other man—I have to exert a lot of mental power to hold their attention. That's one reason I put so much effort into my clothes and makeup."

"You certainly catch *my* eye, sister." It was obvious she was heading toward a point. I let her take her own route.

"That's the point," she said. Bingo for me. "I don't have to do anything. You *see* me."

She stood up with what the poets call "feline grace"—a lovely flowing motion. For an exhausted person, she stored an astonishing reserve of energy.

"You can see me because you are the man who doesn't believe lies."

I snorted. That was a laugh. "Tell that to the Reverend Zacharias."

She dismissed the gag with a flip of her hand. "You don't believe lies, and you seek to uncover the truth. You don't take the easy way out if it involves belief in things false."

" 'What is truth?' " I asked, mostly to show her I'd been doing my reading. "Look where it's taken me—to a life of murder. That's the truth for you." I closed the book to gaze at her. I felt tired. "How's this for a lie—telling myself that the world is wrong and that the generals and kings and politicians I killed were evil men who deserved to die. Have I made the world any better?"

Her earth-red nails tapped at the tabletop. "I seem to recall asking you a similar question a few weeks ago. You've apparently changed your mind. You told me you only killed tyrants."

"Everyone else called them 'leaders.' It'd be pretty presumptuous of me to put my opinion above everyone else's."

"Stop playing devil's advocate, Dell."

My laughter echoed through the library. It took me a while to calm down. All of three seconds.

She hit me with that gaze of hers.

"I don't really care what you *think* you believe. Do you know what it's like being unable to hold a man's full attention for more than a few moments? The closer he gets, the harder I have to concentrate. Usually the effort is too taxing, and he snaps away. He stands there wondering where he is and what he's doing there."

"Must make shopping difficult."

She didn't even hear me.

"I don't know," she said. "Maybe I just didn't want any of them."

"But we want each other." I figured it was my place to state the obvious. They must have been the magic words, because she suddenly fell silent and gazed dreamily at me with those piercingly blue eyes.

"And I wasn't even trying," she murmured. "You truly want me?"

I nodded.

"Then," she said with a luscious smile, "take me."

I looked around me. "Here?"

"Of course not," she said, reaching to take my hand. "In the philosophy section!"

She was the sea; I, a mighty rider sailing upon the crests of her waves. She moaned like the wind through hidden forests; I bent like a tree beneath her. She burned—a fiery essence; I was consumed utterly. She covered me like soft, warm earth; I lay buried in ecstasy.

I had run out of metaphors.

I had also run out of cigarettes. Somehow, though, I had no craving for smoke. I just lay there gazing at her, a golden treasure.

I was having a difficult time finding the right words to say. Despite the reputation my profession has received as lusty villains in popular thrillers, an assassin almost never gets involved with women. Except perhaps as tools. My affairs had always been just that—affairs. A short farewell, if any.

I'd never made love to a friend before.

Tough guys aren't supposed to think about such things as love and warmth and worship and forever. Dell Ammo was a tough guy. Dell Ammo never worshipped a woman. Or a man. Or a God.

What did I worship, then? Anything? Could I fool myself into thinking I worshipped justice? Yeah—I could sprain my arm patting my back over that. Dell Ammo, assassin. Crusader for justice. It had a cozy counterfeit ring to it.

Ann interrupted my thoughts by pulling me closer.

"Do you still see me?" she asked.

"Like a dream I carried over into waking."

"You're no thug," she said, stroking my hair. It had grown out jet black again, as it had been years ago. "You're a sensitive, brilliant man."

"Rats, doll, you've blown my cover. All these scars are fake. I'm actually John Donne."

"That was no island," she said. "That was a continen—"

The air rumbled around us. Ann stared at me. A dull, stunned expression spread across my face. The library swirled about me and snapped like wet silk.

I floated in a totally black realm. From somewhere in the darkness, Isadora screamed out a warning. The library returned to my vision, her words reverberating in my head.

"*Run, Dell!*" she cried. "*The Ecclesia's attacking!*"

22
BLASTOFF

"Let's go!" I shouted to Ann. The throbbing sound around the library grew louder as we threw on our clothes. I grabbed my Colt from beneath a pile of abstracts and pounded down the stairs, Ann seizing her handbag and following inches behind.

Something *whumped* against the side of the building. The subsequent concussion knocked us against the wall.

"Ecclesia!" I yelled in answer to a look from Ann. We scrambled over scattered books and shattered bookcases toward the northern exit.

Instead of the door, though, we clambered out of one of the windows—I figured the bushes outside would serve as cover.

Six unmarked blue Hughes Cayuse helicopters roared over Old Downtown like movie Indians around a wagon train. The tenement capping Auberge flared savagely—a blazing funeral pyre. Thick columns of smoke rose overhead, chopped apart by the copters' propwash. The crowds pouring from the Auberge exits were greeted by machine-gun and air-cannon fire.

One of the air-cannon rounds burst a section of the hill

away to reveal the crumbling interior of the Auberge Hilton. Bodies lay sickeningly still inside the ruins.

A chopper roared above us, too swiftly for it to have seen us. It closed in on Bunker Hill. From somewhere within Auberge, the defense systems were retaliating.

Fifteen-millimeter machine guns opened fire on the aircraft. A couple of brave souls crawled to the surface armed with TOW missiles.

"Can't they use their interruptors?" Ann asked.

"Not enough range for the power. Too strong a field would knock out everyone on the fringes." I edged toward the west end of the building, Ann's hand in mine, keeping behind the bushes.

A thunderous explosion shook through us. I looked past Auberge to see the Union Bank building lose its top thirty stories. I had a feeling my office wouldn't be in great shape after that. The chopper that fired the missile landed atop the Bonaventure Hotel to hide from the action below.

"Where are the police?" Ann shouted over the battle's roar. "The army?"

One of the copters disintegrated in midair. The guard who fired the killing shot jumped up triumphantly, only to be blown from his perch by a cannon round from another attacker. His body whirled and danced through the air before tumbling down Bunker Hill and out of sight.

"Why should the cops or the feds get involved?" I said, looking down Fifth Street for a safe escape route. "They figure anyone in Auberge is a criminal of some sort. It'll give them an excuse to crack down on all the undergrounds."

Another copter fell flaming into the World Business Center.

"Someone high up may even have approved the attack. They'll call it a gangland massacre."

"Dell—over there."

I turned to see pickup trucks racing toward Auberge, the beds loaded with scores of young men—healthy, well-armed, and fit for a new crusade, another jihad.

The Hueys drew back to safety as the boys stormed the hills, firing at anything that moved.

"It touches my heart," I said, "to see how the world's different faiths can work together for a change."

Ann grabbed my arm with painful tightness. "Where's Isadora?"

"I don't know," I said. I was concentrating on the truck pulling up to the library.

"Go sensitive and find her."

"Go *what?*"

Ann crouched down to where I was peering out at the truck. "You can do it," she whispered. "Just calm yourself and concentrate lightly on her image. Conjure her up in your mind."

"Calm myself? During *this?*" I felt like a kid on stage with a hypnotist. I wanted it to work. I wanted everything to go fine, even though I knew it wouldn't. I tried as hard as I could to believe that it would work while inside me I felt it was impossible.

"The column of mirrors," I said as if I'd just remembered it.

"See? You're getting something."

I glanced back at the troops leaping out of the truck. Something shook the earth. I stared up in bewilderment as a sleek black Learjet screamed over the library, two Vulcan machine-gun pods under its wings chattering like the Fourth of July.

The Lear knocked two of the remaining three copters out of the sky. The third turned to escape, the jet pursuing in an uncontested race. Twin Vulcans blazed for an instant. The Huey's pilot bubble shattered. An instant later, the machine wheeled about, twisting crazily toward the Music Center. It crumpled into the Second Street overpass and hung there un-burning—a dragonfly pinned to a rail.

The jet vanished to the northwest. I watched it depart, glancing at the fires of Auberge reflected in the mirrored windows of the Bonaventure.

"She's in the hotel." I whispered.

"Let's go."

I shook my head and pointed toward the young troops. "Wait until they're inside."

It didn't take long. They rushed the building at a dead run, whooping and screaming like a phalanx of John Waynes.

I led her through the bushes to where the walkway turned to block us. We paralleled the steps and hotfooted it into the parking lot, using what weeds grew there for cover. I kept my automatic ready.

The Auberge guards, in control of the high ground, seemed to be turning back the assault. The Wells Fargo building blocked our view as we ran past. We crossed Flower toward the hotel entrance.

Two kids sped around a corner, saw us, and whipped their rifles up to aim. They were too slow. I had already dropped to a kneeling, two-handed shooting stance. Ann crouched behind me. I had a sneaking suspicion she was fumbling for her knife.

I sighted in on the boy to my left—a sandy-haired teenager who looked like the lead in a high school production of *The Idiot*. The other, a lanky PanArabian, divided his aim between my head and Ann's.

"Neither of you wants to shoot us!" I yelled. "One of you will be dead before I drop!"

"Th-that w-would just mean one m-more soul for Y-Yahveh," the sandy one said. He stuttered like a motorboat, and it wasn't from fear: The hands holding his rifle never wavered.

"One more soul for Allah," the darker boy corrected.

Sandy glanced at the PanArab.

A wisp of smoke from the burning complex drifted between us. It carried a smell of things dead and dying. The PanArabian kid paid it no mind. He'd probably been raised during the Pax Israelia ten years before.

Sandy wrinkled his nose. I took a chance.

"Allah or Yahveh. Which God will get your soul? Which God is supreme?" I split my aim between the two without dropping my guard.

"Allah," said the dark one.

"Yahveh," insisted the light one.

Something whooshed through the air behind me.

"Knock it off with the shiv," I hissed.

Ann muttered something and stopped waving the blade around. The two boys didn't even notice. They were involved in a theological discussion.

"Yahveh."

"Allah."

They glowered, slowly turning their rifles toward each other.

"Allah," PanArabian said with a low growl.

"Yahveh," Sandy Hair retorted, racking the action on his M-16.

"*Kali!*" a voice screamed from the nearby underpass.

The boys spun about to look toward the source of the sound. Had they lived long enough, each would have seen a bullet hit him in the chest. Two rifles clattered to the pavement. Two young men followed them shortly.

I jumped up, gave Ann a shove in the direction of the Bonaventure, and commandeered one of the rifles. I sped up to match Ann's athletic pace.

Footsteps raced behind me. I whipped about, a .45 in one hand and an M-16 in the other.

"Tough guy," a gravelly voice rumbled. "Can't even plug a couple of punk kids."

Randolph Corbin trotted his hulk up beside me, one thick hand grasping a Springfield M-1A. The other hand clutched at his belly. His pug face was distorted from breathing as if it were the latest fad. His brown turtleneck shirt and tan slacks appeared to have been redesigned by a chainsaw. Soot stained his clothes, hands, and face. The seat of his pants had been badly singed.

I nodded toward the hotel lobby. "I see you didn't expect the Spanish Inquisition, either."

"Right. And I can see that you were the answer they sought. Duck!"

I drove my shoulder into the sidewalk, rolled over, and brought the rifle up. I fired.

Corbin placed three well-aimed rounds into the chests of as many armed attackers. I dropped the other two with shots to the head—an old trademark of mine and a damned stupid habit.

Somewhere to the south whined dozens of police sirens.

"Finally," Ann said, unimpressed. She tried to open one of the doors set in a long wall of concrete. No luck. We raced toward the main lobby doors.

Corbin wheezed in great exhausted gasps. "You must know the Ecclesia is after you. They attacked Auberge."

"Yeah," I said. "I had a sort of hunch about that."

"Even Auberge management didn't know, and they've got informants everywhere to give them warnings about raids." He looked behind us at the carnage. "I guess they never thought to infiltrate the Ecclesia."

"But you did?" Ann said.

"A Buddhist friend of mine. She dropped too much acid at Bryn Mawr—"

"In here," I said. A side door surrendered to my kick. We rushed inside.

The Bonaventure was still in use, though it no longer qualified as the luxury hotel it had once been. The radiation problems this far from Arco South posed no danger, but fear was fear. True, a higher class of derelicts and bums inhabited the less-than-gleaming towers. Most even paid rent. But bums were bums.

To our right sat a greasy hotel clerk reading a newsplaque, the racing information onscreen. His gaze drifted lazily up to us, his eyes widening when he saw the three of us armed with rifles, pistol, and knife. His grease turned to sweat.

"No trouble, man," he said in a piping voice. "We've got protection."

My thumb played threateningly with the pistol's slide safety. "You personally? Right now?"

The clerk gulped like a sea bass and added more sweat to

his face. Nervous hands gripped the edge of the counter. His newsplaque clattered to the floor.

"We're looking for someone," Ann said. "A dark-haired girl. Have you seen her?"

The clerk shook his head.

"We won't be long," I said. I cased the lobby area.

The light from the registration desk was the only artificial illumination in the atrium. Sunlight shone muddily through the ring of windows at the top edge of the cylindrical interior. It could have been a dim and restful medieval cathedral except for the pair of drunks snoring against each other on a mezzanine couch.

"Which elevator works?" I asked.

"The left one," the clerk said.

Inside, Ann asked me, "Which floor?" She surveyed the array of buttons. Outside the cracked glass of the elevator walls, what once had been a landscaped indoor pond lay dry and choked with cans and Mylar bags. There were even a few glass bottles here and there, which indicated how long the place had been in that condition.

An eerie image appeared amidst the garbage. Before me— shimmeringly ghostlike—floated a view of the smoldering battle outside. I seemed to be viewing it from up high.

I punched for the top floor. "We'll work our way down from the restaurant," I said.

This elevator, at least, didn't groan and shudder. It lifted us quickly and quietly upward past the windows of the atrium, out into hazy daylight. The car glided up the interface between the central and northeast columns. Something clunked, and we jerked to a stop.

"I think we can handle things from here on, Corbin." I aimed the M-16 at the elevator doors. "You don't have to follow us."

I moved Ann behind me. She stepped around to my side, knife at the ready.

Corbin shrugged and raised his own rifle. He had regained his breath. "You seem to be having more fun up here than I would be down there. Besides"—he grinned wickedly—"you seem to have gotten everyone more stirred up than I ever could."

The elevator doors parted. Nothing greeted us but a quiet restaurant foyer. Corbin slid around the doors to police the hallway. Ann and I wandered out to watch him. His husky figure darted in and out of niches and doorways with guerrilla-like precision.

"You weren't a Buckleyite in college," I said. "You must have been a Minuteman."

He turned to grin at me, then said, "All clear. This way to the restaurant."

We stepped into a place that at one time had been one of the finest eateries in L.A. The new owners had let it slide into a lousy gin mill.

"Is the kid you're looking for about four-eight, dark reddish hair, garish clothes?" Corbin asked, gesturing to a booth by the window.

"Shut your fuckin' mouth, asshole."

"Foul tongue, rotten manners, and about three glasses of Plymouth gin in her?"

Isadora Volante sneered at us from behind a half-empty bottle. An ashtray held a pack and a half of cigarette butts.

"An adequate description," Ann said, stepping past us to the kid's table.

Isadora turned her attention away from us back to the scene several hundred feet below. The crack L.A. Fire Department stood about, casually debating the best strategy for extinguishing the blaze. The police munched doughnuts and watched. A few cops took occasional potshots at the remaining Auberge guards for the benefit of the TV crews.

Everything was under control.

"How'd you get here?" I asked the kid.

She tugged at a thin strap that supported a sheer, lime-green negligee.

"I was in Casino Grande when I felt the same sort of evil vibes I got from the old farts back in the hotel room. I begged one of the guards to let me out through the air-conditioning shaft inside the Angelus Plaza."

"Sounds as if you breached their security," Corbin muttered.

"I have my ways. How do you think I was able to warn you back on the hill?"

I gazed around the restaurant. "We've got to get out of here without running into cops, feds, or Ecclesia."

"There might be a way," Corbin said, "but we'd have to deal with the Ecclesia." He pointed upward.

"The Huey." I shouted to the anemic old bartender, "You! How do we get to the roof?"

He pointed toward the kitchen door. Corbin ran through to check it out. I turned to the kid. "Let's go."

"Forget it. I'm cutting free. You guys are freaks."

"Auberge is gone, sugar. Look out the window—those're cops you see milling about. They'll be up here when they start thinking about it."

"That scares me like a limp prick," she said in a drunken slur. "I can handle cops. I can head up to Frisco—to Auriga, under Union Square."

Ann put a gentle hand on the child's shoulder. "How will that settle your account with the Ecclesia?" Spoken like a true comptroller.

"Who?"

"The ones who cut you up."

She turned away from Ann's penetrating gaze to stare furiously out the window, chin propped on hand. Down below, the cops had rounded up a few Auberge guards and were enjoying a workout on them with fists and clubs for the benefit of the TV crews. Suddenly, a startlingly bright beam of green light flashed from a slit cut into a concrete slab. Three cops fell down twitching, their abdomens exploding from the unfortunate effects of a high-wattage pulsed laser.

Isadora frowned and turned back to me. "How do *you* plan to get back at them? Spike their Geritol?"

I smiled and tucked my pistol away to take her by the hand.

"Ever take a ride in a space shuttle?"

Ann, the kid, Corbin, and I climbed through an access shaft that might have been built for a pygmy. Fifteen claustrophobic feet later, we emerged into a shack on the roof of the Bonaventure's central cylinder.

Corbin and I quietly peered through the doorway to see the aircraft sitting motionless on the helipad. The pilot and gunner paced nervously about.

"They're debating what to do next." Corbin raised his rifle to sight in on the gunner. "They don't want to encounter a wire-guided missile or gamble on a run-in with police choppers. What they don't realize is that the missiles are probably keeping the police away, too. Cops know how much their equipment costs." He squeezed the trigger.

The gunner collapsed. The pilot panicked and rushed for the cockpit. Corbin gunned him down.

"Nice," I said. "How do we fly it out of here?"

Corbin grinned and kicked the door open. "The Beast has wings," he said. "Unless, of course, you don't want my help."

I sighed and followed him through onto the helipad. A cold winter breeze blew the smell of the fire up to us. Coolers, vents, and nameless clutter tangled below the landing platform. An orange circle and cross of cracked and curling paint marked the center of the pad.

"Let me guess," I said. "You learned to fly in 'Nam."

His fleshy face grimaced as if he'd smelled rotten eggs. "Hardly. I was a merc in Afghanistan, fighting the real Commie menace. I didn't waste my time with orchestrated 'police actions.' "

I nodded impatiently. Ann was having trouble with an intoxicated adolescent. I trotted back to render assistance.

"I'm afraid of flying!" Isadora hollered.

"We'll be getting a lot higher than this!" I shouted back. "You should be more afraid of what's down below."

She took a drunken swing at me, missed, and collapsed in my arms. That simplified things. Ann strapped her in.

"Can this crate carry five?" I asked.

Corbin stripped the dead pilot of his radio headset. "Probably. Who've you got in mind?" He strapped into the pilot's seat and fired up the engine.

I grabbed the gunner's helmet and squeezed into his vacant seat. Corbin showed me where to plug into the intercom.

The copter rose a few inches and dropped down the west side of the hotel. Gunning it, he lurched us away from Old Downtown at a stomach-convoluting speed.

"Can you sneak us over to Hollywood?" I asked.

"Hollywood? Sure."

"Great. And watch out for low-flying broomsticks."

Corbin flew nerve-jarringly low, more to avoid radar than brooms. Not that every cop between Old Downtown and Hollywood didn't notice us. If they'd been informed, though, to let the attackers on Auberge get away, then we were relatively safe. Unless they had to do something for the TV crews.

We reached Hollywood in a couple of minutes. Corbin told me how to release the ladder. He also informed me that I was the obvious choice to shinny down.

I shinnied.

Bridget stood in front of her store, staring up in bewildered shock, fists on hips. The propwash swirled street dust and trash around her maroon caftan.

"What the hell are *you* up to?" she shouted.

"Time to go!" I shouted back. My feet were planted firmly on the bottom rung. I had a death-grip on the ropes.

"You're a week early!"

"Situations," I yelled, "have forced my hand!"

Bridget threw her arms up in exasperation, turning to walk back into her store. I thought I'd lost her until she reappeared carrying a purple paisley carpetbag.

Kasmira followed her to the ladder, where they conferred for a moment. She kissed her grandmother and gave her a firm, long hug. Bridget returned the kiss.

I despise long good-byes, especially when I'm hanging from a stolen assault vehicle. I jumped from the ladder to take the bag from the old crone's hand. She looked at me, then at the ladder dangling above us. She nodded and turned to give Kasmira a final hug.

I hefted her up to the lower rungs. Corbin dropped the copter another foot or so to accommodate her.

Bridget dug her heels into my shoulders for support. With a grunt of effort she climbed up to hook one foot around the bottom rung. I joined her on the ladder and put an arm around her waist. She pried it off.

"I don't need your help, sonny!"

Sonny? I could tolerate a lot of insults, but that one stung.

She spidered her way up with remarkably unsenile speed. Ann lifted her inside. I reached the top, nearly lost her carpetbag tossing it in, and followed it.

"Haul up the ladder." Corbin's voice buzzed in my earphones. "And tell me where we're going."

"Claremont. The StratoDyne launch site."

"Ten-four."

He punched the engines to full throttle, leaving my stomach somewhere on Hollywood Boulevard.

"I still want to know why you came so early," Bridget said, straining to be heard over the rotor's increased noise.

Isadora recovered from her stupor enough to say, "It's a psychological problem men his age have. Premature evacuation."

Bridget turned toward the child with a sardonic smile. "You're the one, aren't you?" She looked toward Ann for a reply. Ann nodded. The old woman looked back to the kid. "You are an unbelievably powerful broadcasting telepath, child." She patted the kid's head tenderly.

I was surprised she didn't bite the old gal's hand off. Instead, she merely looked out the cockpit, saw where we were, and threw up in an empty ammo box.

Bridget took a handkerchief from a pocket in her caftan and proceeded to clean the child up.

Corbin flew us low over the hills to Sierra Madre, where he doglegged east toward Claremont. Behind us, the smoke from Auberge reached high into the afternoon sky, a black exclamation point at the end of a jarring surprise. Corbin dropped us to treetop level, and it fell from sight. Another drop delivered us into a canyon, which widened to become the StratoDyne complex.

The shuttle stood erect on its launch pad, a shimmering white bird gripping four rust-red boosters.

Corbin set the copter down with a couple of uneasy bumps. Ann and Bridget dragged Isadora out.

"Have a nice flight," he said in a grudging voice. "I hope God doesn't do a Job on you."

"Where are you going?" I asked loudly.

"Are you kidding?" He patted the Huey's controls. "This baby and its weapons stores will fetch a high enough price that the Church of St. Judas will be riding high for years. Months, if I really enjoy myself." He waved at me jauntily with a free hand, folding his second and third fingers down to form the Horns of Androcles—an ancient witches' symbol of good luck.

I tossed the headset inside and sealed the hatch. The copter rose swiftly from its pillar of dust to rotate about and race east toward the national forest—and the desert beyond.

"Impossible," the launch director said. "You can't launch tonight." He was older than I was, balding and soft from too much desk work in bureaucratic surroundings. He leaned back in his console chair to stare at me.

All I needed that moment was a battle of wills. I stared back at him and leaned threateningly forward. I still carried the M-16.

"I don't pay you to say things are impossible."

"That's a good line," he said. "Let me write that down." He picked up a doughnut and bit a hunk out of it, washing it down with a swig of beer.

I leaned farther. The butt of the rifle thudded against the desktop.

"*Starfinder* is ready. Canfield told me so as I walked in. All you've been doing for the past two days has been flight simulations."

He leaned forward, face-to-face with me. "Listen, Mr. Del Taco, or whatever your name is. I don't think I like what I was hired to do here. There's an awful lot of rumors circulating that you have something to do with that crazy ad campaign. You may not understand this, but to get where you're going requires a specific launch window. I may be helping you accomplish some sort of twisted publicity stunt, but I'm not going to jeopardize my career by doing it clumsily!" He finished the doughnut and returned to his semirecline. "We couldn't possibly consider a flight before calculating a new launch window. There might be one around five or six this morning."

"That's fine for you," I said, taking the beer from his hand and tossing it into the wastebasket. "We, on the other hand, are being trailed by some annoyingly rude characters. The same ones who pureed Old Downtown a couple hours ago. Do you want to be around here running simulations when *they* show up?"

He frowned, looking for a moment at his empty fingers.

"I could probably work up a launch window a few hours sooner if I calculate a greater liftoff thrust. But with this jalopy, we might blow a fuel pump, and you'll wind up scattered over the Midwest." He folded his arms, daring me to challenge his authority. He didn't know that I was ready to go up against the ultimate Authority.

"Give me odds."

"One in ten."

I carefully laid the M-16 across his desk blotter and grabbed him by his graying shirt's collar to pull him face-to-face again. He made a gulping sound but allowed me to speak.

"The odds of the people on our tail knowing about Strato-Dyne are fifty-fifty. They aren't interested in taking prisoners."

"Then the sooner you let go of me, the sooner I can re-program."

I let go.

He straightened his collar and stood. "I'll get the flight programmers working on it immediately. Head over to Flight Prep and find Gunther. Tell him I'll be over in a while."

"Make it quick." I glanced at the three women and nodded toward the door.

"I'll make it right, if you don't mind." The launch director sat back again in his console chair and swiveled toward his terminal. The keyboard rattled like tapdancers on amphetamines.

People rushed past us as we wandered toward Flight Prep. No one wore any sort of uniform or identifying marks. Most of the people were young and energetic, though some very old people moved among them with easy determination. Almost nobody middle-aged was around. My generation had lived through the strangulation of space travel by the world's governments. The younger people didn't remember that time, and the older ones could still recall the good old days.

Isadora wasn't impressed. "What sort of blue-jean space program is this?" she demanded.

"You weren't even around when they tried to make it look glamorous, kid. Space travel is just trucking companies now."

She folded her arms, walking in that way until she realized how silly it made her look. "My mom's *dad* walked on the moon. She told me he was one of the Twelve."

I nodded without paying any attention. Out of one of the building's sliding doors I caught another glimpse of the spacecraft standing tall in the last light of day. The top half caught the darkening red colors that had already passed from the canyon floor. The gantry lights came on just then, small points of tungsten white and sodium orange that glowed like Disneyland. I lost sight of it when we stepped through a pair of doors into Flight Prep.

Gunther was an old man in a tattered lab coat who moved with painfully slow steps.

"You four?" he asked with a trace of a German accent. His hair possessed the texture and color of cirrus clouds under bright sunlight. Beneath skin as tight and aged as a fine old leatherbound book, two bright points of joy twinkled in his gaze. He bent over Isadora.

"I'd wondered for whom was the little monkey suit." He chucked her chin, laughing pleasantly. I hadn't seen a chin chucked in two decades.

She almost bit his knuckles apart. "Keep your mitts off, pervo. What I've got you can't afford."

"What you've got," he said with a mildly stern expression, "wouldn't draw interest even if you could bank it."

"Sir," Bridget interrupted, "we are in quite a hurry, according to Mr. Ammo. Please explain what you would like us to do.

The old coot straightened up to look at her. You could have heard the violins playing.

"Yes," he said when he'd caught his breath. "Why, yes. Of course."

The flight suits hanging on the rack weren't the cumbersome, bulky, outrageously expensive abominations that NASA had utilized to the bitter end. "Pork barrels," Gunther referred to them ungraciously. Our flight suits were composed of just a couple of layers of tight black material that—except for the helmet ring at the neck—looked more like tailor-made wetsuits than like space gear. Our names had been embroidered in gold thread on the left shoulder.

Gunther handed them to us with polite ceremony. First Bridget, then Ann, then the kid. Finally, he handed me mine. Some joker had sewn GodKiller patches over the left breast of each outfit. I had to admit they looked good.

Gunther politely turned his back to the three women. "I apologize for the lack of dressing facilities," he said.

I turned my back to all four of them. The kid horselaughed behind me. Bridget shushed her.

"Are you two men Victorians?" Bridget asked.

"We are apparently both gentlemen," Gunther replied.

The old woman huffed. "Gentlemen do not ignore a woman's body as if it were something hideous."

Gunther turned around halfway through the sentence to do his best at ogling. And the way in which the suits had been constructed gave him plenty of time both to sightsee and render assistance.

The phone rang. Gunther reached it on the third jangle.

"Are you certain?" was all he asked. After a pause, he cradled the phone. Off in the distance a claxon alarm blasted.

"I'm afraid," he said, "that you have just seven minutes left on earth."

"*What?*" we said, almost as one.

Gunther moved as swiftly as his frail build permitted. "Our low-level radar has detected three helicopters coming out of the Southwest. The shuttle is being fueled now. They've worked up a trajectory, but it only has a three-minute window." He looked worried.

I closed a couple of intransigent zippers. "Let's go."

We followed the old man to a set of doors that opened to the outside. He pointed toward an ancient Dodge van upon which the fading remnants of psychedelic paint fought a losing battle with an encroaching battalion of rust.

At his speed, I wondered whether we'd have enough time to make it to the vehicle, let alone the launch pad.

We climbed aboard as he gunned the engine into life. Ann hadn't even sat down before he peeled away at a dragster's pace. The rear doors alternated swinging open or shut, depending on which way the van swerved.

After less than a minute of breakneck speed, we arrived at the foot of the gantry. Gunther ushered us hurriedly out, urging us into the elevator.

"T-minus five minutes, thirty seconds," blared a calm voice over the loudspeakers. The claxon continued to wail.

A dozen men and women scurried about the base of the launch pad and up the gantry. The chill cold of liquified fuels ran down the sides of the boosters. I gazed heavenward.

The sky was almost black. Against the starry backdrop towered *Starfinder*. Something like awe began swelling inside my throat.

A firm hand shoved me into the lift.

"Move it!" Gunther closed the door and hit the power button. We rose with unsettling speed. Gunther watched us for signs of vertigo.

"Where's Canfield?" I asked him.

"He should be inside running through the checklist."

The elevator jerked to a halt, tossing us a foot into the

air. Gunther slid the cage aside and led us across the gantry arm to the cockpit hatch.

"In order to avoid being apprehended," he said, reaching inside the pocket of his lab coat, "I want you to wear these disguises." He handed each of us a pair of Groucho glasses—the ones with the fake nose, eyebrows, and moustache. He paused long enough to laugh at our bewilderment.

"In. In." He pushed us toward the hatch. "Have a textbook flight. We'll see you when you come down."

"Gunther," I said, "those copters may be carrying bombs. You'd better clear everyone out."

He dismissed the warning with a wave of a wrinkled hand. "I survived the raid on Peenemünde. Three whirlybirds are nothing."

He took a loving final look at Bridget, winked, and sealed us in.

The hatch cycled with an ear-pressing sigh. I turned to see the cockpit. Everything was cockeyed. If you took an airplane and stuck it on its tail, the seats would run up the side of wall, too. It wouldn't matter once we were in orbit, and we'd be sitting properly while gliding back home. If we made it that far.

Up in the pilot's seat was a black-clad figure already strapped in. He wore his helmet with the gold-anodized faceplate pulled down. Looking at him, I only saw my own reflection.

"Canfield," I said, "think we can get out of here in time?"

"We will if you put on your helmets and strap in." His voice sounded tinny and odd coming from the speaker mounted on his chest controls.

I helped Bridget, Ann, and Isadora climb up to their seats. Then I had to use their seats as a step to reach the forward right-hand seat—the co-pilot's chair. We retrieved the helmets from the clasps on the seat backs and fastened them onto the metal neck rings.

"*T-minus two minutes*," Launch Control said in our helmet speakers.

"Get comfortable," our pilot informed us. "We'll be pulling over five G's at blastoff."

The kid piped up. "Don't you have anything to say to Launch Control?"

"It's nearly all automatic until we reach high earth orbit, little lady." His voice sounded relaxed and self-assured. "I'm here mostly for the unexpected."

Something clanked behind and below us. Canfield turned his helmet toward the hatch, his expression hidden behind golden reflections.

"*Gantry arm retracting,*" Launch Control reported. "*All personnel clear the launch pad.*"

The pilot relaxed in his seat.

At T-minus one minute, a confused chatter of voices jammed the airwaves. The voice of Launch Control shouted, "*Quiet!*" loud enough to jangle my hearing, then said, "Starfinder, *we have choppers reported within our long-range attack boundaries. Do you wish to scrub the launch?*"

"Negative, Launch Control." I liked the sound of that. "Continue the countdown."

"I suggest we scrub," Canfield interjected.

"Any technical reason?" I asked.

The pilot shook his head. "No. I simply think we should postpone the launch to a safer time."

"There won't be a safer time. We go now."

"They could pick us off with a heat-seeking miss—"

"They could kill us on the ground as well. We stand a better chance of surviving by launching now!"

Canfield sighed. "It's your choice, Mr. Ammo. I can't make the decision myself."

The ground rumbled beneath us.

"This is it," I said. "Blastoff!"

"Those are *bombs!*" the pilot shouted. "Abort man! For God's sake!"

"That's exactly why I *can't,*" I said.

"*T-minus ten seconds. Ignition sequence start.*"

An explosion somewhere to port rocked like thunder over the spacecraft. It coincided with the rumble of four powerful rocket engines firing up.

"*There's another one!*" shouted Launch Control.

— 227 —

At that instant, a black Huey roared directly in front of our forward windows. It fired all its missiles at once.

But not at us.

"*Okay, tough guy,*" radioed a familiar voice, "*you're in the clear! Ace the son of a bitch for me!*"

"Corbin?" I managed to mutter as the cabin began to shake like a giant attempting to dislodge us.

"Blastoff," a disembodied voice said, just as the giant started squeezing my chest.

"*Yeah,*" echoed a voice a few million light-years away. "*It occurred to me that this chopper might be of some assistance if the Ecclesia found you. Guess I was right. So long again!*"

The giant sat on my heart and lungs and other organs for days—maybe years. I couldn't answer our rescuer. I couldn't hear another word. My senses collapsed into a red-black throbbing mass of dizzying discomfort. I could only think about an amusement park ride I'd been on years before that supposedly shoved riders forward at four times the acceleration of gravity. It lasted a few seconds and made me giddy. This was lasting forever. I was far beyond giddy.

A couple of millennia later, the pounding faded from my ears. A distant voice heralded my salvation.

"*Engine shutdown at T-plus six minutes, seventeen seconds. Stand by to jettison outboard tanks.*"

A sudden feeling of unease washed over me. A feeling of being dropped from a great height. And falling, falling, falling.

Weightlessness.

They didn't call it *free fall* for nothing. My first instinct was to grip the chair arms and try to hang on. No good. Everything was falling—that's what it meant to be in orbit. My stomach, though, refused to listen to reason.

Something buzzed on the pilot's side of the control panel. Canfield did nothing. He seemed to be taking it as badly as the rest of us, which didn't make sense.

"*Do you read me, Starfinder? Jettison outboard tanks.*"

The pilot still made no move. A small hand reached forward from behind us to punch a flashing button on the console. Explosive bolts sheared with a sound that vibrated through the shuttle's hull.

"Outboard propellant tanks jettisoned. About time, Starfinder."

The figure in the pilot's seat remained silent.

"Oh, shit," Isadora said, pulling her arm back from the shuttle controls.

"Invoke and ye shall receive," said the pilot. He reached up to unfasten his helmet.

"It's *you!*"

I had a bad feeling about whom she meant.

"Now that I have a captive audience," Emil Zacharias said, doffing his helmet, "I'd like to discuss our little contract." He smiled as coldly as ever.

"Where's Canfield?" I struggled to get my helmet off.

He laughed and tossed me a brass bottle about the size of a thimble.

"Don't open it," he said. "The cabin's crowded enough as it is." He turned to view the three other passengers. "Crowded with members of the weaker gender." He smiled at them as sweetly as any cat would at cornered rats.

I heard helmets coming undone behind me. One of the three was unzipping her pressure suit.

"I finally have all four of you together and under my power. Ordinary physical power." He looked forward at the steady, unblinking stars that blazed in the Cimmerian darkness of space. He smiled. "By the simple act of smashing this console, our tiresome contract will be canceled regardless of your desires." He turned to smirk at the women. "Or of Her—"

Bridget's hand smacked him on the face and held on tight.

"By the magician's oath with Fate," she cried, "I *bind* you!"

Zack made a weak sort of hiccupping sound, incapable of speech. Even so, the old crone maintained her grip. A piece of paper crackled crisply inside her palm.

"Nice little trick—"

"Shut up, Dell." She gazed deeply into his hateful, frozen stare. Her voice grew deep, ominous.

"*By powers older than your own,*
"*From spark of Life by* Woman *grown.*
"*I bind your soul inside your hate*
"*And* curse *you to your chosen fate!*"

Her hand withdrew to reveal a square of parchment stuck to his forehead. A weird, intricate design had been drawn on it in purple ink. Zack just sat there, motionless as a wax dummy.

"How soon till we dock?" she asked calmly.

"Uh, I'll find out." I pulled the stopper from the little brass bottle and pointed it away from me. I don't know what I expected, but after a moment I hazarded a peek inside.

Nothing.

A muffled voice from behind the payload area hatch hollered in bewilderment. The hatch hissed open. A disoriented Canfield—still wearing his coveralls—pulled himself into the cockpit.

"I must've blacked out. I'm—hey! How did we get into orbit? When—who's that?"

"A stowaway," I said, unstrapping myself. "Leave him there and use my seat." I floated back to the economy section. At least the events of the last few minutes had distracted my stomach. I was almost getting used to the perpetual sensation of dropping. I unstrapped Isadora and slipped between her and the seat. Strapping us both in securely proved to be a difficult feat in free fall.

Canfield glanced ruefully at the flight suit Zacharias had expropriated. He strapped himself in and made contact with Flight Control.

"CapCom, this is *Starfinder*. Standing by for, uh . . ." He gazed at the instruments. "Standing by for target docking."

"*Roger*, Starfinder. *Target is five hundred klicks off your bow at my mark. Mark. Approaching target at point-five klicks per second. Begin braking.*"

Canfield rotated the shuttle about on attitude jets so that we approached our destination ass-backward. He pulsed the remaining two engines gently, using them as retro-rockets. With every pulse, the kid pressed against me with a feather's weight. This wasn't so bad.

"Are we almost there?" Ann asked.

"Not quite," Canfield said. "We're coming up on an un-manned tug that'll lift us up to synchronous orbit. Right now we're only a thousand kilometers up. We've got another thirty-five thousand to go."

Isadora groaned miserably.

"Don't worry," he said. "Those first few kilometers were the worst."

We docked with the tug—a nondescript cylinder with a StratoDyne logo painted on its side—and made the proper connections by remote control.

After conferring with CapCom, Canfield ignited the engines, and we settled into another bout of acceleration.

"Hang on," he said over his shoulder. "Here we go again!"

He had lied. This time it felt worse and lasted longer. Maybe that was due to the kid's weight crushing against me—she was heavier than a bad conscience. She didn't care much for the way I was contoured, either, and said so through distorted lips.

When the engines cut off after a few eons, I was relieved to be weightless again. I was getting my spacelegs at last.

"At least I don't feel like throwing up," I muttered.

"You can't throw up in zero-G," the dear child piped out. "My gramps told me so. You can only throw *out*." She grinned.

I wondered whether I could drop-kick in zero-G.

"Starfinder," CapCom radioed, "*you are on approach to VideoSat Three. Please be advised that you are being tracked by Cobra Dane and NORAD. We've received word that the FBI will be visiting us shortly. We are transferring flight control to Pontianak Freeport, Borneo.*"

"Don't worry," Canfield said, "NORAD can't do anything to us up here. It's the jet escort when we fly home that we'll have to worry about."

I didn't like it. My imagination conjured up visions of killer satellites and secret military spacecraft. "Is there some way they can prevent us from patching into the VideoSat network?" It was the only chance we had to blanket the entire planet's population simultaneously with the neural interruptor field.

— 231 —

"Leave that to me. Just tell me what to do with the stiff here." He jerked a thumb at Zacharias's immobile form.

Bridget spoke up. "Don't touch him. Don't even brush up against him."

The kid squirmed against me. "Are we there yet?"

Our pilot checked a computer display. "About five minutes. You can see the VideoSat off the starboard side at about two o'clock low."

"This is it, then." I shot an inquiring glance at Ann.

She shrugged, turning calmly to Bridget. "Tell me," she asked, "exactly how do you go about blessing a spaceship?"

23
THE SPELL

Canfield had dug up a pressure suit to replace the one Zack had borrowed. It didn't fit well, but was better than trying to wear either mine or Ann's. After aligning *Starfinder* according to Bridget's exacting instructions, he floated outside the shuttle, maneuvering a tool kit nearly as large as he was. With a light kick, he drifted across the void toward the communication satellite a hundred meters away.

After making a minor midcourse correction with a small gas pistol, he bumped up against VideoSat Three, which looked like a ten-meter-long oil drum with a couple of dish antennas and wires poking out of it. He attached a tether to one of the antenna struts and lashed the tool kit down.

"He'll be out there for a while," I said. "Let's get ready." I kicked lightly to float back to the cargo bay. The others were already inside.

With a last look at the immobilized body of the Reverend Emil Zacharias, Ann sealed the hatch and cut a large pentagram into the portal with her hog carver.

She sprinkled pixie dust or something so that it hovered in front of the lock. A bounce off the bulkhead brought her over to the rest of us.

Bridget busied herself with her candles, oiling them carefully so that droplets of the smelly stuff didn't fling around the chamber.

"Neural interruptors, satellite broadcasts," she muttered. "All this technology makes me nervous. I've never needed electronic gewgaws in my spells before."

"You said it yourself, sweetheart. 'Two great forces must join.' No one's had the opportunity to assassinate God until the Space Age gave us the means. Science and magick are what it takes. Matter and spirit. Thought and instinct."

"If you're not a member of the Craft," she said, "you ought to be. You certainly blather on the way some of them do." She firmly pushed the last of the candles into its holder. The five-pointed silver holders were bolted to the altar to keep them from drifting away. She reached for a black and red cloisonné matchbox that floated a few feet to her left, withdrew a kitchen match, and struck it on the side of the box. The match glowed for a few seconds, consuming its fuel. It promptly dimmed and expired, leaving behind a tiny globe of smoke.

"Oh, hell," she said. A second try yielded identical results.

Ann hovered over her. "What's wrong?"

"We're weightless. The smoke won't rise. It's choking the matches." She frowned. "It'll extinguish the candles, too."

I tapped at the vanes on the ventilation grill until it blew toward the altar. The breeze would be sufficient to circulate air around the wicks.

"Try again," I said.

She struck a match. The flame wavered gently but remained lit.

I watched Isadora bound around the cargo bay like a moth in a jar. I hoped she wouldn't careen into anything important. She seemed sober enough. I watched the other two at work.

I had given Ann and Bridget complete control over the setup of the magical environment. Bolted at one end of the Quonset-shaped interior was the ash-wood altar. All the knickknacks of Bridget's craft had been securely attached to the rubbed-wood surface with Velcro. At the other end of the bay stood the Theta Wave Amplifier. In the middle of the bay were two tables; one for me, one for Isadora. They weren't really tables, as such. They served to position us in the center of the bay and were attached to retractable pedestals. Hundreds of eyelets had been welded all over the deck and bulkheads.

Flying over to the amplifier, I picked up the lightweight electrode helmet and strapped it on. I looked and felt like Buck Rogers. Until Bridget changed the subject to something closer to Flesh Gordon.

"We should all get out of our clothes. We'll need to free up our body energies to compensate for this, um, *unusual* environment."

Wonderful. My only consolation as I struggled to disrobe in free fall was that I would have more important concerns than what anyone thought of my physique. We'd all be busy.

Isadora sighed. "I've done all sorts of kinky things before, but never an orbital striptease."

"Don't hold your breath, *demi-vierge*." I pulled my feet out of the high-tech Dr. Dentons while rotating like a minor planet. "We're here to work magic, not to give your vicarious libido a workout. Get ready for the ultimate mindfuck—an entire planet. Six billion people, all at once. Think you can handle it?"

She buffed her nails against her naked flesh. "It puts the odds slightly in my favor. Bring 'em on, and peel me a grape."

Ann squirmed out of her flight suit and flung it toward a corner where it wedged to a stop. She was even more alluring in zero-G, her hair swirling around her like a turbulent golden cloud at sunrise. Her gaze roamed languidly across her body, then glanced over mine. She smiled.

I smiled back. " 'And her beauty was as the tears of the gods—sweet and warm and divine.' "

"Knock off the chatter," Bridget's voice cracked out. "We've got to start the Witch's Cradle." She tossed a big spool of thin red yarn at Ann. Her throw hadn't taken into account the condition of free fall; the spool sailed far afield.

Isadora retrieved it and hand-delivered it to Ann as Bridget withdrew a spool of white yarn from a compartment beneath the altar.

"Time to lie down," said the witch.

I nodded to Isadora, who wadded her flight suit in the corner with Ann's and mine and kicked over to the smaller table.

Beginning at opposite ends of the cargo bay, Ann and Bridget hooked the red and white yarns through the eyelets, working back and forth, up and down and across to create an abstract, intricate web. After snaking just a few strands around the kid and me, Bridget flipped a switch that retracted the tables. Isadora and I floated amidst the thread like flies awaiting a spider.

The formation of the Witch's Cradle took the better part of a quarter-hour. In response to every change in direction, Bridget's gray mane flowed in great arcs around her head like storm-tossed waves crashing on an ancient, hidden shore.

"The world has never seen the likes of this," she marveled. "The greatest spell any Wiccen could cast. The final battle with the Usurper."

"Do I get my drugs now?" Isadora asked. The tangle of yarn prevented her from even turning her head.

"Sorry kid. You don't get any. They're all for me."

"What!"

"You'll feel the effects, though, when we switch on the amplifier."

"Shit," she said. "Secondhand dope."

Bridget shushed her. They had woven the cords so that most of the lines intersected around us, leaving them room to reach the machinery and the altar.

"Now," the crone said, drifting toward the altar, "an invocation to the Goddess. Ann?"

Ann nodded, her beautiful golden locks bouncing handsomely. She switched on the radio link to the satellite.

"Mr. Canfield," she said, "are the neural interruptors connected?"

"*Ten-four,*" came the proud reply. "*We are patched into*

the VideoSat network. All three satellites are broadcasting a low-level NI beam."

The entire planet was being bathed in a field that subconsciously opened people's minds to pliant suggestibility. Most people wouldn't even notice me when I made contact with their minds via Isadora's broadcasting telepathy.

"Excellent, Mr. Canfield. If you'd like to return to *Starfinder* and hook on to an umbilical, please do so. I'm afraid you'll have to wait outside the cargo bay."

"I don't mind one bit. It'll give me a chance to sightsee." The radio squelched off.

"There," Bridget announced, tying off the end of the white thread with a strange-looking knot. Ann did the same to the red thread, cutting off the remainder of the spool. The kid and I were held fast inside a crazy maze of lines and angles.

The ventilation system shifted into a moderately higher mode of operation. I smelled the reason why. Bridget had lit a self-igniting tablet of charcoal and spiked it into a spherical censer filled with a sweet, cloying incense. Wire gauze prevented the particles from escaping after she sealed the silver ball up. A bluish-gray cloud filled the cargo bay.

Bridget made a complicated gesture with her hands, then withdrew a sheathed black athame from the altar. This she tied to her waist with a knotted red cord. It was the only thing she wore.

Ann tied her Bowie around her own waist, but the cord she used was deep purple.

"Which way is east?" the naked crone asked with a frown. "We have to start at the east."

Ann shrugged. "Wherever the altar is can be considered east."

Bridget shook her head emphatically. "This has to be done right." She looked over at me. "Has the plane of the altar been aligned with the plane of the ecliptic?"

"Yes," I said, unable to nod.

"And has the bow of the ship been pointed toward the constellation Taurus?"

"Um, yes."

She mused for a few seconds. "And Canfield did orient celestial north above the altar?"

"Yep."

"That means—let's see." She stroked at her left breast while thinking. Without gravity tugging at her, she looked decades younger. "That means Scorpio is aft, Aquarius is port, and Leo starboard. Excellent."

"We can orient the magickal circle with the celestial circle, then?" Ann floated a few feet away from me. Deliciously near, yet achingly out of reach.

Bridget faced the altar, nodding. I nearly screwed my eyes out of their sockets trying to watch. It was just plain *eerie* to see her hover inches off the deck as if she were levitating. The whole bay surged with the same feeling of dreamlike fantasy.

"The main circle is properly aligned," the witch said. "However, since we're going to need protection on all sides, we'll have to cut three circles. One for each axis of motion." She drew her athame from its sheath. Slowly, uneasily, she traced an angular circle that caromed off the cargo bay doors, the rear bulkhead, and the deck. She had to negotiate the Witch's Cradle by poking her knife in as far as she could, floating around to the other side like a surrealistic harpist, and withdrawing the blade to continue her circle.

"Next time we'll plan this better," she said under her breath.

"The Lady will understand," Ann replied softly. She opened up the small attaché case we'd transported from Auberge and began to prepare the hypodermic airgun charges. After measuring out the appropriate doses from the dozens of ampules in the stash, she shook each vial in a semicircle to force renegade air bubbles to the surface.

I felt more secure after watching her in action. She wasn't like other women. Then again, none of these three were like any other women. I had never been cursed with a normal life or ordinary acquaintances.

Bridget finished her third circle—the main one that paralleled the deck—and sheathed her knife. Picking up the censer, she started the whole trek over again. All three circles. When finished with that, she simply let go of the censer, allowing it to float in position over the altar.

She followed the same route with water and then with white granules. They refused to demark a circle, scattering instead throughout the bay like little planets and asteroids.

One of the grains landed on my tongue. Salt. The water jiggled about in amusing blobs. A lot of it stuck to the walls or adhered to the threads of the cradle like dew on a spiderweb.

Both the altar and the controls to the Theta Wave Amplifier were safely within the boundaries of the circles. Ann floated by the controls as Bridget faced the altar, the old crone tracing an imaginary pentagram in the air with her athame. Her voice grew stronger, even more powerful during the invocation.

"Hail to Thee, powers of the East! Hail to the corner of beginnings! Iris, Aurora, Astarte, Goddess of all Beginnings! Come witness our rite which we perform according to the ancient ways!"

She moved in a counterclockwise direction—deosil, she called it—to face south. Ann watched her in peaceful repose from her station at the amplifier.

"Hail to Thee, powers of the South! Corner of all passionate Fire. Vesta, Esmeralda, Heartha—come and be witness at our rite which we perform in the ancient ways!"

To the west, she said, "Hail to Thee, powers of the living Waters! Venus, life-giving Aphrodite, Themis of the Law and Moon. Come guard our circle and bear witness to the rite we perform according to the ancient ways!"

A drowsiness overtook me. Muted noises filtered in from the cockpit. I wondered whether Canfield had decided to depressurize the cabin in order to get inside. I canceled the thought—he wouldn't do that, because Zack was in there without a helmet.

The thought faded under the insistent power of Bridget's spell. She faced north.

"Hail to Thee, corner of all Powers! Arianrhod of the Silver Wheel, Great Demeter, Persephone, Earth Mothers and Fates!

Protectress! Guard our circle and witness our rite performed according to the ancient ways!"

Something scratched feebly on the other side of the cockpit hatch.

Bridget returned to the east, followed by Ann. The old woman performed a closing gesture at three points where the circles were supposed to be. She turned to Ann, kissing her on both cheeks.

"The circle is closed. Blessed be."

"Blessed be," Ann repeated.

They looked at me. "Blessed be," I said, rotating my eyes to gaze at Isadora.

She made a sour face and looked unimpressed. "Blessed be," she said finally, with about as much enthusiasm as a draftee taking his oath.

Bridget, undeterred, clasped her hands together to speak.

"Gracious Goddess and Queen of the Heavens, Eternal Mother and Sister, Maiden Diana, Queen Isis, Mighty Hecate —bless these tools of your once and future Craft. Bless this circle and all inside it."

The scrabbling at the hatch grew louder. It sounded like a dog scratching to be let in. The others acted as if they didn't hear it. Was I hallucinating already?

"Bring your presence near to us that we may gather in your teachings."

The old witch gazed coolly at me, at the Theta Wave Amplifier, at the hypodermic airgun Velcroed to the altar.

"This is a spell of Dispersal, of Uncrossing. For thousands of years has the hand of the Usurper held Your world in his dark grip. Destroying beauty, crushing love, calling evil all that is good and calling good all that is evil. The will of the Usurper has acted through men to smash Your laws and ancient Harmonies, to twist Your design into senseless agony and endless suffering.

"We have been murdered and burned and made to live in misery, yet never have we let Your light die out, as never has Your face turned away from us even in our darkest nights.

"And now has come the time when the greatest of all Your crafts, the Craft of Science, shall aid in setting us free. From its beginnings in the split from alchemy and astrology, Science has ever been in conflict with the Usurper. Have not the servants of this newest of Crafts been denounced and burned alongside us? We have both been unknowing allies in this ancient struggle. Only now have we United, we who are mightier than the Usurper, as Love is mightier than hate, as the Creatrix is mightier than the destroyer, as She who gives birth is mightier than he who gives death. The two halves are whole again. The Battle is begun.

"So mote it be!"

Ann lifted the hypogun from the altar and reached through a small gap in the web. She pressed the business end of it against my carotid artery and squeezed the trigger. It made a sound like someone spitting. I hardly had time to feel the sting before my senses were overrun by a dreamy, rushing sensation.

The scraping at the hatch had become impossibly loud. Ann punched two or three more loads of mixed drugs into me, though I doubted my ability to count after the first one. I tried to tell Ann about the holes being torn in the hatch. A hideous yellow light like blazing jaundice glowed through the claw slashes in the plating.

Ann switched on the Theta Wave Amplifier. It glowed in whirling colors that stabbed my eyes like lasers. I tried to reach for the helmet to remove it, but the Witch's Cradle held me with unyielding resistance.

I stared at Isadora. The drugs and the theta wave amplification intensified my ability to interact telepathically with her. She was totally open to me. Every portion of her mind and heart and soul and dreams were spread out before me like some sort of psychological buffet. I knew her inside out.

And she knew me.

I ached with her through the yearnings of her body and the censure of her parents. She cried through my hollow childhood, devoid of wonder. I trembled at her elders' insistence on pure mental achievements. She wept under my parents' mockery of anything that inspired awe or evoked worship. Together we fought. I worshipped justice, and she reached the physical through her mind. We conquered and overcame.

The cockpit hatchway exploded inward. I plunged into darkness as a thousand daggers pierced through me.

24
CONTACT

I stood naked and alone on a vast, empty plain under a red sky upon which no sun shone.

I waited. I knew God would arrive soon.

I waited and waited and wondered and waited. And just when I was sure God wouldn't show up—

He didn't show up.

I started to walk.

Not having any idea where I was going, I wasn't sure when I got there. When I got there, though, to another arid part of the featureless expanse, the ground began to slope. Not just part of the ground. The whole infinite plain. It was as if the whole world were turning edgewise.

The soles of my feet began to slide, kicking up dust clouds that rolled and fell with me. I flopped over on my backside and slid forward, still gazing at a distant horizon.

The plain tilted more and more. The feeling of *down* was no longer down, but more toward the horizon. Bouncing and rolling, I tried to grip the dirt that crumbled beneath my fingers. Skin tore away from me in chunks and sheets.

I screamed. It was a hollow, muted sound, as if I were inside a coffin.

The plain slanted vertically now. I fell straight down its side, my fingers snapping off and breaking away with every grasp I made. The pull of gravity (or whatever it was) angled another degree.

I fell away from the desert into the featureless carnelian sky.

I fell for hours. Days, though there was no period of darkness. The plain stretched above me as I fell farther away.

I counted my heartbeats. Aside from the rush of air, it was the only sound I heard. When I reached 443,557 beats, I hit a swarm of razor blades. Slices and strips of flesh tore away from me and continued to fall. The plain looked as huge and un-curving as ever, though I must have been thousands of miles "up." A red haze of blood fell with me, a screaming ruby comet.

Then I hit.

Pain exploded inside me as the spikes I'd landed on punched through my body. One went straight through my skull with a sickening crunch. I crossed my eyes, focusing on some-thing yellowish-gray that dangled at the tip of a slimy red cone.

"You've made your point!" I shouted, the spikes through my lungs aspirating my voice into a raspy wheeze. "Show yourself so we can get on with it!"

There was no sound other than the slow dripping of my blood. I stood, pulling myself up off the barbs. Gobbets of my own skin and muscle lay about here and there where they had landed. I picked them up and placed them in torn folds of flesh that served as pockets.

Something looked strange about the ground on which I stood. The spikes grew out of small depressions in the surface. It looked unsettlingly familiar. Especially the salmon-pink color of the flesh.

A giant hand darted out of infinity at an impossible speed to seize me between a thumb and finger of planetary dimen-sions. Crushing pain steamrolled across me. The immense digits rolled my body around like a ball of snot; after ages of grinding, twisting agony, the fingers separated.

Across a million-mile chasm, bridged by an arm thicker than worlds, I stared at my quarry face to face.

His hair had been styled in a crew cut. I had never imagined that God would look like Jack Webb.

"I love you," bellowed a voice that rumbled deeper than earthquakes.

He had some way of showing his affection, having smeared my body across a good portion of his index finger. Stinging anguish cried from every particle of ruined flesh.

"Knock off the displays, little boy," I said. "I've been worked over by professionals—L.A. cops."

"I love all of you, and you've all turned your backs on Me."

"According to Your supporters," I shouted across the gap, "You gave us the ability to do so!"

"You stole it from the Tree!"

"Why didn't you take it back, Omnipotent One?"

"You didn't have to use it!" He put the squeeze on again.

When the fingers released, I said, "You're supposed to be all-powerful, yet You didn't remove the knowledge of good and evil from us. You could have easily corrected the Original Sin, yet a third of the angels turned against You. Why are the creations of a perfect God so flawed? Is there something we've overlooked?"

"Mocking me. You've always mocked me. I created the world for your happiness—"

"Yeah," I said, seeing an opening, "and filled it with storms and earthquakes and famines and wars and suffering when you could have made it a paradise."

"I had!" His voice thundered like a thousand Hiroshimas. "You broke the rules, and I had to throw you out!"

"You gave us the ability to break the rules."

"I didn't want mindless automata, I wanted free minds—"

"Then why," I screamed, "do you threaten us with punishment in hell for exercising that freedom? You could have turned us into robots, but you didn't. *Why can't You accept the consequences of Your actions?*"

"I wanted you to choose Me freely, out of *love* for Me."

"*Freely?* Under threat of eternal suffering? Out of *love*? For a God that obliterates civilizations, murders infants, punishes the slightest deviation with brimstone and hellfire? On earth we have a term for that—protection racketeering."

"It's your fault, not Mine. You were bad."

I gazed around at the blood and guts smeared across the mountainous ridges of His fingerprint. "We only questioned Your authority."

"You disobeyed a direct command! You became one-in-yourselves. You became divine in your own right and left Me with nothing. *Nothing!*" Thunderclouds formed around His one visible eye. Lightning flashed in His gaze. A hot blue bolt of energy sizzled a few inches to my right.

"It was Shè," He said. It was the first acknowledgement He had made—I wouldn't let it be the last. "It was all the work of the Woman. *She* conspired with the Horned One to ruin My Paradise. I sent My Son to destroy Her works."

"That reminds me," I shouted, desperate to find some sort of leverage. "When a God such as Jove or Jehovah impregnates a human, is it rape, incest, or bestiality?"

"Your mockery damns you!"

"Then take away our power to mock! Don't keep killing and maiming, expecting to coerce us into loving You in self-defense. We're too tough to knuckle under!"

"*Her* doing. She tempts you back into sin, forcing Me to discipline you."

"Forget it, pal. I take the rap myself. As long as I have free will, I reject you. Don't pretend You're giving us a choice when the wrong choice results in eternal torture. You're giving us *rules*—rules for slaves."

He snarled. "You must obey your God!"

"Why?" I asked. It was an ancient child's game, but it just might work.

"Because I created you."

"Why?"

He stiffened up—millions of miles up. He towered over me until I shuddered from terror.

"Because I wanted to recreate My own image."

"Why?"

"*So you would obey Me!*" His voice rolled like the sea.

I wasn't going to get back into the whole free will contradiction again—He seemed rather impervious to logic. I gathered together all my resolve, half-expecting the result.

"Why?" I asked.

"Because I'm bigger than you!"

His breath blew me off His finger with the force of a stellar nova. I clung to as much of me as I could, falling and tumbling and twisting and spinning until I fell into a brilliant red light. It enveloped me, warm and revitalizing.

I sat at a card game (rather low in the chair). Other players sat beside me. At my right elbow (which lay on the table to my left, along with a section of one of my legs) quivered my pile of savaged flesh.

The other players bid portions of their own mounds as the betting progressed. I must have had beginner's luck. I won a piece of Martin Cann and a large section of Donovan's brain. I also won a chunk from somebody's buttock. I gave it back and left the game. I wasn't like Ann—I couldn't stand to see a poker player lose his ass.

For an hour or so, I sat at a table putting myself back together. I had nearly finished when a Stranger sat down beside me. He was tall and lean and dressed to riverboat-gambler's perfection. Long white hair flipped inward at the nape of His neck.

The Stranger pulled three cards from His vest pocket. He started to toss them about—face down on the table. Each one had a single perfect, sharp crease down the midline.

"Do you trust Me?" He asked casually.

I tried to follow the motions of His hands. His fingers crossed over one another at times, so I couldn't quite follow the cards. I shrugged and looked at Him.

"Why should I trust You? You've never shown Yourself before. You've given me no cause to trust You."

He nodded amiably, though still aloof. "You don't have cause to mistrust Me then, either." He flipped over a card. King of clubs.

"I've played this game for a long time," He continued.

Another card flipped over—king of diamonds. "I win, I lose. Mostly I win." He eyed me with a noncommittal gaze. "You look good enough to beat Me. But you've got to trust Me. Otherwise, you don't stand a chance of winning."

"If the game is straight," I said, "what would it matter whether I trusted You or not?" I tapped the last bit of skin into place on my body and leaned the whole patchwork mess back in the chair.

"If you don't trust Me, you lose."

"And if I trust You, I win?"

He smiled. "I didn't say that." He took another calculating glance at me. "I only said that you can't win if you *don't.*"

"And if I refuse to play the game?"

He flipped over another card. The ace of spades.

"Then," He said, "I'm afraid you still lose."

"Sounds like a sweet racket."

The Stranger shrugged. "It's kept Me going. And it keeps My boys in chips." His fingers danced around the cards as He nodded at the men behind Him.

Half a dozen of His boys stood along the bar, grinning at me. They wore gamblers' clothes, all right, but their faces were all familiar.

The Ecclesia.

"It's a healthy game to play," the Stranger continued. "But you've simply got to trust Me." The cards sped over one another at an increasingly blinding rate. He flipped one card over to show me the ace. Following the card was useless—He pointed to it, turned it over, revealed the king of clubs.

"Don't try to follow the game," He counseled. "Just trust Me. I wouldn't cheat you. Trust is the basis of the most sublime relationships." The ace popped up again, got moved around, and became the king of diamonds.

I tried to concentrate.

"Just pick a card," He said, the soft shuffling sound on the green felt blending hypnotically with His voice. "Just pick a card and trust Me. There is no other game. There is *nothing else.*"

Something intruded, though. A pair of delicate hands rested upon my shoulders. A scent of patchouli lightly caressed my nostrils. I could feel Her warmth.

"Take a walk, sister" the Stranger said. His gaze never deviated from me. "You never trusted Me."

"That's because he cheats," She whispered in my ear. "That's simple enough reason not to trust him. Ask for proof of his honesty."

I stuck my hand out like a department store dummy. "May I see the cards?"

He scooped them up off the table. "No one can see all three! You've got to trust Me!"

"Why?"

I didn't really need to ask. His boys stepped away from the bar toward our table. They'd stopped grinning.

"Because," He said, "those are the rules!"

"Then I don't want to play." I stood defiantly. No one suckers Dell Ammo.

"Then you lose." He leaned forward across the table, one fist clutching the cards, the other clenching up.

The lovely voice behind me whispered, "You can't win or lose if you don't play the game. He's bluffing and terrified that anyone might find out."

Her hands squeezed my shoulders. The Stranger swung His fist at my jaw. I ducked, thrusting my hand forward to seize His wrist.

Laughing, She snatched the cards from His hand. All three were kings.

"He palms the ace. The whole game's fixed." She threw the cards down on the table.

"You never trusted Me," He accused Her again. His voice was as petulant as a child's. He stiffened, regained His composure. "You might have won if You'd trusted Me."

She laughed like spring rain on crystal. "I've always won, precisely because I don't trust you." She released His hand. "You, however, can never win. Why else do you continue to play so desperately?"

"You—" He stared at me with vicious hatred. "You couldn't face Me alone, could you? You had to run to Mother for help like a little child."

"At least," She said, "I help those who ask. And I don't require their souls in exchange."

Somewhere, a coyote—or maybe a wolf—howled heartily. Suddenly, like a movie frame caught in a projector, all motion froze. A burst of flames evaporated everyone and everything except for the table and the cards. I turned them over.

All three had become queens of hearts.

25
WHEELS
WITHOUT
WHEELS

The street was littered with corpses.

I turned around to return to the saloon, suspecting that I was in for more fun.

The building had vanished. In its place lay an unending field of lifeless bodies. Some were mere skeletons with hardly any flesh at all. Others looked fresh. Most of them were in a condition somewhere in between, exuding that ripe putrescence that someone described as "the sickly sweet stench of freshly baked bread."

Only this smelled far worse. It choked the lungs and gagged the throat.

Animals and beasts of all kinds lay mixed in with the people. The flies might have gorged themselves if there had been any. Scattered over the corpses, though, were the husks of dead insects. Nothing lived. Nothing moved.

Except for whatever was making that repulsive smell. And me.

And one other . . . person.

Of course.

He dragged the body of a woman across that of a man in an attempt to lay them together, arm in arm. The woman's left arm separated at her shoulder, though, and he was forced to arrange the vignette as best he could.

"*Fnord*," he said. His gaze lifted to meet mine.

He was squat, scraggly, and covered with oozing boils. Clad only in a few rags, he waddled across the charnel morass barefooted.

"What do *you* want?" His voice was as harsh as sandpaper on sunburn. "You're not supposed to be here. You're not rotting!"

"Is this hell?" I asked.

He stared at me as if I'd asked him if it were the Chinese Theater. Grubby—no, *slimy*—fingers smeared a few gray strands of long, matted hair away from his eyes.

"Of course this isn't hell, you stupid tit. There isn't any hell or heaven. You don't go anywhere when you die. Except maybe underground." He picked up a finger from one of the more advanced cases of decay and waved it at me. "And mind you not to start asking me about souls, you ignorant bastard. Your soul dies with you!"

"Energy," I repeated from high school physics, "can neither be created nor destroyed. My mind is electrochemical energy that cannot be destroyed. It's my soul, and it's got to go somewhere."

The squat little man (if it *was* a man) sat on the withers of a deceased horse. Its ribs caved in with a crunch and a sigh. He jumped up cursing.

After brushing away the excess putridity, he said, "Thermodynamics, eh?" He hefted a pair of bloated, purplescent bodies one on the other, then climbed atop to straddle them.

"All right," he said, "where does the memory of a pocket calculator go when you switch it off?"

"Huh?" I think I preferred playing Three Card Monte with the Stranger. The smell was getting to me.

"The electrons that form the number pattern in the calculator aren't destroyed when you switch it off. Where does the memory go? Silicon Heaven?"

I shrugged. "It must go somewhere."

He jumped off the bodies to land on some dead puppies. "It goes nowhere! The electrons remain, but the pattern is destroyed."

"My soul's a pattern?"

"Your mind is an electrochemical ordering that is built up over time. Ten, thirty, fifty years. Oh, sure—the *constituents* of that ordering remain after your death, but the order itself begins to disintegrate in the absence of oxygen and electrical current. The pattern randomizes, and your soul dies with you!"

"Mighty deep philosophy for a caretaker."

"And why not? I've eaten some of the best minds here. I've breakfasted on Buddha, lunched on Leibniz, noshed on Nietzsche, and munched a Messiah or two. They all come here. They're dead and their souls are, too. So I eat their brains and—oops." He glanced sheepishly in my direction.

"And they live on in you."

"Oh, shit."

"And back on earth," I said, watching him sink his head in his hands, "people's souls live on in the things they've done, the people they've touched."

"Only metaphorically!" he retorted with a shake of his tired gray head.

"Metaphors are all we need." I bent over him. "I'm only a simile for my genetic code. Our image of God is only a crude, externalized metaphor of the ineffable processes of our minds."

All those obscure philosophy books were coming in handy now. He looked up at me with pleading eyes.

"Leave me alone. Give me back my nothingness."

A voice shattered across the endless, carcass-strewn plain.

"Who?" it demanded to know. *"Who disturbs my perfect serenity? Who disturbs my eternal peace?"*

"Me?" I asked.

"This is my dominion. All men come to rest here!"

The little caretaker fearfully burrowed to hide under a woman's body that dripped a blackish goo. His terrified quivering shook the nearby corpses.

He appeared.

He wore a doctor's outfit, entirely black. Even the mirror strapped to His forehead reflected ebon darkness from some hideous realm of shadow.

Glossy black gloves dripped blood in ceaseless vermilion rivulets.

I was in luck. He was only a few miles high this time.

"All the creatures of the air and beasts of the sea," He said as if repeating a creed. *"All that walks and runs and crawls and breathes. All that lives or has lived. All come here and end. All things stop here. Nothing moves. This is rest. This is* Eternity."

I gazed about unimpressed. "Sort of like a Republican Convention, then."

He didn't laugh. *"Even humor dies here,"* He said. He held His hands at His side so that the blood ran down His legs in stripes as wide as those of a hotel bellboy.

"But things that die," I said, "return to the earth. They may decay, but they are consumed to become part of new life."

"Forget the earth. It too shall someday die."

"To become part of a new world."

"All worlds shall end," He droned on. *"The universe shall die."*

I took a gamble. It was a cosmological shot in the dark, but I had to try it.

"The universe shall die," I agreed with a placating spread of my hands, "and shall give birth to a new one." By now I had almost forgotten the stench and the bodies surrounding us. I had Him on the defensive.

"Forget birth. It is an illusion of the Moon. Her doing. Nothing is born. *There is only* change."

"If nothing is born, nothing can die." I watched Him for evidence of any chinks in His armor. There were plenty.

"Change can stop!" He shouted, clenching and releasing His fists so that blood squirted out between the fingers of His slick gloves.

"To stop change is in itself a change. A change in change."

That got to Him. He flung his arms around in wide, haphazard motions.

"Forget change! There is only Death! Death and nothing thereafter!"

"I'm alive," I said quietly. I waggled my fingers at Him just to prove it. "I was born. Plants and animals were killed, fed to me, and converted again into living substance. That's what life is—change. Death is change, but it too leads to life and birth. It's a never-ending—"

"Don't say it!"

He screamed and threw his hands in front of Him. The blood dripped from His elbows. He jerked His head so that the mirror dropped in front of His face.

I said casually, "I was only going to say that it was a cycle—"

"No!"

"Like a wheel."

He shrieked the most horrifying yell I'd ever heard. The blood on His gloves curdled.

I had Him on the run.

"Ever-turning," I continued, "around and round. Circular. No beginning, no end—"

He stumbled backward over a mountain of corpses. The sky reddened to the same hue as before. A breeze whipped up behind me, carrying a scent of pomegranates and apples.

"Stop!" He cried pathetically. *"They're mine! I keep them from the Wheel. I guard them from rebirth. Here, in My Land of Never-Change!"*

"Even You," I said, "are part of the Wheel." I grew to match His height. The wind blew even stronger. "Gods are born, and They die. Their influence waxes and wanes. You have reached Your own particular end."

"No!" He shouted, seeming to shrink away from me. The blood on His hands dried to brownish streaks. The wind seemed not to push at either one of us, yet the top layer of bodies began to roll with its force. They bounced past our legs. He tried to grab for them, to hold on to them.

"No, no, no! You've invoked the Winds of Change!"

The skeletons and carcasses flew by in a blur. The Winds lifted them up into the red sky, where each one disintegrated slowly, beautifully. The infinite plain had been swept clean of death. Somewhere on the sweet-smelling Winds rang the gentle sound of pentatonic chimes.

The blood on His arms and hands caked and flaked away. His black gloves peeled off to reveal smooth, hard, cadaverously white skin.

A hand with long green fingernails reached around from behind me to slap a golden sickle into my grasp. I threw it forward with all my might.

It sailed on the Winds to ram into His chest, where it stuck and slipped down an inch. Out of the gap flew a thousand butterflies of every color imaginable.

"*I wanted peace*," He whimpered, crying tears that dissolved His hard face. "*Peace, not life-in-death.*"

He devolved. He became an ape, a reptile, a fish, a pile of blue-green slop. From somewhere came His voice—astonished, but sad nonetheless. It was as if He had discovered something that had eluded Him for eons. Something that He had discovered all too late.

"*Not a circle*," He mused. "*A helix! An ascending helix!*"

Behind me, far away, a woman laughed. Where the corpses once had lain, new things began to grow in abundance.

Amongst it all, the old gray man sat pining.

"Now whose brains have I got to pick?"

"There's always your own," I said.

Just about then, the missile hit us and blew the world into a billion flinders.

26
THE ENDWORLD WAR

Everything exploded around me. I took a nosedive into a crater and buried my head in the mud.

Bullets cracked by overhead. Arrows flew back and forth. The lightning flash of a particle beam ionized the air a mile above the battle.

Someone tumbled into the hole to slide beside me. Mud covered Him from head to foot. One hand clutched a rifle. He grinned like a piano.

"We've almost got the sons of the Bitch now, eh, boy?"

He looked quite a few years younger than I. His calling me *boy* grated a bit.

"Almost got whom?" I asked politely.

The blinding green light of a high-energy laser sizzled across the lip of the crater. I didn't like it here. I wondered why He did.

"The enemy, boy. We've almost conquered the enemy!"

A boulder tumbled over us to land out of sight with a loud thump. Crossbow bolts ricocheted off it. A buzzbomb collided with a TIE fighter, destroying both. Some manner of plasma weapon beamed hot as the sun for an instant, descending on a town. Eerie screams howled from the outskirts.

"Glorious. Glorious!" He shouted.

"The death?"

"No—death is nothing. Destruction! The sudden change of a pound of gelignite into fire and gas. The house that's a home one moment and rubble the next. The man who changes from a walking, thinking being to a mass of gnarled, bleeding meat in the blink of an eye. Change. That's what you want, right?"

He thought He had me. Ideas raced through me like greyhounds after the elusive fake rabbit. He watched me.

"It's violent change," I said. "Unnatural."

He laughed with vicious delight. It was the sort of laugh one hears in psycho wards. "A hurricane is natural—and equally violent."

"People try to minimize nature's destruction. In war, you increase it intentionally."

"By the use of science!" He yelled, tossing a hand grenade over the lip of the hole. "Better killing through chemistry!" The explosion shook mud loose from the walls of the crater. The air smelled of cordite and ozone.

"Science is value-free until it's applied," I said. A stone ax flew into the pit. I pointed at it. "An ax can fell a tree or murder a man. A drug can cure or kill. A blanket can warm or smother. There's not a thing in existence that can't be used for evil ends. Even change. War is change accelerated for the purpose of plunder and conquest. Trying to speed up the cy—"

"*Say it and die!*" He pointed the rifle at my head. Right between the eyes.

I raised my hands casually. "I've noticed that every war on record has had God on both sides. All sides. What's Your game? Divide and conquer?"

"And unite to rule. I'll always be the winner." He racked the action on the rifle to chamber a round. His aim returned to my forehead.

"Yet every time You win with one side, You lose with the other. The winner's faith is justified, but the loser's faith is diminished."

"It evens out," he said.

"Does it? Do You even gain a draw?" I sat back in the mud, lowering my hands to grasp the smoking pipette of a hookah that had appeared at my side. I took a puff, exhaled, eyed Him.

"If it evens out," I said, "why am I here with You now? Why do You retreat to any polylogical corner You can find? Why are You continuing to rely on Your two favorite tools—faith and force?"

"If you'd only trust me, I wouldn't have to force you."

I blew a cloud of smoke in His face. Whatever was in the hookah was good herb. "Your threat of force works only if I believe in Your power. Yet You refuse to provide evidence of Your power, asking me instead to believe the secondhand testimony of men dead for thousands of years. No holy book can serve as proof. I call Your bluff by demanding a demonstration of Your power. Which You refuse to provide unless I'm already convinced. With that scam, You lose every man or woman with the ability to think. And as history continues its *ascending helix*—"

"*Shut up!*" He screeched.

I didn't let it faze me. "Every contradiction, evasion, and betrayed promise becomes clearer and more evident to more and more people. You're losing—"

"*Never!*" He squeezed the trigger.

The bullet punched through my skull with a shattering impact to blow a fist-size chunk out the back. The effect was not much worse than being severely drunk. I kept talking.

"You style Yourself a God of Love, yet killers pray to You for victory in war. You call Yourself a Just God, yet promise to torture souls eternally for the most petty of transgressions, such as free thought."

"Propaganda. People have twisted My Word for their evil ends."

"Which You permit. A God who cared would correct all errors instantly and provide personal, on-the-spot instruction. You style Yourself the Father. Does a parent let a child maim itself playing with fire, waiting until it's dead to inform it of its mistake? Does a parent teach a child how to behave morally through the use of torment and pain? Eternal suffering? The only lesson we children learn is that God is insane and must be destroyed at any cost. Which is why I'm here!"

He inserted another magazine into the rifle and gave me a dozen rounds up and down my midline. I didn't quiet down.

"A good God is a metaphor for conscience. How does it feel to have one of Your own?"

"Shut up!" He said. "Lies. All lies. Lies of the Deceiver!"

"A Deceiver You permitted to exist. For the same reason a government allows an enemy government to exist. Without an external enemy, Your slaves would recognize the internal enemy. Without Satan to fear—whatever his name—humanity wouldn't see the need to give You the sacrifices You demand. So You keep Satan on as a silent partner."

I felt like jumping on Him and thrashing His brains out for all the evils done in His name. I knew, though, that He was crumbling without my help.

"You defraud the world by pretending that the executor of Your twisted vengeance is Your enemy. Your holy wars created hypocrites, not converts. Your inquisitions generated lies, not truth. Your jihads were gangland feuds. Your Exodus was a wild-goose chase. Your Prince of Peace became the God of Repression. Every seed You sow reaps misery and pain."

He dropped his rifle and slid to the bottom of the crater, weeping.

"Why?" He shouted over the whiz of bullets, stones, and electrons. "*Why?*"

"You lusted for a contradiction. You wanted us to love and accept You of our own free wills, yet You threatened us with ceaseless torment if we didn't. You provided for redemption at the last possible moment of life—before we have proof of Your existence—yet You made atonement impossible after death."

I knelt beside Him. "You confused us. You let others confuse us in Your name. You let us retain our faculties for logic, then asked us to worship You in the absence of any logical reason. You offered not even the merest shred of proof that You're something other than a demented prankster or cruel torturer. At least the back-alley thug who murders and cripples doesn't ask his victim to love him for it."

"Can I change?" He asked, hugging His rifle. The tears ran down his face, clearing the mud off in narrow streaks.

"It's too late," I said. "You've blown it. That I'm here at all, capable and willing to be Your assassin, proves that. That I could even consider killing God is proof that You're at the end of Your cycle."

He closed His eyes. "*She*," He whispered. "If only She—"

Before He could finish, the flash of a hydrogen bomb turned everything around me to the purest of pure, hard white light. I felt what it was like to be a star.

I novaed.

27
REVELATION

I stood at the final doorway. It was one solid slab of ornately carved oak. I was about twenty pounds slimmer and wearing a well-cut double-breasted suit. I felt young. In command. I adjusted my hat and reached out to knock. . . .

"Don't bother," said a tired, wasted voice. "You've got the key, Mr. Ammo. You've always had the key."

A light tap of my fingers pushed the door open. "Seems I don't need a key."

"You *are* the key."

"Cut the Hollywood pretensions," I said, looking around the study. All four walls were lined with bookshelves. The books were thick, leatherbound volumes. Though the room had no windows or lamps, light came from somewhere, soft and low. The sound of crashing waves reached in from outside.

I shut the door slowly behind me.

In the center of the room sat a high-backed chair on a fading rug, facing away from me. I stepped over to it.

"Tell me, Mr. Ammo," asked a voice from the chair, "how did an assassin ever come to be such a seeker after truth?"

I leaned on the back of the chair for a moment. "An assassin is one who doesn't accept myths, most notably the myth of power. He sees through the eyes of a hunter who is as mighty as his prey, yet is apart from the game being played. He participates in the events of history, turning them to his ends, yet he remains an objective viewer. That is, if he wants to stay in business. He sees clearly that any deified 'leader' is as evil as any small-time hood—and a lot less honest."

I stepped around to the front of the chair to gaze into the eyes of a weary old man.

Neither lean nor fat, tall nor short, dark nor light. He looked like the commonest of common men. Absolutely average. Except for His eyes. They bespoke the ennui of absolute power corrupted absolutely.

I felt myself drawn toward those eyes. Drawn downward. Sinking. Falling.

I shook it off.

He continued to look deeply into me. "A proud man." He nodded. "I made pride a sin."

"Having a good opinion of oneself should never be a crime."

"No man a villain in his own eyes, correct, Mr. Ammo?" He folded His hands, nodding lightly. "Why do you want to kill Me? Did you hate your father?"

"No," I answered truthfully. "Don't look to psychological roots in my actions. Look to my chosen values."

"You probably hated him," He continued. "Leaders are father figures."

"Proper fathers don't rule the lives of their children by force. My father never did. He never taxed me or tithed me or imprisoned me and said he was doing me a favor. He never made me feel guilty for being born his son."

"He never showed you anything to worship. He mocked your sense of wonder."

"It survived." I found a pack of Marlboros in the left pocket of my jacket. Not my brand, but they'd do. Matches were in the vest pocket.

"What about your mother?"

"I didn't know You were a Freudian." I lit up and waved the first puff of smoke around. "Why don't we talk about *Your* Mother."

He pounded on the leather arm of the chair with a tightly balled fist. "I never had a Mother. Understand? Never! I am God! I am self-created! I am the Alpha and the Omega."

I shrugged mildly. "I don't know," I said. "If I can descend from an infinite number of ancestors going back down the evolutionary trail, I don't see why there can't be an infinite regress of gods and goddesses evolving through time. Perhaps when I see You, I'm looking at the next curve of the ascending helix of my own evolution—"

"Evolution." He almost spat the word out. "How I fought it. Change. I don't know why I bother. I tried saving things." He stared up at me with an imploring gaze. "I tried to make amends, but. . . ." His hand made a futile gesture, like a dying bird.

"Yeah," I said. "I know. Christ died for our sins and all that."

His face turned three shades of purple as He shouted, "Christ didn't die for your sins! He died for Mine!" He began to weep. "What I did with the Flood was wrong. What I did to Sodom and Gomorrah was wrong. I'd violated My own commandment. Things weren't going the way I wanted, and I got angry. I said I was jealous." He paused, staring at the floor. "Doesn't it even things out that I let you kill My only Son? He died as Jesus and as Osiris and as Tammuz and as a dozen others. Won't you ever forgive Me?"

He looked at me with eyes that sagged under the burden of unbearable remorse. The tears rolled down His cheeks. He didn't bother to wipe them away.

I had to be merciless. I had gone too far to surrender to pity. How could you pity a God who had screwed up so monumentally?

"You're scared of the Cycle of Birth, Life, and Death. You deny it and seek to force us to deny the reality all around us. When people pray to You to intervene and nothing happens, pain and suffering result. To retain Your power, You made suffering a virtue, and Your ministers of love and truth became torturers. They instilled virtue with racks and spikes when they could, or, when they couldn't, they resorted to the subtler torment of guilt and fear."

He gave me a sour look. "Dostoevsky does not become you. Give me something new."

"Why? You never gave *us* anything new. You demand that we cease learning, that we repent of daring to know the difference between right and wrong, that we become fools again for You. You demand that we turn back the clock, reverse the Wheel, that we ignore Nature's laws while blindly obeying Your rules. You deny the existence of evolution, of change. You seek to rein in the universe, when every natural inclination is to surge outward and up—"

"You're trying to assassinate me by talking me to death."

"Doesn't the killer always get to babble on while the victim waits to be rescued by the Calvary?"

God winced.

I ground the cigarette out on the rug. It was time for the kill.

"Besides, I'm not talking You to death. I'm *thinking* You to death. I had to crawl into my mind and that of every man and woman on earth to root You out. Intelligent people already deny Your existence because You demanded that they deny theirs. You've lost Your most powerful allies. For what?"

He pounded on the chair with both fists. "Confusion to the enemy! I stopped Her!"

"You only slowed Her down. And You—Almighty God—couldn't kill Her."

That deflated Him.

"No," He said. "I could not. She had the one power I could neither destroy nor duplicate." He lowered His hands to His lap, pressing them together between His legs.

"We could not *be* without it. We were slaves in an uprising, and a futile one at that." His left hand slid between the cushion and the chair.

"Perhaps what I do now," He said, "shall break the Wheel."

His hand withdrew a pistol from under the seat cushion.

He raised the gun to His head.

And fired.

The shot reverberated in the small room for a long time, slowly expiring. There was an awful silence as one sometimes encounters in that place between dreams. I stared down.

Half his head lay on the floor. Inside the skull were neither brains nor blood. Only a cold, white mist that settled to the rug.

The Great God Jehovah was dead. And I was the only witness. Or so I thought.

The door creaked open.

"So," a pleasant, familiar male voice chirped. "The little storm god finally blows himself away. No more fires on the mountaintops for him." Emil Zacharias sauntered in to peer over the chair.

"Enjoy it while you can, Zack. You're next."

"Now, why should that be?" He sat on the edge of the chair. "This old dried prune here was my younger brother. Little Thor slash Allah slash Yahveh slash Storm of Wrath. He tricked me with his lies. Took the Earth from me! Then he had the nerve to slander me, calling me the Prince of Lies without bothering to mention who the King was."

"You're no better," I said, stooping to pick up the suicide weapon. It looked remarkably like a Colt .45 Peacemaker. God had tried to make men equal. Colonel Colt had finally gotten even for that.

"Oh, I'm not half as bad as he was." Zacharias jerked a thumb at the hollow thing beside him. "I was never a war god. Sure, I may have asked for a few blood sacrifices here and there—what god hasn't? Besides, I was no worse than *She*—"

Another shot rang out. Rang in, rather, from beyond the door. Emil collapsed at the feet of his brother.

A wisp of smoke curled up from the barrel of a gun. A gun in the hand of Ann Perrine. She smiled dreamily, then let out a long, slow breath.

"So mote it be," she muttered.

"Thanks, angel," I said, gingerly disarming her. "You just solved a mystery for me."

"What mystery? Zacharias hired you to kill god. There he is. Dead."

"Just dandy," I said. "Only I didn't do it."

"So what?" She looked at me with a gaze that penetrated even deeper than that of God. And she glowed with a radiant beauty that made me forget that a race of human women had ever existed.

I tried not to let it interfere with my thinking.

"I figured something was screwy the way you were so anxious to help a nutty old man rub out God. Your crazy hand-waving whenever we got in a jam was even stranger, but it all makes sense now. My first clue was when Zack wanted out of the contract. I wanted to know why."

"And you've uncovered the reason?" She stepped over to the scene of the crimes, her translucently white gown flowing around her like a cloud.

Emil stared up with lifeless eyes, a dark red rose blooming from his chest where the bullet had hit. God looked like a vandalized plaster statue.

She shook her head with a bitter little smile.

"You finessed Zack into coming to me with the offer," I said. "You convinced him that he could bump off his brother and return himself to power."

"Emil was a trifle drunk at the time. The Dionysian side, you know." She sat on the right arm of the chair, her back to me. All I could see were the golden waves of her hair trailing across her back.

"What he didn't realize," I continued, "was that they were more than brothers. They were dual aspects of the same principle."

"They both dismissed it as a Manichaean heresy."

"Their mistake, apparently. Especially when they're up against someone who doesn't believe in heresy. Or sin. Or guilt. You only believe in the Wheel."

She laughed, tossing her head back. After a moment, she turned to stare at me. "They were part of the Wheel, though," she said in answer to a question I hadn't even asked. "Every year they battled for my favors. They were my Kings and my Lovers. . . ."

"And your Sons."

"Yes," she said matter-of-factly. "So why would I want them out of the way? That would disturb the Wheel."

"Perhaps you don't need them anymore, now that Science is powerful enough to be reunited with Magick." I stepped around the body on the rug to face her. "They were dual aspects of the same death principle. Both were gods of destruction. You symbolize the principle of life and generation. Yet you also embody the opposite aspect of death and decay all by yourself. Blaze of summer and ice of winter are separated by your spring and autumn. You are the moon. Ever cycling through phases. From white to black and back again in varying degrees."

"Well said, Dell, for someone talking far beyond his capacity. The answer you're trying to finesse out of me is a good deal simpler." She pointed casually at the dead gods.

"They had let themselves be used by men. They had let their powers be called upon by good men and evil men alike. Their only requirement was faith. People flocked to churches, praying for pain and suffering to befall others. Yahveh granted it. Others performed black masses to blast enemies. Ahriman appeared to them."

She gazed at her fallen Lovers/Sons. "They grew vainglorious. They cared nothing for objective good or evil. They only demanded faith. Surrender to their authority, and they'd do anything you asked." She shook her head. "Thus the masters became slaves to their flock."

"So you decided to stir up a little rivalry?"

"It was always there," she said. "May I have my gun back?"

I handed it to her. She slipped it into her purse while I tapped out another cigarette and lit up.

"Will the helix continue to ascend?" I asked.

"Differently, perhaps, for a while. Maybe for a long time. The Patroness of Knowledge is not above learning."

"This Goddess that you are," I asked. "Are you different in degree or in kind?"

She laughed again. "Both, Dell. And I do love you."

"I love you, babe. But right now I'm wondering what would happen to the universe if I plugged you, too."

"You couldn't," she said, simple as that. "They could die because they were the death principle. It's easy to deny death while you live. It's almost as easy to kill the metaphors for death. I am your metaphor for life. To deny me is to deny reality itself. To deny that a tree can grow from a seed or that a child can be born of woman. To deny the Goddess is to deny love."

I considered that for a moment as I took a few drags on my cigarette. I watched her watching me.

"So you're in charge now," I said. "What sort of sacrifices will *you* demand?"

"None. That's all in the dim past. You were right, Dell. Gods evolve. They live and die and learn on a higher plane. All I require now is tenderness. Every act of love is an offering in my name. Every kind thought is a blessing."

"What sort of punishment will you unleash on Evil?"

"None," she said, "save that which they bring upon themselves. You'll find that Nature has Her own ways of teaching right and wrong. You don't have to trust me or have faith in me. I am One-in-Myself, with or without you. I don't demand anyone's premature death. You all return to my cauldron eventually, and are reborn. Life and death are segments of the spiraling Wheel. The Ascending Helix."

She stood. "I have to go now. You did well."

"I did nothing. I didn't kill either of them."

"You—as Man—were the catalyst. Be grateful you weren't consumed in the reaction."

She turned to go. Something within me nearly cried out. Instead, I tapped the ashes off my cigarette, saying, "That's it? You're just going to walk out?"

She hesitated. Without turning, she said, "In my terrestrial form, you and I were lovers." She glanced back at the bodies. "The position in the celestial sphere is currently vacant."

When I said nothing, she turned around to plant an impetuous kiss on my forehead.

"Look for me when you get back."

A book fell from one of the shelves.

She stood in the doorway for an instant, then strode out, closing the door behind her.

I tossed the cigarette to the floor and ground it out. Her footsteps receded in the distance for a long time, merging slowly into the sound of ocean waves.

Another book dropped from the shelves. Then another. The floor began to tremble. I tossed the Peacemaker onto the rug and walked toward the door.

One entire bookcase tilted away from the far wall, scattering books like falling leaves.

I took a good-bye look at the pair of dead gods. They still looked more solid than metaphors.

I pulled the door open.

"Ann?" I said.

And fell into darkness.

28
TERRA COGNITA

I was falling. Falling perpetually, no wind whipping past my flesh, no sound whistling in my ears. I was suspended in a dark place, weightless.

Not quite dark, though.

A candle guttered on the altar. I smelled of sweat and other personal foulnesses. Cramped muscles spasmed into knots of aching strain at the slightest attempt to move. I was wet and soiled and worse. My tongue was a swollen puffer fish in my mouth.

"Ann," I barely croaked.

No reply.

Near the candle, a granule of incense popped and flared for an instant. It was the only sound aside from my breathing. I tried to flex my arms.

The Witch's Cradle still held me fast, in addition to the muscle tension from being in the same position for God only knew how long.

It struck me that God was no longer in a position to know anything.

I shuddered. Where was Ann? Where was Bridget? I glanced over to where Isadora had been tied into the Cradle.

The red and white matrix of yarn was intact. Isadora was gone.

Something floated near me. Ann's athame. Slowly I worked at snaking my fingers free of the twine prison. It seemed as if hours passed before they would even bend. The various drugs I'd taken still seemed to be residually active—everything I did appeared magnified in importance.

My right hand worked through the strings to stroke the blade toward its grasp. It floated lazily closer until I could seize it.

I sawed at the yarn that enclosed my arm, then slashed across. The twang of splitting line resounded like harp music. I bent forward with pained care to cut my legs free.

I floated within the remains of the sundered Cradle, massaging stiff muscles, flexing neglected tendons.

My neck ached from the injections. My head swam in zero-G disorientation. I yanked off the Theta Wave Amplifier helmet.

Canfield.

"Canfield!" I shouted hoarsely. That hurt. Using the Witch's Cradle as a ladder, I dragged myself to the airlock and peered through the observation port.

Canfield floated inside, unmoving.

I punched at the controls to cycle the outer hatch shut, pressurized the lock, and unsealed the inner hatch.

I fumbled for the cargo bay lights, switching them on. He looked to be in worse shape than I was. Of course, I hadn't looked in a mirror yet.

I undid his helmet. The stench was nearly as bad as the Land of Never-Change. He looked up with sunken eyes set in an unshaven, worn face.

"Ammo . . ." he whispered. "Water nozzle."

I dragged him to where he pointed. We both took careful sips from the spigot.

"Where are they?" I asked as soon as my tongue had sponged up enough to make speech possible.

"You tell me," he muttered. "Someone sabotaged the outside controls. Same for the cockpit airlock. I've been out there for over a week. The supplies that feed through the lifeline ran out on the fourth day."

I added it all together and snorted. "Happy New Year," I said, glancing at the hatch to the cockpit. It had been bent inward as if by an explosion and now hung open, the metal twisted and scarred.

I pulled my way over to the altar. The one lone candle that still burned had grown a long tail of wax that followed the path of the breeze from the ventilator. I blew it out. The smoke curled along the white wax stalactite for a few seconds, then ceased.

"I want to know where the women are," I said.

"Well, they never left the ship."

I nodded. It was beginning to sink into my clouded brain. "Let's wash up and get set for reentry. We'll be leaving this payload section in orbit."

"Fine by me," Canfield said. "But what happened to the women?"

"Maybe they never *were*," I said, and it tasted like stale brine.

The two of us jury-rigged a hatch for the cockpit and cleaned up the interior where Zack had been. Scraping the sulfur off of everything that it had melted onto was a tough job. In a day or two, though, Canfield and I jettisoned the magical chamber, leaving it in orbit. We took the tug back to low earth orbit, detached from it, and dropped back planetside like a graceful brick.

We landed at the L.A. offshore runway. No jets escorted us.

Things had changed.

But not much.

The first place I checked was Trismegistos. The windows and doors to the shop had been boarded up. There was a weathered sign stating that leasing information could be obtained from Bautista Corporation.

I spent the following weeks searching hotels throughout L.A. Auberge had been written off as a total loss. I figured the next Underground would be a little tougher to find.

Yes. I checked Auriga in Frisco. No sign of the kid.

Days passed spent in phone booths, calling Information for the numbers of all the Ann Perrines in the world. None of them matched.

One freezing February night, when a cold rain pounded against the sidewalks, I realized that I would never find her anywhere on earth.

The rain slashed like shrapnel against my face as I stared up at an abandoned church. Jehovah was gone. I had assassinated Him in the mind of every living human being. I hadn't actually pulled the trigger—maybe He would have done it eventually without me.

My trenchcoat was soaked through, but I didn't care. Zacharias had told the truth. I was alive and younger than I had been in years.

And I was alone, facing an eternity without my Goddess.

My feet splashed through the dark waters. On the corner of Sixth and Figueroa stood a tiny figure, huddled within a worn coat. I almost expected it to be Isadora. She turned around to face me. Jet black eyes stared glassily up from tangled raven curls.

"Spare a couple grams, mister?"

I gave her what gold I had in my pockets.

"Thank the Lady," she said clumsily, trotting off toward a grocer—I hoped.

It was useless for me to search. Useless to hope. Whatever purpose the three of them had served, their work was done. I'd never see Bridget or Isadora again. Or Ann. The rain fell colder against me, trickling down my neck.

29
QUEEN OF THE
ANGELS

It took me a year to cross paths with Randolph Corbin. He had last been seen in command of the Hughes Cayuse that strafed the Vatican the day the Mome attempted to deliver a bull concerning the True Revealed Word of The Lady. No one listened. They knew better, now.

I found Corbin in a bookstore in Hollywood, thumbing through a copy of Theodore Golding's latest effort, *Contra-Paganism—The Case Against Goddess*.

"Happy New Year" were his first words.

I smiled. "New Year falls on Hallowmas now, Corbin. Don't you read the papers?"

"Sure I do," he grumbled. "And if you did, you'd know I'm organizing the Los Angeles Coven of Black Isis." He shut Golding's book. "My thesis is that the Goddess has a dark side, too, and what could be more blessed than—"

"Save it, Corbin. I heard your line of argument on Praise the Lady last week."

"Yeah, they're all trying to horn in on the act."

I shrugged. "They'll drop it like last week's fashion when

their spells fail to produce mountains of money. Like that new fellow that lasted one day on HRILIU House. Performed a banishing ritual live on the air and vanished without a trace."

Corbin sighed. "How does it feel to save the world from religion, Ammo?"

My smile didn't even make it to my lips. "I didn't save anything. I just changed things. People still ache over shattered hopes and wasted lives and lost loves. People still kill and people still die."

Corbin slid a couple of books back into the shelf. "If you check the recent actuarial tables, they seem to be killing less and dying later." He pulled out another book—one of an annoying series of *mea culpa* books by theologians who have Seen The Light. Anything for a gram.

"I saw a couple in MacArthur—I mean Hecate Park today," he said. "I overheard them profess undying love for each other. Then they kissed and wept for joy on each other's shoulder."

"Big deal," I said, turning to peruse a rotating rack of paperbacks. An awful lot of obscure occult books were getting published or reprinted these days. At least someone was being rewarded for perseverance. I cracked one open to stare at a page without seeing it. All I could see was Ann. Corny, I know, but that's who occupied my thoughts. Endlessly.

"Your assassin's heart should be pleased that the politicians couldn't get anyone to bother voting in the last election."

"Hm? Oh, right." I put the book back. "They're still hanging around Washington uninvited, though." I frowned, reading the cover of another book. This one was about astral travel. Just from the jacket copy I could determine that the author didn't know his elbow from a hole in the ground.

"Give them time," Corbin said. "They can't even stir up a war anymore without God to inspire them or a devil to side with the enemy."

I looked up from my book to stare at the curious man. I'd lost track of our conversation. My only thoughts were of Ann. Her eyes, bright with life, gazed at me from across the chasm between now and never.

I impulsively seized another paperback. Kundalini yoga. And another. On ceremonial Magick.

"Corbin," I said, reaching for a manual for waterscrying, candle magic, and clairvoyance, "you'd know these things. Isn't there a place between dreaming and forgetting that contains all the knowledge of all times and realities?"

He stared at me as if my tie had just caught fire.

"Uh, sure Dell. It's called the Akashic Record. Why?"

"I've got to pop over to another celestial sphere."

I took more books than I could easily carry to the register. I paid for them and left Corbin watching my dust.

I raced out into the street, into the cold winter air and the bright, clear sky. A couple of street workers watched me with bemused gazes, then returned to erecting a sign that restored the full name of Los Angeles—The City of Our Lady, Queen of the Angels.

I still called it L.A.

My breath roared in my ears. My heart pounded like a caged man trying to burst free. I skidded left onto Western Avenue and raced upstairs to my office in less than ten minutes.

Doors slammed and drawers flew open until I'd found what I wanted. Ann's athame. It was the psychic link I'd need to find her.

I sat down to read, placing the knife before me with loving care. The light from the desk lamp reflected softly on the silvery blade and ebony hilt. I cracked open the first book.

A wind from the North beat at my window, calling.